SENECA FALLS

By the Author

The Chase

Seneca Falls

SENECA FALLS

by
Jesse J. Thoma

2014

SENECA FALLS

ISBN 13: 978-1-62639-052-2

This Trade Paperback Original Is Published By
Bold Strokes Books, Inc.
P.O. Box 249
Valley Falls, NY 12185

First Edition: April 2014

CREDITS
EDITORS: VICTORIA OLDHAM AND CINDY CRESAP
PRODUCTION DESIGN: SUSAN RAMUNDO
COVER DESIGN BY SHERI (GRAPHICARTIST2020@HOTMAIL.COM)

Acknowledgments

Writing for Bold Strokes is a wonderful thing. The community of authors, editors, and team members is second to none. That being said, a few special individuals deserve mention. As a writer, I would be nothing without Victoria Oldham. She is a wonderful editor, friend, and mentor even when I think I can hear her tearing her hair out across the pond. Cindy Cresap, thank you for trying so hard to make me get along with the comma. I'm a work in progress. Sheri, once again the cover is a work of art. Finally, the leadership Radclyffe provides makes her easy to follow.

My family and friends are a wonderful support. I especially thank everyone who gave me such positive feedback after my first novel was published and encouraged me to keep writing. To tiny Mr. T, I could not ask for a more enthusiastic cheering section, but buddy, you should probably wait a few years to read Aunty's book.

And to my wife. Our life together is always my sweetest romance and my grandest adventure. Thanks will never be enough.

Dedication

For Alexis
Love Rocks when we're together
Love Rocks, gonna love you forever
Love's got me rockin' and I only wanna rock with you

PROLOGUE

Seneca King stepped off the bus into a glorious New England fall day. The trees were just beginning to hint at the explosion of color that would draw tourists from all over the world in a month or so. The air was crisp and fresh and crackled with fall electricity. The slight breeze stirred her hair, and she smoothed it back to keep it from sticking up, which it occasionally did. She could see why people so easily called New England home. It was beautiful, and the small college campus was putting on a good welcome show. The old ivy-covered buildings were majestic, and the hint of a pond glimmered through the trees directly in front of her. The air contained a sense of mischief, and the buildings looked worn enough to convey that Sophia College wasn't a stuffy Ivy League institution, no matter what ranking it received in *U.S. News and World Report*.

Despite her best efforts to contain it, Seneca sighed. Maybe this place would finally feel like home, a concept so foreign she wasn't even sure she would recognize the feeling. She adjusted the straps of her backpack over her shoulders, picked up her half empty duffle bag, and glanced at her campus map to locate the building that would be her home for the next four years. At Sophia, all students lived in small dorms called houses and dinner was served in dining rooms in each house. She would have preferred the anonymity of large, impersonal dorms and massive dining halls, but she was happy to have a chance at college, whatever the setup.

Gingerly testing her damaged right leg, she was pleased to find she could bear more weight than she had expected after the long bus trip. She knew the wooden cane strapped securely to the handles of her duffle could help, but it also made her stand out, and she didn't need that on her first day in town. It was convenient to ignore the fact that a bum leg and a cane strapped to her bag weren't exactly standard-issue for college first years. She had made the mistake of calling herself a freshman, but was quickly corrected, they were all first years. There weren't any men on campus, so there weren't any freshmen. She could be walking through campus buck-ass nude with a party hat on singing a song about freshmen and people wouldn't stare more than they did because of her bad leg. She set out purposefully across the small campus, trying to normalize her gait, refusing to acknowledge the pitying stares her limp elicited.

She was tired of showing weakness and receiving everyone's sympathy. Someone's pity is the only reason I'm here, she thought angrily as she climbed the three brick steps and limped through the door of Razor House. She wasn't stupid enough to throw away a wonderful opportunity when it was offered, though, and free tuition to one of the most prestigious women's colleges in the country was too great a gift to throw away, despite her reservations about why her benefactor had offered her the scholarship. Not many positive relationships were built in a criminal courtroom, but this one was defying the odds. For now, at least.

Once inside the dorm, she took a moment to appreciate her new home. The dark wood paneled walls were warm and comforting, and the books strewn around one corner of the large living room spoke of generations of women finding peace and companionship within the walls. The furniture was well kept but also lovingly worn around the edges. It was meant to be used, not admired.

Seneca fell into the nearest chair for a moment, giving her aching leg a respite. Her pride often caused her more pain than was necessary. Trying not to limp made the pain almost overwhelming, but for the first time in two years, she wanted someone to see her first, not the damn limp. It was as if she was living with a more outgoing, repulsive twin and no one bothered to get to know her after encountering "the limp."

When the throbbing was back to a manageable level, she shuffled through her backpack to find the wrinkled letter with new student instructions and her dormitory room assignment. *Fourth floor. Fantastic. And a roommate. College, what a fabulous idea.*

The climb up four flights of stairs took longer than she would have liked. She leaned heavily on the rail, but even so, she knew by the time she reached the top, her leg would be almost worthless. The charming old building would have looked even cuter with an elevator. Almost every limping step had brought offers to help with her bags by students shooting past her on the stairs, but she politely turned them down. When she reached the second floor, she stopped again to rest.

"What floor are you on?"

"What? Oh, fourth," Seneca said.

"Great, I'm going that way. You keep the backpack. I'll take this. My name's Britt." The woman extended a hand, shook Seneca's, and started up the stairs with Seneca's duffle bag before she could protest.

Seneca didn't like losing possession of her duffle bag, but walking the rest of the way up the stairs was much easier without it.

When they reached the top, Seneca regained possession of her duffle and thanked Britt. "I'm Seneca. Thanks for that. I was close to being clocked with a sun dial."

"You're welcome," Britt said. "I like to wander around at move-in time. I get a little extra cardio helping carry stray bags. You looked like you had it all under control. I should be thanking you. I'll see you around."

As soon as Britt was gone, Seneca found her room and collapsed onto one of the two single beds but almost immediately jumped up again. *Sheets, shit, I forgot to get sheets.* She grabbed for her backpack again and pulled out a tattered notebook. She found a blank page and wrote *sheets* on the top line. She added *pillow* and *blanket/sweats* under *sheets*. It depended on the price. She checked her wallet and grimaced at how little cash was there. A good bit of her money had been spent on the bus trip. Under blanket, she wrote *job*.

It wasn't long before her new roommate appeared.

"Hi," the young woman said, clearly trying to sound cheerful. She sounded terrified instead.

"Hello, I'm Seneca King. I guess we're going to be roommates."

The girl's handshake was weak and limp-wristed like a floppy fish, but Seneca tried to keep an open mind. She's young, she reminded herself. *And you look like hell, and probably have the poor girl scared out of her mind.* The girl bounced around the room, unpacking, and Seneca felt as though there were a world of difference between them, even though they probably weren't all that far apart in age.

Seneca was twenty-two, not a typical age for a college first year, but not exactly out of place, either. Even though it was tradition that all undergrads lived on campus all four years, Seneca had wanted to beg out and get an apartment downtown. When it became obvious that her scholarship wouldn't cover off campus housing, she was forced to acquiesce, as there was no way she could afford an apartment on her own. She tried to snap herself out of grumpy old man mode and smiled at her roommate. Maybe they could be friends. Britt had seemed nice. Maybe everyone was like that.

"What happened to your leg?"

It always amazed her how other people felt it their business to inquire about her limp. People either uncomfortably ignored it, obviously waiting for Seneca to make a statement about the nature of her injury, or they flat-out asked. She debated her answer, knowing she had to live with the young woman for the next year.

The truth didn't always set you free, and often a boldface lie was best. However, she didn't think lying to her roommate was the best way to start off their relationship, so she told the truth.

"I was shot," she said flatly, giving away none of the turmoil that was swelling in her gut or how hard it was to say the words at all.

As expected, that was the end of the conversation. Her roommate suddenly had something very important to do across campus.

Fuck, what have I gotten myself into?

Chapter One

One Year Later

Seneca leaned against the back wall of the dimly lit bar and surveyed the crowd. The liberal Massachusetts town Sophia College resided in didn't really need a gay bar, since almost all the nightspots catered to women, both gay and straight, but this dive on the edge of town was frequented mostly by locals and women not associated with the college. That was what Seneca counted on.

Although technically a sophomore, she was taking far more than the required four classes a semester and was well ahead of her graduation schedule. The new academic year started in three days, and she was looking for a much needed stress reliever before she was immersed in her studies.

She was a fairly frequent visitor to the bar, stopping by when loneliness outweighed her desire to avoid personal entanglements. In this crowded bar, she was all-powerful. The women watched her from the moment she walked in and tried all sorts of outrageous things to capture her attention for the evening. Even without the direct stares, she knew she was the center of attention. The bar provided her with another necessity, control. She dictated who took her home and also the rules by which their encounter would play out. Seneca offered the promise of a pleasurable night, but nothing more. There was no commitment, no phone calls the next day, and certainly no lingering conversation over coffee. It was strictly sex, no strings attached. In the bar, she became more than her usual awkward, introverted self. There, she was charming, witty, and charismatic, and she enjoyed that almost as much as the companionship. Although everyone knew her, they didn't really know anything about her, and that was freeing. Everyone, including her, had one goal in mind during their interactions.

Seneca surveyed the options for the evening, noticing more than a few previous conquests who looked willing for round two. However pleasurable, Seneca usually avoided choosing the same woman twice. There were too many complications involved, and although most of the women were okay with her not getting fully undressed on their first hookup, they tended to get upset when she wouldn't take them off a second time. It was easier to find someone new. The arrangement didn't always chase away the lingering demons or loneliness that Seneca had come to associate with living, but it provided an enticing way to pass the time. She enjoyed not only the other woman's pleasure, but was also bolstered by being the one in control of the situation. She'd been the one without control in her past, and it would never happen again.

Despite the many gazes on her, roaming over her body and trying to catch her fancy, Seneca was also aware of the unspoken resentment toward her. Although almost any woman in the room would gladly take her home, even the chosen ones wondered at her detached nature and unbending rules. She had gained a reputation as a playgirl, and some even went so far as to call her a jerk. Only the bartender, a woman named Suzy, seemed to see through her tough exterior. Seneca was pretty sure she stood up for her when the gossip reached critical mass. She had no idea why, but she appreciated it. As weird as it was, she needed this place.

She studied the faces in the room and leaned heavily against the wall, willing her aching leg to stop its endless throbbing as she nursed her first beer. Her gaze finally fell on a group of women directly across from her, next to the bar. Facing her was an incredibly beautiful woman with shoulder-length wavy red hair and fiery green eyes. She was deliciously curvy, and Seneca felt the familiar twinge in her belly, and slightly further south, that always indicated the catch of the night.

This time, however, the sexual twinge was accompanied by a pang of loneliness so acute, she almost turned to leave. As she caught the green eyes, she wondered what it would be like to be known, truly known, by the person behind the gaze, and that thought scared her more than she wanted to admit.

❖

Dylan Walker couldn't believe she had let her friends convince her to come to the one gay bar just off Sophia's campus.

She felt out of place, but that was true on campus these days as well. She had been back from her junior year abroad for less than a week but was starting to wonder if she would ever fit back in. Her time away had opened her eyes to a world she hadn't ever imagined possible, and being back here, as wonderful as it was, felt claustrophobic. It didn't help that the women she remembered as her closest friends now seemed ridiculous and shallow. They were currently prattling on about some hot mystery woman who frequented the bar.

Dylan caught Gert's eyes. Her best friend obviously wasn't having a good time either. Gert nodded toward the door, clearly eager to find something else to do with the evening. Dylan agreed. No woman could possibly be hot enough to have to endure this crap. And even if she were, Jess, Viv, and Mary were acting like they were at the zoo, here to see an exotic animal. The whole thing was making her a little nauseous.

She looked up from her Cosmo when one of her friends elbowed her hard in the ribs.

"Ow, what the—"

She stopped mid-sentence, transfixed by the amazingly good-looking woman approaching her, her eyes clearly locked on Dylan. She had closely cropped brown hair; strong, angular features; and a tall, lean frame, accentuated by broad shoulders and a narrow waist, but her eyes were what Dylan couldn't turn away from. There was invitation and desire, but also pain and fear. The fear surprised her. Maybe this woman was worth acting like a teenager at a pop concert after all.

"That's Seneca King," Mary said. "She's coming this way."

"No shit," Gert said.

The whole point of the evening, at least for a few of her friends, had been to catch the attention of Ms. Seneca King, and now that she was making her way toward them, the table was silent.

"Your sudden, total silence isn't weird at all," Gert said. "Most groups of five women sit in silence at bars on Saturday night. Say something, you idiots."

Despite Dylan's annoyance at her friends' swooning, it was hard to take her eyes off Seneca. She exuded confidence and really was hot. As striking as she was, however, the obvious limp drew Dylan's attention.

"Ladies, good evening." Seneca's voice was charming and seductive. "Mind if I join you?"

She took the time to greet each woman and shake her hand as they all hurriedly introduced themselves. Dylan felt like Seneca lingered a second longer over their handshake.

"I'm Dylan."

"Like Bob," Jess said, leaning forward to catch Seneca's attention. Dylan shot her a nasty look, but Seneca smiled, almost tenderly.

They all chatted idly for a few minutes. Based on how Dylan had heard this evening would go down, Seneca would soon reveal which of them she wanted to sleep with. Other bar patrons were staring daggers at the group, probably jealous that their table had been ignored. Dylan thought it was the most ridiculous display of an intricate mating dance and exaggerated preening she had ever seen. Seneca King was only one woman, a very good-looking one with sad eyes and a damaged leg, but just one woman, all the same. *Right, then why can't you take your eyes off her if there are so many other intriguing women here?*

"Bob?" Seneca asked quietly, pulling Dylan out of her daydream.

Dylan flushed red and once again glared at Jess. Jess smiled sweetly and nodded toward Seneca, who was waiting for Dylan's reply. Dylan looked in her direction, gasping slightly at her beautiful face and intense eyes.

"Would you like to dance?"

Seneca offered her hand and Dylan took it without thinking. About halfway to the dance floor, she realized dancing with the mysterious Ms. King would send the wrong message. She started to pull her hand out of Seneca's grasp, but she gripped tighter and steered them onto the dance floor just as a slow, romantic tune drifted from the jukebox.

"If you chose me tonight, I'm sorry, I'm not going to sleep with you," Dylan said quickly as Seneca pulled her close and began leading them around the floor.

"It's just a dance, Bob." Seneca's expression was amused. "And you shouldn't listen to everything your friends tell you. Sometimes I'm capable of simply asking a beautiful woman to dance."

"I've been back in the country for less than a month, and already I know you never *just* ask women to dance. I'm willing to play along though."

Seneca pulled Dylan a little closer. "International adventurer? If I weren't convinced before, now I know I chose the right dance partner."

"My adventures consisted of taking as many pictures of dingoes, kangaroos, and koalas as possible. Probably not quite as intriguing as what you had in mind."

"I know I've got no shot against the koalas, and I'd say my odds are fifty-fifty against the kangaroo, but I've got to be cuter than a dingo, right? At least a better companion? I've never eaten a baby."

Dylan couldn't help but laugh. This wasn't what she expected from the overly hyped sex machine her friends had described. "Is dancing hard for you?" Dylan asked, curiosity getting the better of her.

Seneca stiffened slightly, and Dylan thought she might pull away.

"Not so much. Just makes me a little jerky. Is it bothering you?"

Dylan shook her head and smiled, happy Seneca had answered so earnestly. She wanted to know more about her, and she sensed talking about her injury was probably hard. A less loaded question as an icebreaker might have been a good idea.

"See, now you know what they mean when all the gossipers say I'm a jerk. I told you not to believe everything you hear." Seneca wasn't as stiff as she had been, but her expression was guarded.

Dylan flushed, wanting to assure Seneca she never assumed she was a jerk, even if that's what everyone in the bar—all of her friends and a few disgruntled customers on the front steps—had insinuated.

"I never, I don't even know—"

"Sure you did. Everyone does," Seneca said, seemingly unconcerned. "Most of the time it's true. So on almost any other night you would have been perfectly reasonable making that assumption. Tonight, though, no jerk; just a jerky dancer."

"All right, jerky dancer, then you better use one more song to convince me to take your word for the new and improved you. I'm a tough sell," Dylan teased back, enjoying the feel of Seneca's arms around her. Even the uneven steps of her partner felt natural, after the initial adjustment. Dancing with Seneca was a wonderful experience, especially now that they had established the ground rules.

Seneca smiled and moved them further onto the dance floor as another slow song played. The dance floor was crowded, and other dancers bumped into them occasionally. When one particularly exuberant couple rammed into Seneca's back, Dylan was shocked at the effect it had on Seneca. The impact caused her entire body to recoil, to the point she was almost standing on Dylan's toes. Her shoulders sagged and she cowered slightly as if awaiting another blow. Her eyes were wild and pain filled, although the force of the bump didn't seem like enough to hurt her.

Dylan pulled her close and steered her away from the offending couple. Her shoulders were still hunched, as though she were trying to make herself as small as possible. Her eyes were slightly closed, and her body was tense. Dylan tried to gently reassure her by stroking her cheek, but Seneca reacted as if Dylan had slapped her. She pulled away violently and opened her eyes, fear clearly blurring all other emotions.

"Hey, it's okay. We're out of the crowd. It's just me. Bob." Dylan hoped the use of her silly new nickname would jolt Seneca back from wherever her mind had taken her. Dylan put her hand on Seneca's shoulder, trying to comfort her, but she only succeeded in making Seneca flinch away again.

"Dylan, I'm sorry." Seneca finally seemed to pull herself out of whatever horrible place she had been. The look of fear faded a little, and her breathing slowed to the point that Dylan wasn't looking for a brown paper bag.

"Don't be. Are you okay?" Dylan felt completely helpless. She was afraid to touch her again, so she stood with her hands in her back pockets, rocking awkwardly on the balls of her feet.

"Fine, I'm fine. I think I might have to cut our evening short though. Thank you for the dance."

Seneca turned and limped away without a backward glance. Dylan watched her as she stopped at the bar, said something quickly to the bartender, handed over money, and quickly exited. She looked wound tight, her uneven gait far more pronounced than when she'd wandered over to their table.

"What happened? Did you tell her the saintly Dylan Walker doesn't sleep with someone on the first date?" Dylan's friends asked when she returned. She knew she probably looked shell-shocked.

"Yes, I did. But that was before we started dancing, and I'm not a saint." Once again, she wondered where the wonderful supportive friends she remembered from their first two years together at Sophia had gone. They were also drunk, which never helped matters. At least Gert, who had even less patience for this bunch than she did, looked sympathetic.

"Well, why did she run out of here so fast then?"

Dylan didn't want to tell them the truth. Somehow, what she had witnessed felt private. She had a feeling that whatever past events caused her reaction, Seneca wouldn't want them broadcast to the group of women who routinely spent the evening trying to get in her pants. She invited the attention, Dylan reminded herself. Even so, whatever mysteries her past held, Dylan wouldn't be the one to lay them out for speculation.

"I think she got a call. She said she had to go, thanks for the dance, but she had to head out. Looks like she paid for our drinks before leaving though."

Dylan stared at the door thoughtfully, trying to decipher the past twenty minutes. She had gone from stating matter-of-factly that she wasn't going to sleep with Seneca to wondering if she was okay and if she would ever see her again. No wonder women were intrigued by her. Seneca King was a fascinating enigma.

CHAPTER TWO

Seneca wound her way quickly through the quiet streets, making it back to Sophia in record time. She searched the shadows as she walked, something she rarely did anymore, and felt uneasy until she was safely back in Razor House. She chastised herself all the way up the stairs for her weakness, repeating over and over that those days were behind her. She was safe now. Despite her own assurances, she still felt raw and her right leg throbbed painfully, a steady reminder of just how much her past had cost her, and continued to cost her.

She made it to the fourth floor, stumbled through the door, and flopped onto the bed. Britt looked at her curiously.

"Thought you were on the prowl tonight. What are you doing here?" Britt looked like she had more questions, but she stopped with the one.

Britt was the fifth roommate Seneca had lived with since enrolling at Sophia. The first had lasted through a total of three nights of Seneca's nightmares before begging the housing coordinator for a room change. The three roommates that followed didn't last more than a month. Seneca was surprised Britt had managed nearly a year.

After chasing away the fourth roommate, Seneca had been called before the housing committee and her house president. They originally thought she was playing some kind of bizarre joke to get rid of roommates and force them to put her in a single, but they quickly realized the nightmares were out of her control. She didn't like the terror-inducing, screaming, sweaty dreams either, and they certainly weren't an act. Each of her four previous roommates had testified for her, saying she wasn't making anything up. They just couldn't live in the same room. Seneca didn't blame them. If she could get away from that version of herself, she would too.

The easiest solution would have been to place her in a single occupancy room, a pleasure usually reserved for upperclassmen, but Razor House didn't have any available rooms and Seneca wasn't eager to transfer to a new house. She had moved around enough in her life and didn't relish the idea of starting over with another group of young women. After a couple months, the residents of Razor House had welcomed her into the fold, allowing for her oddities, and encouraging her to socialize. For the first time in a while, she felt the glimmer of belonging.

Just when moving seemed like the only option, Britt had come along and actually volunteered to room with Seneca. Seneca's fourth roommate got Britt's single, and Seneca got a friend. She didn't know why they hadn't given her the single and had the other two women share a room, but she was happy it had worked out the way it had. Seneca wasn't sure how she managed, but having Britt's calm presence in the room each night had eventually helped quiet the nightmares, and many nights they both slept peacefully.

"Got turned down." Seneca shrugged, rearranging the sheets and her pillow, trying to find a comfortable position. She finally gave in, yanked the pillow from under her head, and shoved it under her right knee and thigh. The pain diminished enough that she thought she might be able to sleep.

"Excuse me?" Britt asked, incredulous. "You, Miss Queen of the Sleaze Bar, got turned down? By who?"

"By Bob." Seneca enjoyed the memory of Dylan blushing crimson as her friend rudely suggested the comparison. Seneca cringed, realizing Dylan might not like being called Bob. *See, they told you I was a jerk, Bob.*

"You picked up a guy named Bob and he turned you down? What was a guy doing in your gay chicks' bar, and when the hell did you start to hit on men?"

"*Her* name was Dylan," Seneca said.

"You hit on a girl named Bob Dylan? Good Lord, Sen, how much did you drink tonight?"

"Bob's not her name. Her name is Dylan. Dylan…I'm not sure what her last name is, actually. A friend of hers said her name was Dylan, like Bob, and I thought it was cute. We danced. I came home," Seneca said, remembering the feel of Dylan in her arms. "One drink, Britt, only one. You know my limit."

"Only one drink, just a dance. Tell me, Sen, what does this surreal creature, Dylan-I-don't-know, look like, and when are you seeing her again? I want to meet her."

"She's about this tall," Seneca said, holding her hand just under her own nose, "has red hair just below her shoulders, really bright green eyes, and the best curves you've ever felt." Seneca sighed. That just about summed up Dylan on the outside, but there was something about the way she looked at her that had her more unsettled than being bumped on the dance floor. She remembered the dance floor incident and flushed with embarrassment. "I'm not seeing her again. I don't date, remember?" she said regretfully. "That sort of thing only leads to getting hurt. And she strikes me as the kind of woman who dates."

Seneca rubbed her damaged leg absently, used to Britt's scrutiny when she was thinking about something. Britt let Seneca chew things over, but she was the only one at Sophia willing to push her, a little. Again, Seneca could tell there was more Britt wanted to ask, but she kept quiet. Britt was the only person she considered a friend, but tonight it felt too raw.

"You might need these tonight," Seneca said as a way of good night, tossing a pair of earplugs across the room without looking at her. She had bought a figurative lifetime supply, hoping to offset some of the strain being her roommate entailed. "I had a bit of an incident at the bar."

Seneca heard Britt catch the earplugs and sigh at Seneca's withdrawal. She also heard Britt shove the unopened pack next to the other twenty pairs she had accumulated since moving in. Seneca had found them one day while looking for a pen in Britt's desk. She hadn't asked about them because she didn't know how to. But it lent credence to the feeling that in the midst of her nightmares, it was Britt's voice that helped her find her way back. Seneca had no idea why Britt would do that for her. Or how to repay her. Maybe one day she'd figure it out.

CHAPTER THREE

Seneca lay on the grassy hill overlooking the Sophia soccer field. The athletic fields were ringed with trees, each one beginning the annual competition of outdoing the others with brilliant displays of fall foliage. It was still early in the season, but a few of the trees had jumped the gun and were blazing red and orange against the backdrop of blue sky and green fields. Past the softball field was the school pond, good for lazy rowboating and illegal skinny-dipping. It was a remarkably beautiful setting. She felt at peace in a way that was rare.

It was the first day of classes and the last tune-up practice for the soccer team before the season. Seneca had been coming to watch practices, and sometimes games, since her first day on Sophia's campus a year earlier. After her first roommate had abandoned ship, Seneca had sought solace in the one place she had always found it in the past, the soccer field. Seneca thought perhaps she should try her hand at coaching one day. She loved watching a team grow through the practices, suddenly understanding what their coach had been saying over and over as they came together as a sporting family. She imagined it would give her great satisfaction to be the coach who helped that happen.

She settled against the soft hill, content to focus on the intricacies and strategy of the beautiful game. By the time practice ended, she was so lost in the flow of the scrimmage, the shouts of the players, and the thump of foot on ball that she didn't notice the new athletic trainer approaching until she was standing next to her.

"Seneca King?" It didn't really sound like a question.

Seneca jumped. She didn't like being snuck up on. "Yes."

"Follow me," the trainer said, before heading back down the hill at a steady pace. She headed toward the small field house, clear on the other side of the athletic complex.

Seneca scrambled up and followed, much to her annoyance. *Always following. A woman snaps at you to follow and here you are tagging along like a good little puppy. Shit, she hasn't even slowed down or turned back once. She knows I'm going to follow.*

Although it was a little annoying that the athletic trainer assumed she would follow, Seneca realized how important it was that the woman hadn't slowed down. She didn't do what almost everyone else did when they knew about Seneca's limp, which was to taper her pace to an absolute crawl. Either the athletic trainer didn't know about the injury or she didn't think it was an excuse to slow things down. Intriguing.

When they reached the field house, the trainer opened the door to the small, stuffy training room and motioned for Seneca to take a seat on the rolling stool. Seneca did as directed and took a moment to study the athletic trainer, who was busy fumbling in the scorching water of the hydrocollator for a hot pack. She wore a navy polo shirt tucked neatly into a pair of khaki shorts despite the chilly evening. A blue Red Sox cap covered closely cropped, dark curly hair and a small black bag hung cross-shouldered in front of her body. When she finally extracted the hot pack with the help of the hook end of a coat hanger, she handed the pack and two towels to Seneca.

"Put this on your leg. Use the straps to tie it on. You're going to need your hands."

"Excuse me?" Seneca asked, completely confused and defensive at the thought of someone else telling her how to treat her damaged leg.

But the woman's smile was kind, and completely devoid of pity. She leaned down and gently wrapped the hot pack around Seneca's leg, almost directly over the injury.

"Did I get the placement right?" she asked, her blue eyes gentle and nonjudgmental.

"Almost," Seneca said, shifting the pack slightly higher. "Who are you exactly, and what am I doing here?"

Seneca needed some shred of information to calm her churning mind because the heat felt amazing, and despite her misgivings, the woman was quite likable and had an air about her that Seneca found hard not to trust. The combination of being in the dark and being, paradoxically, comfortable, was making her distinctly *un*comfortable.

"Kate Smith. I'm the new trainer. I assumed you would have known that already. Sorry for not introducing myself. I wasn't sure I could get you to follow me if we spent time shooting the shit on the field."

The laugh escaped before Seneca could censor it. Kate had an infectious smile and had easily assessed Seneca's standoffishness.

"Oh yeah, it's all fun and games now, but wait till the little monsters come in from the field. You, go over there." She shoved the rolling stool Seneca was perched on with one foot, sending her flying across the tiny room toward the ice machine.

"What am I doing here?" Seneca asked.

"I needed some help today, and I thought you might be the woman for the job. I would explain it all to you in great detail except I see the first of our tormentors on their way now. Bags are to the left, that big roll of plastic. One scoop of ice and make sure to suck the air out before you tie off the bags." Kate demonstrated the correct ice bag making technique and left Seneca to begin her task. "Make about ten and we'll go from there. No telling how many are going to need ice tonight."

Seneca did as she was told, and soon the soccer team, or the little monsters, as Kate had called them, were cramming into the small room seeking treatment, ice bags, or scissors to cut off ankle tape, or Kate's ear to complain about a new ailment. In a whirlwind of fifteen minutes, all was quiet again.

Kate's athletic trainer kit, as well as the much larger full duffle sized kit, had been pillaged, and Kate quickly restocked each before removing the heat pack from Seneca's leg and replacing it in the hydrocollator.

"So," Kate said, leaning against the back counter and looking intently at Seneca, who was flexing her leg gently, enjoying a few pain-free moments, "how did you like your first day on the job?"

"My first day on the job? I already have a job, and this isn't it."

"You wash dishes in the alumni house and tutor kids who don't bother to go to class at the high school who then panic about their upcoming tests. And, this one I don't get, you're a security guard at the pond. Do you ever bust anyone for skinning-dipping, making out, fornicating, stealing boats, or any of the other mischief you all get up to at the pond?"

"No. But I never said I was any good at those jobs," Seneca said.

"Well, hopefully, you'll be proficient at this one. I thought we could consolidate your jobs a little. You would also get to stay near athletics, which you seem drawn to. You've been here almost every practice, and I hear it was the same last year. Either you've got a girlfriend on the team"—Kate held up her hand to stop any protests—"which I hear isn't your style, or you just love this game. If the leg screwed up your chance, why not help other injured athletes? And you get to work with me, which is clearly a pretty big plus."

Kate was grinning so devilishly Seneca laughed. "You hear quite a lot for someone who just started this job," Seneca grumbled half-heartedly, not attempting to hide her amusement. She wasn't usually quick to trust, but Kate Smith didn't seem to have an ulterior motive, and her eyes were sympathetic and caring. "I've got a scholarship," Seneca said, realizing the one thing that could scrap the whole crazy proposal, "but no work study, so you can't hire me."

"Work study doesn't pay for shit. That wouldn't replace the three jobs you've already got. I'm not talking about a work-study position. I happen to be in charge of hiring an athletic department lackey, which is a fancy word for a personal slave that I rent out every now and then to other people in the department. It won't get in the way of your class work and—"

No. No fucking way. Seneca was out the door faster than she had moved in a while. The heat had limbered up her leg, and her limp was less pronounced as she ran from the field house. Kate was out the door almost as fast after her and grabbed her arm to slow her down. Seneca could feel Kate approaching and knew contact was imminent, but she still cowered at the touch and flinched when she faced Kate, expecting her to be angry. Instead, she found concern and caring and more than a little confusion.

"Sorry." Seneca pulled out of Kate's grasp and saw Kate's look of surprise. She wished she could get out of the situation. She was checking for an escape route, but there wasn't anywhere she could easily go. She would disappear if she could. Over and over, her body betrayed her at inopportune times, like the other night dancing with Dylan. "I don't much like to be touched."

"Of course. I apologize," Kate said. "I didn't mean to offend you. Can we start over? I really do want you for the job."

Seneca was sure Kate had no idea what had just happened, but she appreciated Kate's willingness to let it drop. It wasn't Kate's fault that she had used the word "slave." As they walked back to the field house, Seneca realized she had overreacted. *She didn't mean anything by it, and she has no way of knowing what Shannon did to me.*

"Why are you offering me this job? And how did you know my name? Actually, you seem to know a lot about me. Why?" Seneca refused the offered stool, preferring to stand, feeling too emotionally stirred up to sit down. She had been happy and relatively relaxed earlier, but now her protective shield was once again firmly in place.

"As to your first question, I have friends in high places, and as to your second, I also have friends in low places."

Seneca was trying to decide whether to be offended, or just what Kate meant, when she continued.

"Your bartender friend Suzy? I've known her since we were ten."

"So this is some kind of pity offer? Suzy tells you about poor Seneca King who comes into the bar to pick up women, looking like a homeless person most nights, who works three jobs, and you feel sorry for me, so you pull some strings and get me a job where I can be your slave. And I'm supposed to accept with gratitude. Do I have to sleep with you, too?" Seneca was practically shouting, confused, defensive, and hurt. She didn't want anyone's pity, and she didn't want anyone owning her either. She would rather work three jobs than be indebted; debts could be collected in all kinds of unpleasant ways.

"Oh man," Kate said, taking off her ball cap and running her fingers through her short hair. "Suzy said this would be hard, but I didn't think it would be this hard." She looked at Seneca for a long moment, obviously studying her. It made Seneca uncomfortable, but she didn't look away. It didn't seem like a challenge, more of an exploration, or an invitation. "I don't want to own you. This position already existed. And the only string I pulled was getting to be in charge of the hiring process. I wanted to hire you, and a certain member of the board of directors thought that was a great idea. And just for the record, I already have someone to sleep with. If you're lonely, the bar opens at six. Which I suspect you already know. What I would like to do, is be a friend. Every butch girl needs an older butch lady looking out for her until she finds a hot femme to take care of her for the rest of her life. I'm available for the job. Someone looked out for me when I was young and lost."

Seneca bit back her immediate reaction, which was to scream "fuck you" and storm out of the field house. She wasn't even entirely sure why that was her gut reaction. "That seems awfully presumptuous on so many levels," she said. Seneca didn't bother to reply to the bar comment, since there was no way to deny that part of her life even if she wanted to. Suzy worked the bar every night and had probably told Kate plenty of stories. She went to the bar to find companionship and to feel connection, but on her terms. It was a controlled environment, and if the women she approached didn't want to play by her rules, she could find someone else. She was in charge, and that was important. *Except for last night's little episode...*She shook off the thought and paid attention to Kate.

"You not into girly girls then?" Kate asked.

"I never said that," Seneca said, hearing her somewhat frosty tone melting a little.

"Ah, well then, you might not know it yet, you're young, but we run around, all butch and tough, and full of vinegar, but good Lord does it feel good to find your lady and let her be in charge. It's exhausting trying to prove how macho you are all the time."

"And that's where you come in? To help me out until I find a woman to tame me?" Seneca asked.

Kate nodded, her smile suggesting she knew just how goofy that sounded.

"I think that sounds insane."

"You want the job or not?" Kate asked.

Seneca thought about her three part-time jobs, how little sleep they afforded her, and how much she missed the smell of the grass on game day. "Fine, what do I do?"

Kate looked relieved and smiled a huge, winning smile, her eyes sparkling. "Can you be here tomorrow at four? We'll go over what you need to do and fill out your paperwork then. I'll have some polo shirts for you. Do you have any khaki pants?"

Seneca shook her head, embarrassed again. She worked hard to earn the money she did, but most of it was used to buy books, school supplies, and to save money for the summer when her housing and meals weren't paid for.

"No problem. After work tomorrow, I'm taking you shopping. We'll get you a few pairs of pants and you'll be all set."

"I can get—"

Kate interrupted her, holding her hand out, one finger up in a mock warning. "I know you can get them yourself. This isn't pity, and this isn't charity. You have to come to work dressed a certain way, which makes it a kind of uniform. I'm going to help you with that. We can take it out of your first couple paychecks if that makes you feel better."

Seneca nodded. It would make her feel better, and it was nice of Kate to recognize that. Despite their rocky start, Kate was quite likable. She was looking forward to working with her.

"I have to get to class," Seneca said, backing out the door. "I'll see you tomorrow."

"Sure will, kid. I'll be here."

Seneca made it through the outer doors before she realized she had been rude. She turned and poked her head back into the small training room. "Kate?"

"Yeah, kiddo?"

"Thanks."

CHAPTER FOUR

Dylan waited impatiently for her Ancient Inventions class to start. She tried not to look out the window where summer was making a last run at relevance. It wasn't a day to be cooped up inside. She looked at her watch, counting the time between the end of class and when dinner was served in her house. Missing dinner wasn't a good idea because there weren't many other options for food on campus.

If class got out on time, she might have enough time to head down to the pond and read for a while and still make it back for dinner. Maybe Gert was free and they could continue their discussion on how they were going to make it through their last bit of time on campus. She flipped idly through the book she had purchased earlier in the day for class. The subject matter looked interesting, but in reality, she had enrolled simply because a friend of hers had taken the class last semester and promised they got to use the machine shop to re-create one of the ancient inventions at the end of the semester.

Dylan wasn't particularly handy, but the idea of being able to tell her mother she had learned how to weld had been enough incentive to sign up. Her mother wouldn't approve, and she'd probably be downright horrified. Walker women did not weld. It just didn't happen. They threw dinner parties, knitted, and looked fabulous on the arms of their wealthy and powerful husbands.

There wasn't time for calluses, freedom of expression, or personal growth, except in the form of a bank account. She knew that was probably selling everyone short, but her family legacy was starting to feel stifling. Especially now that she was getting so close to graduation and was faced with figuring out what she wanted to be when she grew up.

Scandalizing her mother had become a personal project, and Dylan's rebellions had gotten more and more brazen as she got older. It started by playing baseball with the boys in the yard and had culminated last year in Australia when she had the audacity to date a woman and not really make any progress on defining what world-changing contribution to society she would make after graduation. That was another thing Walker women did not do. They didn't date. Period. And certainly not women. They were courted and then they married. The only requirements were wealth, status, and of course, male. It was all very eighteenth century.

When she was feeling particularly cranky, Dylan had only to recall the conversation with her mother, when she *accidentally* revealed the name of the person she had been seeing, to be instantly cheered. The sheer volume of the shrieking coming from the other end of the phone would have been enough to bring a smile to Dylan's face, but the multitude of tones, lengths, and expressions of the shrieks her mother emitted had Dylan reaching for a tissue to wipe away tears of laughter. She'd always been into girls, but it really had been worth it to wait and tell her mother when she did.

Lady Walker had, of course, threatened to pull her out of school, bring her home, and not let her out of her sight until a suitable man could be found for her to marry, but even she knew she didn't really have much power over her daughter, especially not a world away. Although technically her father controlled the tuition payments being made to Sophia each semester, the money actually belonged to Dylan, left to her by her grandparents years before she was even born.

Even if that weren't the case, Dylan highly doubted her father would go along with her mother's threats. He had never really understood her, as he spent much of his time out of the house and worked hard at providing the kind of life to which his wife had grown accustomed. Perhaps it was misunderstanding, or maybe even a desire to make up for what he hadn't given her in her earlier years, but he always came to Dylan's defense when she and her mother got into a particularly nasty argument. The irony of the entire ridiculous situation was that, overall, she had a great relationship with her mother and loved her dearly. Most of the time they got along really well, as long as Dylan didn't buck her mother's plans too noticeably. She just hoped for an understanding that didn't seem as if it would ever be forthcoming. Things had actually been better for the year she was a world away, excluding the dating a chick hiccup.

Lost completely in her thoughts of family and home, Dylan didn't notice as her classmates slowly filled the room. She was sitting a few rows from the front, torturing herself by being near a particularly large and ornate window that dared the interior world to find something more beautiful outside. She dimly registered a slight change in the cadence of footfalls as students shuffled to their seats. The gentle tap on her shoulder quickly followed by the sharp thump on the floor wasn't enough to pull her completely from her thoughts until a deliciously familiar voice dragged her back to the present.

"Bob?"

Dylan whipped around, happy to see Seneca. Dylan surprised them both by hopping out of her seat and wrapping her in a hug. She felt Seneca stiffen at the initial contact, and Dylan chastised herself for not being more sensitive. Their dance had given her a hint that Seneca didn't like unexpected contact. But Seneca didn't pull away and awkwardly returned the embrace, even if she wasn't able to fully relax into it.

Dylan pulled out of Seneca's arms, reminded of how nice they felt around her from their dance a few nights earlier. She felt her face flush, which was embarrassing. She had no idea what had possessed her to hug Seneca, but she wasn't disappointed that she had. The other women in the class stared, open-mouthed at the display. Dylan was sure most of them knew of Seneca, and not one of them could ever imagine working up the courage to say hello, much less hug her in the middle of a classroom. Seneca didn't exactly give off a warm, fuzzy vibe. Dylan's friends had been giving her the Seneca 101 crash course. Or at least the rumors about her. Dylan didn't believe most of it.

"I was worried about you," Dylan said, returning to her seat and nodding to the open seat next to her, inviting Seneca to take it.

Seneca hesitated a second, looking conflicted. She lowered herself heavily and seemed to unconsciously rub the leg she limped on.

Dylan watched as Seneca tried to ease the pain of her injured leg, but didn't say anything. It wasn't any of her business why Seneca didn't use a cane or crutches, or what had happened to her in the first place, and she figured she got asked about it a lot. She really wanted to know, however.

"Why were you worried about me?" Seneca asked, looking genuinely confused.

"You seemed upset before you left the other night. I hope I didn't do or say anything to offend you." Dylan was pretty sure Seneca's reaction had had nothing to do with her, but she really did want to make sure she was okay. It seemed out of place to just ask.

"You were worried from the other night? You're still worried about that?"

Seneca's confusion nearly broke Dylan's heart. "Of course. You were upset."

Dylan watched Seneca trying to wrap her head around Dylan's concern. *What happened to you? Why can't you believe anyone would be concerned about you?*

She didn't have a chance to ask, although she wouldn't have expected a response even if she had. Class started and they were swept back in time to the land of the Egyptians, to Aristotle and Archimedes. Dylan felt Seneca slipping back into herself the longer the class wore on, and for some reason, that bothered her. She quietly tore out a page of her notebook and scrawled out a note. "So where are you taking me after class?" She put it on Seneca's desk.

Dylan saw Seneca read the note and then try everything she could think of to get Dylan's attention, but Dylan stayed laser focused on the professor yammering on about their first reading assignment. Seneca was going to have to figure this one out on her own.

CHAPTER FIVE

"Bob? Bob, what does the note mean?" Seneca was trying her best to look sweet and innocent, her eyes exaggerating her plea. In reality, she was a basket of nerves, not sure what to make of the strange note. Perhaps it was nothing, but she wasn't sure, and it made her uneasy. She was much less sure of herself outside the confines of the bar.

"Relax, Seneca," Dylan said. "I want to grab some coffee, and I wanted you to go with me. You know, to make up for not finishing our dance the other night. Don't worry," she said, seemingly reading Seneca's mind, "no sex."

"Dylan, I told you not to believe everything your friends—"

"Seneca!" Dylan said, interrupting before Seneca could really get going. "I was not implying that you had nefarious intentions. I was simply reassuring you that this afternoon my own intentions lean more to coffee than the bedroom. I'm a little obsessed with my afternoon coffee break, and today I want you to come with me. Agreed?"

Dylan looked like she was holding her breath. It was very cute and not something that Seneca expected. Why would Dylan be nervous about having coffee with her?

"Nefarious?" Seneca said, actually enjoying the teasing. "I never have nefarious intentions. Let's go, Bob. I have to warn you, though, I've never understood the appeal of froth and foam and little pretty pictures on the top of my coffee. You have some convincing to do."

"Do I really seem like the afternoon latte type? Am I that transparent? Fine, well, I'll buy and change your mind. You'll see."

Seneca couldn't for the life of her understand why she was agreeing to coffee. It felt too much like a date, too much like the type of thing she avoided at all costs. There was something about Dylan though that made her feel, not *un*safe. Even that small admission scared her out of her wits, yet her boots continued to follow as if the damned things had a mind of their own.

For almost an hour, they sat in pleasant conversation. Dylan kept up a steady stream of stories about her parents and her youth, each more entertaining than the last as they progressed from slightly silly to downright ridiculous. Seneca had never met anyone remotely like the woman Dylan described as her mother, but she was fascinated all the same.

"Would your mom take one look at me and head for the door, screaming?" Seneca asked. "I can't imagine she finds too many women like me roaming around her neighborhood or joining her book club."

Dylan seemed to find the thought amusing. "My mother does belong to a book club. She was brought into the group by a family friend who is much older, and my mother is the youngest person in it by thirty years. At least once every sixth month they get interrupted during the book club, or the meeting gets cancelled altogether, because someone has to go to the hospital. No one is under eighty. I was trying to picture an octogenarian with your haircut reading *War and Peace* with my mother."

"Does she like the book club?"

"She hates it. It's terrible."

"Why doesn't she find a different one? Aren't there a hundred of those things around? I hear people talking about them and see signs in places like this." Seneca waved at their coffee shop surroundings.

"Of course she could, but it's expected she remain in the one she's in. Socially, it's important and it would be rude to leave. There are a lot of expectations on her, on all Walkers. Anyway, that's lame conversation. Tell me something about yourself."

"I'd really love if you would tell me about Australia. I haven't done much traveling," Seneca said, enjoying Dylan's company and her stories. Maybe this was what a normal friendship felt like. If so, it was sort of nice. Seneca vaguely remembered this kind of thing happening before her life went to hell. It helped that Dylan was willing to hold up most of the conversation, meaning Seneca could simply sit back and enjoy the sound of her voice without having to reveal anything about herself.

"Oh, Australia was amazing, the most beautiful country. I could bore you with the details for days. I took pictures and wrote my mother letters, but all she'll ever talk about is Kathleen. The woman has a one-track mind."

"Who's Kathleen? Girlfriend?" Seneca asked, truly intrigued.

"Girlfriend might be a bit strong, but in a sense, yes, girlfriend fits. Kinda the junior high, lasts two weeks and then you want to throw spitballs at them, kind of girlfriend. You know what I mean?"

Seneca had no idea but nodded anyway. "So, the celibate Bob does sleep with women after all. And just what does one have to do to become the junior high school girlfriend?"

"You offering yourself up for the job?" Dylan asked, her eyebrow cocked.

Holy shit! Was I just flirting with her?

Seneca must have looked terrified because Dylan's face softened and she gently placed her hand over both of Seneca's, which were crammed together so forcefully it was amazing nothing was broken. Seneca flinched at the contact, but didn't pull away. What was wrong with her? She needed to get better at controlling some of these reactions if she was going to have friendships and normal human interactions.

"I was teasing you, Seneca. But to answer your question, I think my mother is conservative, old-fashioned, and un-enlightened, a little in the vein of Mrs. Bennett in *Pride and Prejudice*. However, she did teach me a few things that I've kept with me. One is that I want to be courted and swept off my feet. I know it seems like a fairy tale, but I'm not big on the casual sex thing. Don't get offended. Everyone gets to make that decision for themselves. I want my knight in shining armor and I want to be wooed."

Dylan caught Seneca's eye, probably hoping to reassure her she wasn't judging Seneca's casual flings. Seneca didn't care if she were. They served her purpose, and she wasn't ashamed that she got what she needed, when she needed it. "Wooed? Is that even a thing anymore?"

"Yes, wooed. And it is to me."

Seneca found it completely adorable that Dylan held on to the idea of a fairy tale love. She wasn't about to tell her there was no such thing.

"What about you—" Seneca's shoulders elevated and she wrapped her arms around herself, and Dylan left her question in mid-sentence. Which was good, because if Dylan continued, Seneca couldn't guarantee she wouldn't bolt out of her chair and be gone. She had been running so long it was a hard habit to break, even when she was having an enjoyable afternoon and there was nothing to run from. At least, she didn't want to think she needed to fear Dylan. She moved her hands from around herself and gripped the seat of her chair. She felt like she was holding herself in place, but at least she was staying put.

"What about your plans for dinner?" Dylan said, tapping her watch, pointing out that they were going to be late getting back to their houses.

"Oh," Seneca said, caught off guard. Her defenses were up, and she hadn't expected Dylan to ask about her stomach. "Uh, I don't have any plans for dinner. Was that really what you were going to ask me?"

"No," Dylan said bluntly. "Dinner with me? Downtown or back on campus?"

"Why didn't you ask me what you wanted to, then?"

"Would you have answered?" Dylan asked, looking gentle but curious.

"I don't even know what the question was going to be," Seneca said, but after the glare from Dylan continued, "but no, I wouldn't have answered, and you certainly wouldn't have gotten the opportunity to be taken to dinner because I would have already been halfway up to campus by now." Sometimes it felt good to let some of the burden go by telling the truth.

"Well then, good thing I didn't ask, because I'm hungry. Now, where do you want to go?" Dylan seemed content to let Seneca dictate how much she shared, which was the only way this would work. Like Seneca's encounters at the bar, she only felt safe if she was in control.

Britt was at her desk as usual when Seneca returned. In addition to being a college student, she was a writer, and her computer had become a natural extension of her fingers.

It was late, but Seneca felt anything but tired. Dinner with Dylan had been wonderful. Their conversation was light and easy, and for the first time in as long as she could remember, Seneca didn't feel the pit of loneliness quite so acutely. Maybe another friend wasn't such a bad thing after all.

"Hey, Sen," Britt said. "Out on the prowl? Unsuccessful again? Even you can't have been studying already."

"No, not studying," Seneca said. "Hey, Britt, you've been on dates before, right?"

Britt looked at her, clearly amused by her question but not about to laugh in her face. "Yes, once or twice. Why do you ask?"

"Well, I never have."

"Ever?" Britt asked.

"Nope," Seneca said. She thought back to what she had always thought of as dating, when Shannon was in her life. She shivered. "How do I know if I've just been on one?"

Britt looked like she was trying too hard to not think this was the most adorable thing she'd ever seen. Seneca wasn't sure if she was amused or embarrassed by Britt's reaction.

"Are you going to put me on a Hallmark card or help me out?"

"I would come over there and give you a big squeeze and gross, sloppy kiss on the cheek, but I know you'd freak out and whack me with your cane so I'm just going to sit here and grin a bit. Does this have to do with the cutie named Bob?"

"Some help you are," Seneca said, although she wasn't really mad. If she hadn't just had a great night, perhaps she would be feeling differently, but Britt always got more leeway anyway. Not enough to get away with sloppy kisses though.

"Okay, seriously now. Was the word 'date' ever used?"

"No."

"What did you do?"

"Coffee, and that led to dinner."

"Kiss? Sex?"

"No and no."

"How did you end up out together and any plans for round two?"

"She wrote me a note in class, and not really. I hope it happens again, though. It was…nice."

"Did it feel like a date? Were you flirting, touching hands? Keeping obnoxiously long eye contact?"

"Is dating really this complicated? She made me try a latte. Does that count?"

"For you, oddly enough, I think so. Keep seeing this one, Sen. I think she has potential."

"I've never seen any others. How would you know if she has potential for me or not? Not that I'm arguing," Seneca said. "Oh, hey, I got a job today."

"Seneca! You already have three jobs. Please tell me you're not serious." Britt looked horrified.

If it had been anyone else, Seneca would have recoiled at the note of censure in Britt's voice. However, somewhere along the way, she had realized Britt's chastisements and suggestions weren't an attempt to control her; they were an indication of her genuine concern. She'd been Seneca's only friend, even if Seneca didn't open up as most friends did. Britt seemed undeterred and never asked for more than Seneca could give.

"No, this job actually replaces the other three. It's with the athletic department. It was an offer I couldn't turn down."

"Sweet," Britt said. "Who you working with?" Britt was on the squash team and knew most everyone in the athletic department.

"Kate, the new trainer," Seneca said, reflecting on her very odd afternoon.

"Ooh, she is so damned hot. Real nice too, from what I hear. I foresee a season of extra sore hamstrings for me and probably every other lesbo on a sports team."

Seneca rolled her eyes and laughed.

"Well, she said she's going to train me to patch up all you injury-prone fools, so you're out of luck, thanks to the instant healing powers of Seneca King."

"Oh no, if you and Kate are in there together, that seals the deal. This is going to be the worst season for mild, nagging injuries in the history of sports. I hope you enjoyed your coffee non-date because you aren't going to have time for any more. You are about to become one of the two most popular women on campus."

CHAPTER SIX

Seneca scrambled down the hill to the soccer field, skidding to a halt next to Kate, trying to look composed. She was three minutes late for her first day of work. Seneca was never late. She knew exactly how much time it took to get everywhere and set off to any destination with breakneck speed, mindless of her protesting leg. Whether that was because she was constantly running from her demons or compensating for her limp, she never bothered to consider. What did it matter anyway? On every other day, it took her twelve minutes to reach the soccer field from her room. Today, it had taken fifteen.

"You're late," Kate said without looking at Seneca. "Why?"

Seneca was caught off guard by the question. She didn't sense anger or rebuke in Kate's voice, just mild curiosity. She had expected a lecture, not an opportunity to provide an excuse.

"I stopped to look at a tree," Seneca said honestly, grimacing at how ridiculous it sounded.

In truth, she hadn't had a choice. The tree was in full spectacular fall brilliance and had looked like it had caught on fire, a slow burn that started from within and reached out to the tip of each leaf. It looked like she felt some days. She was mesmerized and had taken the time to stare at its beauty.

The sight, and her almost physical reaction to it, threatened to bring tears, but tears were a false promise because she hadn't been able to cry in three years, no matter how badly she burned for release. Completely unbidden and mostly unwelcome, Dylan's face had flashed in her mind, her red hair blending with the colors of the fiery tree. She had started to smile at the memory of just how beautiful Dylan was, and that unconscious gesture was enough to spur her into action. She practically flew the rest of the way to the field, trying to leave her competing emotions and Dylan's beautiful face far behind. It had been so long since the thought of a friend had brought a smile to her face that the thought of it felt like the taste of a long forgotten, exotic food.

"The trees are beautiful this time of year. It's important to seek out some beauty every day. If your arboreal pursuits are over, however, would you like your first lesson?"

Kate didn't look like she bought that Seneca was telling her everything about the tree, but she moved on anyway, and Seneca followed her to the locker room. Apparently, when Kate said "lesson" she meant purgatorial level torture chamber of frustration cleverly disguised as a learning opportunity.

Taping an ankle was not nearly as easy as Kate made it look. Seneca watched Kate place the initial stirrup strips and the figure eights, but when Seneca tried, her tape looked like a tangled web made by a drunken spider. Kate had enlisted the assistance of the soccer team's manager for practice, and the girl was remarkably patient. She didn't complain even when the tape was bone crushingly tight, which was Seneca's attempt to keep it even and smooth.

Seneca knew the girl was probably just happy to have her attention focused on her feet. There were hundreds of rumors about Seneca floating around Sophia's campus, each more outrageous than the last. Seneca neither confirmed nor denied any of them, probably adding fuel to the roaring inferno. She imagined having your ankle taped by the notorious Seneca King was probably the most terrifying thing happening within twenty miles of Sophia today, maybe even this week. It was a shame it wasn't closer to Halloween. They could charge admission, dim the lights, and call it "The Scariest Fifteen Minutes On Campus."

When Seneca finally produced a tape job that looked halfway decent, seemed functional, and allowed circulation to her patient's foot, Kate magically appeared by her side, offering praise and subtle suggestions. Seneca felt a tremendous sense of accomplishment, more than she had in a long time.

"Enough learning for today. Keep practicing if you have some poor soul you can bribe into providing their ankles. If not, wait until they fall asleep. I'll give you some junk tape we've got lying around."

"God, I don't know what Britt would do if she woke up to me taping her ankle." Seneca enjoyed Kate's sense of humor. "I've gone through enough roommates already. I can't afford to piss her off." Seneca suddenly looked down, horrified she had shared that with Kate. She tried to cover with a joke. "She does wear earplugs when she sleeps though. I'd have the element of surprise."

"You snore that loudly?" Kate asked.

"Something like that." Seneca realized she needed to get better at keeping her mouth shut if she was going to spend time with people. There was something about Kate's calm, non-judgmental-ness, her quiet strength, and the lack of pity in her eyes that seemed to make Seneca a veritable babbling brook.

Kate didn't pursue any further questions, although she looked at Seneca curiously. The door was definitely open if Seneca wanted to talk. She didn't. She turned and motioned Seneca to follow her to the golf cart nearby. They slid into the seats and both put their legs up on the dash.

After a few minutes, Seneca started to fidget. "Shouldn't we be working?" she asked, concerned. She didn't like the idea of getting paid while doing nothing. If felt too much like charity.

"We are working." Kate's body was relaxed, but her eyes were alert when she looked over at her. "Right now our job is to watch the game and hope no one gets hurt. If anyone does, we go. Until then, we sit in the sun, watch a game, and try to keep the smug grins off our mugs. Everyone knows we have the best job on the planet. No need to rub it in."

Well, ain't this the shit. She had no idea why Kate had really offered her this job, but damn if she wasn't right. Seneca would have paid to come sit out here and watch the beautiful game she loved, even if she would never play it again.

❖

An hour after the game, Seneca sprawled on a treatment table in the main training room. The training room wasn't glamorous. It consisted of one large central room, with taping tables, treatment tables, and an island for supplies. Two smaller rooms connected to it, one housing the hot and cold whirlpools and the other the trainers' offices. It was in the basement of the athletic building and had cold, concrete floors, but there was a comfort to the space that put Seneca at ease.

Kate appeared by Seneca's side, a hot pack in hand. She gently set it on Seneca's injured leg, placing it directly over the injured area. "Did the heat help last time?"

Seneca nodded. Her impromptu jog to the field earlier, after her "arboreal pursuits" as Kate had called them, followed by an hour on her feet handing out ice packs and tending to after-game injuries had left her leg aching painfully. The heat was welcome relief.

Kate tossed her a pillow for her head and then gently placed one under her knee as well. She went back into the office and Seneca closed her eyes, letting the heat draw away some of the pain. In a matter of minutes, she was nearly asleep and didn't hear Kate approach.

Kate dropped three pairs of khaki pants on Seneca's stomach. As the pants landed, Seneca jerked awake, jumping so violently that she almost fell face first off the table. She thrust her leg out toward the floor to catch herself, her full body weight landing on her injured leg. Pain shot from the damaged muscles and through her body as if her quadriceps had exploded, sending shrapnel into her blood stream. Even if the pain hadn't been so great, the leg wouldn't have been able to support her weight. She cried out in pain, fear, and anger and fell to the floor, breathing heavily, and trying to get control of her body and emotions. The pain was always bad, but the emotional experience of the pain was probably worse. It brought back too many memories and promised too much struggle ahead.

"Seneca! Oh my God, are you okay? I'm so sorry. I didn't mean to startle you."

Kate dropped to her knees and pulled her into her arms. Seneca struggled against the arms restraining her at first, desperately trying to get away from the blow she knew was sure to come. She couldn't get away though. She was held too tightly and she hurt too much. But the blow never came, and she heard gentle reassurances, not angry yelling. It was Kate trying to comfort her.

"I'm going to get you off the floor okay? Just relax for me. I'll have you back on the table in a second, and then I'll look at your leg."

Although Seneca tried to focus on Kate's face as she was lifted effortlessly from the floor, the pain was overwhelming. Kate collected the hot pack and set it next to Seneca's leg but didn't put it back on.

"I'm going to have to take a look at your leg, Seneca. I'm going to try to avoid hurting you. Tell me if I'm doing too much."

"It's okay," Seneca managed to gasp, turning on her side and pulling her left leg to her body, instinctively curling into the fetal position, but not daring to move her right leg at all. "It will pass… be fine…give me a minute."

Seneca was vaguely aware of Kate settling on the table near her head. She was hypersensitive to people in her personal space so she felt Kate's hand move toward her back, as if to rub it, then stop just before making contact.

After what felt like a lifetime, Seneca finally managed to stretch back out and slowly sit up. Her face felt hollow, like it always did when the pain became overwhelming. She saw the guilt and remorse on Kate's face and was embarrassed by her reaction. She'd had plenty of people explain to her why she was so jumpy and why any unexpected touch created the panic that surged uncontrollably, but she was still ashamed when others saw her so weak.

"I'm very sorry. I didn't mean to do that to you," Seneca said, wanting to erase the sadness in Kate's eyes. It wasn't her fault that Seneca was so screwed up. "What are these?" Seneca picked up one of the pairs of pants, the only one that hadn't landed on the floor when she jerked awake.

"Don't you dare apologize to me. You told me you didn't like to be touched. I wasn't thinking. I'm sorry."

Seneca struggled to smile, her body still shaky from the jolt of adrenaline and pain. "Truce then, no more apologies." Seneca held the pants, shaking, waiting for an answer.

Kate still didn't look convinced she should stop apologizing, but she relented. "They're pants. Your pants, actually. I thought it would be easier to get them for you than wait until we both had a free moment to go shopping. Besides, this was a new and exciting challenge for my wife."

Seneca raised her eyebrows in question, still not completely sure her stomach wouldn't rebel if she opened her mouth.

"She loves to shop. She takes special pride in being able to shop for anyone and not only get clothes they would like, but also get their size perfect. I described you, and she did her magic."

Seneca thought they looked close enough; she had probably worn worse even if they were a little off in size. Seneca couldn't get a great look at them since her arms were shaking so badly she didn't dare hold them out. She had looked weak enough in front of Kate and was still going to have to ask for her help to get home. She laid her head back with a sigh and tried to gently flex her leg. The pain returned and took her breath away.

The swift intake of breath was clearly audible in the quiet room. Kate looked down at Seneca with a no-nonsense look of concern. Whatever she was about to say wasn't for show. "You're welcome to come home with me tonight. My wife and I would be happy to have you. I'll be honest. I'm a little worried about you."

Seneca averted her eyes, touched that Kate would offer, but also ashamed she appeared so weak that Kate would think she couldn't manage on her own. "I'm fine. Well, I will be. This happens sometimes. I'm probably going to need your help getting home though." Seneca figured her face was giving away every emotion. She was conflicted about Kate's offer but also deeply embarrassed about having to admit needing Kate's help.

Seneca could see Kate was a little conflicted too. Or perhaps lost was a better descriptor. Maybe her wife was better at dealing with a puddle of pain.

"Is there someone you would rather I call?"

The pain made her feel so drained even shaking her head was a hardship. She was already dreading having to explain to Britt why she couldn't walk. Dylan's face flashed in her mind, but she pushed it away. She didn't want anyone, especially Dylan, to see her like this. "No, but if you don't mind getting me home, I'd appreciate it."

Kate nodded and indicated Seneca should stay put while she gathered her belongings.

"There's nothing for you to be ashamed of, Seneca," Kate said softly as she approached the treatment table again. This time she moved slowly and alerted Seneca to her presence.

Seneca jerked again, this time because of Kate's words. She kept her eyes closed, but she knew Kate had seen her reaction. After a moment, when it became clear she wasn't going to answer and Kate didn't push her to, she opened her eyes and sat up slowly. Her injured leg felt as though it had a fifty-pound weight attached to it. Thankfully, the excruciating pain had been reduced to a dull ache, but she knew from experience she wouldn't be able to put weight on it yet.

She hated that she needed to lean so heavily on Kate to make her way out of the training room. She thought about the last time her leg had flared up this badly, when she had been completely alone. She had crawled and hopped back to where she needed to be, so emotionally and physically drained that she didn't get out of bed for days after. She wondered if it would be different this time. Now she had people to lean on, at least as much as she would allow, both literally and figuratively. She hated the thought, but Kate's help and reassuring words were comforting. *Is it weak to allow someone to help you?* She couldn't think enough to answer. The pain was too great.

Chapter Seven

Dylan tapped her pen unconsciously on her desk, the incessant rhythm drawing annoyed stares. Her attention was focused on the door to the small classroom. All day she'd been looking forward to Ancient Inventions, and every time she asked herself why, a pleasant fluttering in her stomach accompanied the memory of Seneca King.

There was something alluring about Seneca. She was incredibly good-looking, her face and body lean and angular, but Dylan was drawn more to the parts of Seneca she couldn't see and didn't understand. It wasn't her weakness that drew her; in fact, it was her strength in the face of a certainly difficult past. Seneca was no doubt guarded, but she was also warm, intelligent, and tender. Dylan couldn't help it if she was attracted to the school's beautiful recluse. Besides, the wild rumors couldn't all be true, and given that, it was sort of like being attracted to a movie star, one who had played a wide variety of exciting, dashing, sometimes unsavory characters. Like a hot, female, swashbuckling pirate captain of the high seas.

Although she had only met her twice, Dylan didn't get the feeling Seneca was the type to be late anywhere. She seemed too controlled. As the minutes ticked by and class was about to begin, she became worried. Realizing she had no idea where Seneca lived or how to contact her, Dylan began the pen tapping in earnest. Something didn't feel right. The fact that she was so distraught was confusing, but was comforting at the same time. It was nice to care about someone, especially since she had lost a lot of what she cared about at Sophia since returning from her time abroad.

Two minutes before class was to begin, the professor strolled through the door, her arms filled to capacity with books, posters, and a laptop. She wasn't known for her organizational skills. Dylan sighed and took one final look at the door, resigned to the notion that Seneca wasn't coming. Following close on the professor's heels and stopping now and again to scoop up an item that had made a daring escape from the tangle in the professor's arms, was a woman Dylan had never seen before. She didn't think there was a TA for the class.

Dylan studied her carefully, noting her short stature, shoulder-length black hair, and calm brown eyes. Those same eyes lit with recognition when they met Dylan's, and she started toward her, hand held out in greeting.

"You must be Bob."

Dylan's stomach flipped with pleasure. Seneca was the only one to call her that.

"Yes, or so Seneca has named me. It's actually Dylan. Are you a friend of hers?"

"Dylan, nice to meet you. I'm Britt, and yes, I'm a friend of Seneca's. She asked me to give you this and apologize for not being able to attend class this afternoon."

Britt started to go after handing her a wrinkly note on a torn out piece of lined notebook paper, but Dylan pulled her back.

"Is she okay?"

Britt hesitated and glanced around at the people watching them. She jerked her head toward the door and quickly exited the classroom. Dylan was hot on her heels.

"She's okay. She asked me to give you that," Britt said once they were out of the room. She nodded at the note clutched in Dylan's hands.

"If she's so okay, where is she? And why did you motion me out here if she is really okay?" Dylan asked skeptically.

Britt raised her eyebrows at the note again, clearly wanting Dylan to read it and let her escape the twenty questions.

Dylan held up a finger, silently asking Britt to wait while she read it.

Bob,

I didn't want you to think I was avoiding you after dinner the other night. I had a wonderful time. It will be a night I remember fondly.—Seneca

Dylan looked up, confused, but she was alone. Britt was nowhere to be seen. Dylan glanced back at the note, feeling sick at the finality she read there. Seneca was either very ill and wouldn't be back for a long time, or she had effectively ended any chance at a repeat of their dinner together. Dylan didn't like either option. She made a decision quickly, raced back into the classroom, made a lame excuse about not feeling well, grabbed her backpack, and sprinted out of the building. She scanned the area, looking for Britt. The campus was quiet, most of the students already in their morning classes. She spotted Britt and ran to catch up.

"I don't accept," Dylan said, pulling to a stop next to Britt.

"Accept what?" Britt asked. She looked startled to see Dylan by her side, flushed and breathing heavily.

"This," Dylan said, waving the note. "I'm taking it back to Seneca and telling her I don't accept."

Britt didn't seem to know what to do. "I'm not sure this is up for debate. Besides, I'm just the delivery woman. She asked me to deliver the note, not bring you back."

"Right, that's why I need you to tell me where she is," Dylan said.

"She's not really up to seeing anyone right now."

"She saw you." Dylan wasn't sure why it was so important to see Seneca. Maybe it was because the note scared her. Since she'd returned from Australia, the weight of the expectations in her life were stifling, but Seneca had provided a moment of grounding, and Dylan was desperate not to lose that. She thought Seneca had

had a good time, the note said she did, so she was confused at the way it seemed to shut down their new friendship altogether.

"I live with her," Britt said. "She has to see me, although I don't know if she even wanted me around, to be honest."

"Oh," Dylan said coolly, a surge of jealousy in her gut. *So that's why she doesn't want anything more to do with me. Why does it matter?*

"Shit," Britt said under her breath, looking highly uncomfortable. "Why do you want to see her? If it's to yell and scream and tell her what a jerk she is, forget it. She already knows and I'm not going to let you." Britt held Dylan's gaze, seemingly challenging her to tell the truth.

Dylan suddenly remembered where she and Seneca had first met and looked at Britt with horror. "You don't mind her sleeping with other people?"

Britt looked completely caught off guard, obviously not expecting Dylan to answer her question with another.

"She's an adult, and I'm not her mother. Why would I care?"

"I wouldn't want to share her," Dylan said quietly, not wanting to offend Britt but knowing that wasn't the kind of relationship she could ever enter into.

"Answer my question and then I'll answer yours a little more precisely," Britt said, the challenge back in her voice.

"I don't want to yell at her. I would never yell at her, and I don't think she's a jerk at all. Rumors are just rumors. I only deal in facts, and she's been nothing but wonderful to me. I want to ask her about this." Dylan held the note up again, this time feeling more defeated. She didn't know why she was fighting so hard to see a woman who was quite possibly not into seeing her again. "I really enjoyed having dinner with her the other night. We just had dinner, by the way. Nothing happened. If you two are together then you should know that. I know she goes down to the bar, but it might be different if it's with someone on campus. I was hoping we could be friends, and I'm confused what this means and I want to make sure she's okay. You aren't really convincing me that she is."

Britt sighed, not looking at all happy. She motioned Dylan to follow. "Be gentle with her. She has her reasons for being how she is and she's feeling very vulnerable today. That's not the best time to bring up these kind of issues." She pinched the bridge of her nose and closed her eyes. "Hopefully, she won't be too pissed off with me. Don't make me regret this."

Dylan nodded, planning what she wanted to say. She didn't know what she wanted from Seneca. Definitely the chance at friendship, but she wasn't sure about anything else. It would help if Seneca weren't so damned good-looking. And charming. And, well, all the other stuff.

Britt led the way silently up the stairs at Razor House and stopped outside a fourth floor room. She took a deep breath, clearly steeling herself.

"Hang out here a second. Let me warn her you're here." Britt went inside and closed the door behind her.

Dylan bounced lightly from foot to foot, not knowing what to expect.

"Oh," Britt said, sticking her head back out the door, "we're not together, just roommates. I thought you might want to know that."

"You could have led with that," Dylan said testily, struggling to keep Britt from seeing just how happy the news made her.

She paced in the hall as she listened to Britt's muted voice announcing her presence. Another voice, one barely recognizable as Seneca's, answered and quickly grew louder with anger. *Doesn't sound like she's happy I'm here.*

A few minutes later, Britt poked her head out again and gave Dylan a sad smile. "I didn't think this was a good idea. She said she'll see you in class in a couple days."

"Why?" Dylan asked, unnerved by the worry etched across Britt's face.

"She, she said…"

"If there's no good reason, then let me in." Dylan took a step closer, determined. She knew she had no right to demand entry and wasn't even sure why it mattered so much. She was worried, probably more than she should be, considering she had only spent a few hours with Seneca. There was just something about her that had gotten under Dylan's skin, and she was desperate to see her again, if for no other reason than to assure her own wild imagination that she was okay.

Britt sighed, looked back into the room, and stepped out of the way.

Dylan fought back a gasp when she entered the room. Seneca was lying on her bed, spread limply on the sheets. Her right leg was propped up on two pillows, although she shifted uncomfortably every few seconds. She looked at Dylan and her eyes weren't the same as the ones she remembered from their time at dinner. They had, at times, looked haunted and hollow, but today they looked dead. There was no sparkle at all, nothing to distinguish deep brown iris from dark black pupil. Her skin was covered in a thin sheen of sweat and she looked drawn.

Recognition fluttered briefly in Seneca's eyes, but her expression didn't change, as if the effort it took to breathe and lie still had sapped every useful bit of energy she contained.

Dylan drew nearer, holding up her hand to halt Seneca's attempt to sit up. But she ignored Dylan and got unsteadily to her feet, obviously trying to avoid putting any weight on her damaged leg. She lost her balance as she reached for her cane and was forced to place some weight on her leg. She stifled a cry and started to fall. Dylan rushed forward and caught Seneca before she hit the ground. Dylan felt Seneca tense and struggle against her, but she held tight, because if she didn't, Seneca would hit the floor.

Britt was near her desk, but Seneca had already waved her away.

"Seneca, it's just me, Bob. We're both going down to the floor, okay?"

Dylan made sure Seneca was safely on the ground before she let go. Seneca pulled away immediately and skittered a few feet away, her eyes wild, her body drawn into itself. She looked feral. Dylan had never seen anything quite like it. Whatever had, and continued, to cause Seneca this much pain was something she wasn't sure she could break through. She wanted to hug away Seneca's troubles, but she figured wrapping her in a hug wouldn't be welcome. She settled for poking her gently on the bottom of her sneaker, on the good leg.

"You okay?" Dylan asked. The pain and fear looked like it was squeezing the life out of her. "Do you want help getting your shoes off? Doesn't seem like you need them in bed."

While Dylan waited for Seneca's breathing to return to normal, Seneca avoided looking Dylan in the eye. Her face was red and she looked volatile. Dylan was worried she had crossed a line. Britt looked like she was worried about that too.

"She won't take them off," Britt said. "In case she needs to make a break for it, I guess." Britt sounded annoyed, but Dylan guessed it was concern more than anger.

"Bob, why did you come here?" Seneca asked cautiously, surprising Dylan when her words lacked the anger she expected.

Dylan, still crouching a few feet from Seneca, took a few tentative frog steps forward. "I wanted to see you. You left me that weird note and now that I'm here…what's wrong? What can I do to help?"

"Nothing, I'm fine. Please leave." Seneca's words were stronger now.

Dylan didn't want to leave, but she hadn't been invited over, and if that's what Seneca wanted, she couldn't insist she stay. "Sure, as soon as you tell me about this." Dylan held up the note Britt had given her.

"What is there to tell?" Seneca sounded tired and a little angry.

"You had a nice time at dinner and that's it, never going to happen again? Am I reading this right?"

"That about covers it," Seneca said, pulling herself backward across the floor, back toward her bed.

"Well, I don't accept your brush-off. I had a great time. You admitted you did as well. Therefore, I see no reason not to do it again." Dylan held her ground, knowing it could blow up on her at any minute. She could see the struggle for control, both physical and emotional, playing out across Seneca's face.

"Oh," Seneca said, looking confused. "So if I say no more, but you say yes, your vote wins? I don't understand how this works. Don't I get a vote here?" Seneca pulled herself onto the bed, careful not to put any weight on her leg. "Now all of a sudden what I want doesn't matter? I expected more from you, Bob."

Dylan had expected resistance, but the words still stung. She wondered if Seneca knew what an expressive face she had. If someone bothered to pay even a bit of attention, everything was laid out there for the world to see. Right now, Seneca's face was contorted, not with anger, but with fear. Dylan didn't think now was the time to ask what she was so scared of.

"Have you eaten anything today?" Dylan asked.

"I just said I don't want to see you for meals, Bob," Seneca said, finally sounding angry.

"Given your bad case of the grumpy-uglies, I'm just going to answer my own question in the negative. I'm going to bring you some food. With all you're dealing with right now, you should at least eat something."

"Amen to that," Britt said from her desk. Seneca glared at them both.

"Why would you be nice to me and bring me food?" Seneca asked, confusion back on her expression and in her voice.

"Call me an idiot, but I'm choosing to believe that your personality is a little more along the lines of the you I have class and coffee with and not the ass that is sitting on your bed. I like the Seneca I met in class and would like to continue to be friends with that version of you. When you chase away the grumpies, maybe that's something you'd like too. Let me know."

CHAPTER EIGHT

Seneca saw Kate look her way with annoyance as she released the third long, heavy sigh. She was back at work after her leg calmed down enough for her to walk. It was the end of her shift, and Kate was about to turn over the golf cart for Seneca to put away. She knew she had been agitated and distant the whole afternoon, and it was possible she had lost count of the sighs. They kept sneaking out.

It didn't help that her lunch had consisted of what was left of the food Dylan had brought over. Dylan had left the food outside their door and slipped a note under the door with instructions for Britt to make sure Seneca ate. She'd also left a postcard with a picture of a koala toy, and despite the pain, that cute little creature had made Seneca smile. It wasn't fair how she had treated Dylan, especially since she was only trying to bring her some relief.

"Something on your mind?" Kate asked.

Seneca struggled to find an answer to Kate's question. She knew she had been distracted all shift and she felt bad about that. She felt like Kate would probably have some good advice for her, and the slight exasperation in Kate's voice made her think perhaps she should explain her behavior. In truth, she had been beating herself up about the way things had gone with Dylan, and perhaps Kate could help.

"I think I might have screwed up royally," she said, looking for any sign of recrimination in Kate's face. She didn't find any. "I was an asshole to someone, and I think I ruined any chance I had for…anything."

Seneca couldn't articulate just what she had ruined a chance at. Certainly she didn't want a relationship. She didn't do relationships. Friendships were enough of a struggle. But did she really only want Dylan as a friend? Until Dylan came barging in all heroic and idealistic, Seneca hadn't been able to even consider getting up on her own. But somehow Dylan inspired her to stand up and take a few wobbly steps. She couldn't stop picturing the moment Dylan walked into the room and how beautiful she looked. Britt had told her she was outside, and every fiber of her being screamed for Dylan to stay away, but the moment she walked through the door, she felt nothing—no pain, no anger, no fear. She just saw her.

"Everyone is an asshole sometimes. Have you tried apologizing?"

"I'm not sure I can," Seneca said sheepishly. "I wasn't very nice…" The next thought caught her off guard. "I think at the time I might have meant what I said and felt. Sometimes the pain messes me up in all kinds of ways."

"But now things are different?" Kate asked, giving away none of her thoughts, much to Seneca's frustration.

"I don't know," Seneca said. "I don't think I can tell her I'm sorry until I figure that out. If I say I'm sorry and I still mean what I said, then I'll have to do it all over again. And if I don't mean it any more then…" *Holy shit.*

"Sometimes it's good to apologize for the *way* we say things, even if we meant what we said," Kate said noncommittally. "Do you mind putting the cart away? I'll meet you back in the field house."

Seneca was happy for the time to gather her thoughts. It felt good to talk to Kate. She had never had an adult who gave a damn about her feelings. She laughed when she realized she was technically an adult now too, but Kate still seemed like a much wiser, worldlier woman, and Seneca was afraid she would always feel like a scared little girl.

When she got back to the field house, Kate had already straightened up and turned out the lights. She was pulling the door shut when Seneca came around the corner.

"You doing anything for dinner?" Kate asked.

Seneca hesitated, wondering if this was Kate feeling sorry for her.

"I'm hungry, kiddo, and I have someone who has been asking to meet you. Thought tonight might be a good night. If you don't have plans, of course." Kate seemed able to read Seneca's mind.

"Nope, no plans. Do I need to bring anything?"

"Just you. My car's over this way, and I'll give you a ride back after dinner."

"It's no trouble. I can walk back," Seneca said quickly.

Kate looked at her with an assessing expression. "Don't take this the wrong way, but it's ten miles. I don't walk it, and I'm certainly not going to let you walk it. I'll give you a ride back, okay?"

Seneca nodded. Kate had just told her that her leg condition was a factor in some of her decisions, but somehow that didn't seem as threatening as it once might have. She wasn't sure how, but in a few weeks, her life had started to look completely foreign. For years, she had spent every moment protecting herself physically and emotionally, but suddenly she was breaking all sorts of her rules. *When did that start? Bob. It all started with a dance with Bob.* Seneca groaned.

"You okay? I won't be cooking if that's what you're worried about."

Seneca smiled at the self-deprecating joke; it was very hard not to like Kate. "No, I wasn't worried about your cooking. I think I just realized I need to make that apology."

❖

Kate's wife was a wonderful cook. Seneca couldn't remember a meal she had enjoyed so much, not even the first one after she'd woken up in the hospital and was finally free to eat anything she wanted. Although it was nice to be amidst such domestic bliss, it left her unsettled. She didn't think that was something she desired or hoped for, but watching the way Kate worshipped her wife, falling all over herself praising the meal and even doing the dishes after, Seneca felt her acute isolation.

Loneliness wasn't a stranger, but this emotion felt different. She had been lonely most of her life, never fitting in anywhere, merely taking up space. It didn't much matter to the people around her if she was there or not, and only a few people had ever noticed if she slipped away. Until Shannon, Seneca hadn't realized what it meant to be part of a household, but that had quickly evaporated as Shannon took things to the other extreme.

Watching Kate and her wife, Lisa, Seneca saw what a relationship was supposed to look like, one filled with love, respect, and equality. It was a completely new concept. She had never been around two people quite like them. Much to her annoyance, as she watched Lisa wipe a smudge off Kate's cheek, Seneca's mind jumped to Dylan. The image of her filled her thoughts, the way she had looked the first time Seneca saw her, then again in class, and finally how hurt she had looked standing in Seneca's room, offering her friendship, only to be rudely turned away.

Another loud sigh escaped, and she itched to run from the picture of domestic bliss before her. It was too real and too painful. Seeing what was possible created a heartbreaking ache at the loss of what Seneca didn't think she could ever have. Although she hadn't been to the bar, on the prowl as Britt called it, since the night she had danced with Dylan, tonight she needed something to take the edge off. The arms of a beautiful woman, and the well-defined game played by her rules, had always blunted the edge of dark emotion that filled her.

Even as she thought of the night's potential, however, the idea held less appeal than it should have. What she was feeling now wasn't strictly loneliness and wasn't something an anonymous other could drive away. In truth, she had no idea what she was feeling, and that was more terrifying than anything. Not knowing meant she couldn't find a coping strategy. No strategy meant no control. The whole thing was just fucking unacceptable.

Seneca pulled herself from her thoughts to see Kate and Lisa watching her intently. She wondered how long she had been lost in thought. Kate looked contemplative. Lisa looked worried.

Kate moved next to Seneca and slowly, carefully, and with plenty of warning, put her arm around Seneca's shoulder. "Don't go to the bar tonight, kiddo. There's no answer for you there."

Seneca's head snapped up in surprise. She had no idea how Kate knew what she was thinking. She also knew Kate was right. She nodded slightly, sagging into the couch. She didn't want to spend the night alone, and although she lived with Britt, she had shut her out of her pain for so long she couldn't imagine letting her share any of it now. Britt had been a good roommate and a friend, but Seneca didn't want to scare her away with the reality of just how screwed up she really was.

"I'm not sure I want to be alone tonight," Seneca said, her voice barely above a whisper. She felt weak and vulnerable and had already imposed enough on Kate and her wife's hospitality. She wasn't even sure why she was confessing at all. There was just something about Kate that offered calm in Seneca's constant storm.

"Then don't be. Stay here," Kate said, glancing at Lisa for confirmation. Lisa nodded her consent, her face showing both concern and compassion.

"I can't...I mean I...thank you, but..." Seneca didn't know what to say. She wanted to refuse almost as much as she wanted to accept.

"Tell you what," Kate said, standing and rubbing her hands together happily. "Why don't we head upstairs and watch the ballgame, and you can think about it and decide later. Lisa's also a master baker and you haven't had dessert yet."

Kate raised her eyebrow in question at Seneca who nodded, trying to conceal her happiness. Somewhere along the line, Kate had figured her out with surprising ease. She had said she would show her the way through life, but Seneca hadn't expected her to make it look so damned easy. Panic settled in her chest when she realized Kate and Lisa didn't actually know much about her. They knew nothing about the nightmares, or what had caused them, and she didn't think they would enjoy waking up to a twenty-something screaming on their couch.

"I don't think you want me here overnight. I, um, don't always sleep really well. I have…dreams, sometimes." Seneca didn't want to look like a complete psycho. They had been so nice to her, and she didn't want to ruin it. Her weakness should have bothered her more, but she was too tired physically and emotionally to worry about it.

"Like I said, let's worry about that later," Kate said and motioned for Seneca to follow her up the stairs. "I've got a huge TV up here. It's like you're at the game. Sometimes Lisa catches me wearing my glove like I'm going to catch a foul ball."

Lisa placed her hand on Seneca's shoulder, and she flinched and immediately felt bad about it when Lisa pulled her hand away quickly. Seneca forced control of her breathing. She reached out and squeezed Lisa's hand. She didn't want her to think she had done anything wrong. She took the tray of brownies from the counter. "Do you have an extra glove?"

"She is completely insane about the Red Sox," Lisa said, looking fondly up at Kate, who was eyeing the brownies. "She made us plan our wedding around the playoffs in 2004. I told her it was a good thing they won that year because if it was just another year of the 'curse,' I was cursing her and moving out."

Seneca gawked at Lisa, not sure if she was joking. She couldn't believe they would throw away what they had over a baseball game.

"And so I wrote a letter to the Sox asking them to please win, otherwise my fiancé was calling off the wedding," Kate said with a grin.

Seneca finally started to catch on that they weren't serious. "You didn't actually write to them did you?"

"Absolutely I did. I wasn't about to lose the love of my life because of another Buckner moment. I had to be sure everyone was on their game."

Lisa was laughing now, and Seneca was staring at them in complete amazement. "They wrote back and said they were trying their level best and good luck with the wedding," Lisa said, smiling at Kate and giving Seneca a gentle prod up the stairs. "She framed the damn thing too. It's upstairs. You two enjoy the game. I'll be up to join you in a little while. I'm taking Hank for a walk."

Seneca looked at the eager chocolate Lab and figured he must know it was time to go out. His tail was threatening to punch a hole in the cabinets. As she limped up the stairs after Kate, her mind wandered back to Dylan. She found herself wishing Dylan was there to share in the somewhat surreal feeling dinner party, and she didn't know why. She felt guilty once again about the way she had treated Dylan the last time they spoke and had an overwhelming urge to make it right.

"May I use your phone?" Seneca asked impulsively. "I don't have a cell phone. No one has ever had a reason to call me, and it was just too expensive."

Kate darted into one of the spare rooms on the second floor and grabbed the receiver. She flipped on the lights, revealing a nicely furnished office.

"Take as long as you need. I'll be at the end of the hall in the bonus room. Can't miss it, huge TV, cheering, or cursing, depending on how the game is going."

Seneca called Britt first. She assured her she was fine and asked for Dylan's campus phone number. Sophia was still old-fashioned enough to have room landlines. It took Britt a moment to find it online, and while she was busy, Seneca wondered if she was making a huge mistake.

Britt read off the number and then added, "I think you're doing the right thing. Dylan seems like a great lady."

Seneca wondered when everyone in her life had developed the ability to read her mind, but said nothing as she grunted her thanks and hung up. Her stomach knotted into a nervous ball as she started to dial Dylan's number. She had no idea what she was going to say. Dylan answered on the second ring, and the sound of her voice caused Seneca to lose hers.

"Hello? Anyone there?"

"Bob, hi, it's Seneca," she stuttered, knowing she sounded like a fool.

"Oh, hi." Dylan's reply was surprised and decidedly cool.

"I…I wanted to say I was sorry, you know, for the way I treated you the other night. I was—"

"An asshole?"

"Yes, that's a good way to put it. So I'm sorry for that." Seneca tried desperately to think of something to make Dylan laugh.

"I was about to head downtown for a movie, if you're interested," Dylan said. It felt like a test.

"Uh, I can't tonight. I'm at Kate's house."

"Oh."

Dylan sounded pissed and hurt. Seneca guessed she failed. "Kate's my boss from the training room. She asked me to dinner to meet her wife," Seneca said. "Maybe we could do something later this week?" She resisted the urge to hang up in a panic.

"Oh." This time Dylan's voice was much lighter, but still cautious. "Sure, that sounds good. I'll see you in class. Let me know if you ever want more than that. Have a good night. Thanks for calling."

Dylan hung up before Seneca could respond. She stared at the phone, completely baffled by what had just happened. Maybe some of her uneasiness had come through? Somehow she didn't think Dylan had gotten the "I'm really sorry I was a jerk. Let's start over" message. She seemed more upset after the apology than before.

"Everything okay?" Kate asked when Seneca finally found her way to the bonus room and the baseball game.

Seneca slumped onto the couch next to Kate and didn't answer right away. The emotions swirling within were confusing, and she didn't know how she felt. She again had the uneasy feeling that her life was quickly becoming unrecognizable. This friendship thing was much harder than others made it look.

"I'm not sure. I think I'm confused."

Kate waited for more, seemingly not wanting to push.

"I met this girl," Seneca said.

Kate nodded knowingly and sympathetically at Seneca. "Ah. I see. That right there complicates a life."

"Yeah, I think so too. She was the one I was a jerk to. I called to apologize, but she seemed more upset after."

Seneca was miserable. Although private and solitary, she never wanted to be the cause of someone else's pain. That was a small part of the reason she only hooked up with a woman once. More than that and people could get hurt. She knew she would be worthless in a relationship and didn't want to burden anyone with her pain. Aside from that, she had been on the receiving end of someone else's nastiness and vowed never to complete the circle. And she'd never be at anyone's mercy again either.

"Why do you think that?" Kate asked. "For the record, I have a hard time imagining anyone being angry at you. Frustrated maybe, but not angry."

Surprised by Kate's assessment, she quickly relayed the contents of her conversation with Dylan. She was vaguely aware that she had never shared anything like this with another human being, but instinctively, she trusted Kate to protect her and her privacy.

"She wants a date," Kate said matter-of-factly after listening to Seneca's recount. "She also left it completely up to you to initiate said date. The ball's in your court, kiddo."

"Holy hell," Seneca said, feeling the color draining from her face. "Britt and I talked about dating the other night, and it sounded complicated. I just screwed up an apology where all you have to do is say 'I'm sorry.'"

Kate looked like she was trying not to laugh but was unsuccessful. "I don't think a date should scare you that much.

They're kinda fun. And even the rotten ones usually result in a good story."

Kate's laughter was infectious, and Seneca soon joined in. For the first time in as long as she could remember, she felt a bit relaxed. At least for one night, she allowed herself to let loose and enjoy herself. The date problem could wait. There wasn't anything she could or wanted to do about it right now anyway.

"Tell me about her," Kate said.

"I don't really know her all that well. We danced once and I...left quickly." That was one way to describe it. "We have a class together and we had dinner after it one night."

"I don't need to hear her underwear size or social security number, just tell me about her. Not what you did with her, about her. You two did actually talk at dinner, right? Sometimes first impressions can be quite telling," Kate said gently, clearly hoping Seneca wouldn't close up again. She didn't.

"Okay, she's shorter than me, curly red hair. She spent a year in Australia last year and has one crazy ass mother."

"That's awfully technical and doesn't really tell me anything about her. I think you can do better." Kate waited patiently, her hands folded in her lap, her attention completely on Seneca.

"Hmm, all right. I think she's taking the class we both have to piss off her mom. She dated a girl for a few weeks in Australia, but I think that's it. She told me the first time I met her she absolutely wasn't sleeping with me. Oh, and she pretty much takes my breath away."

"Well, that certainly has potential," Kate said. "Might be worth considering that date idea."

Seneca knew Kate was right. She paid partial attention to the ballgame, Kate, or whatever else was happening around her. Dylan had mentioned a movie, and she sat there thinking of what it would be like to sit in a darkened theater next to her, holding her hand. Her palms started to tingle.

CHAPTER NINE

"You still haven't told us why the hot weirdo ran off so quickly the night she asked you to dance," Viv said, tapping her fake fingernail on the open textbook page she was clearly no longer interested in studying.

"And it's really remarkable I haven't given you every last detail when you ask with such polite grace," Dylan said, not bothering to hide her disdain.

"Oh come on, give us a break here. We all want to know. What's up with you lately?" Mary asked.

Dylan didn't know how to tell them that what "was up with her," was them. Or maybe it *was* her. Going away for her junior year had been a wonderful decision. Coming back, however, had been harder than she'd expected. Now she was a semester away from graduating and felt further from being an adult than at just about any point in her memory. How was that possible?

"Oh dear God, I know that look," Viv said. "You've got the Lady Walker blues. Why were you thinking about your mother?"

The longstanding joke about her mother helped ease a bit of the disconnect she felt with this group of women she had called friends for so many years. Only this foursome would be able to recognize the "Lady Walker Blues" as they called it.

"I wasn't even thinking about my mother. I was thinking about graduating and why anyone thinks I'm ready to be let loose on the world," Dylan said.

"Oh please, you've already been loose on the world. And did quite well, from what I hear."

Dylan wasn't convinced. "That was different. There weren't any expectations there. I could do whatever I wanted and wasn't asked to change the world. I'm talking real world, scary world, what the hell do I want to be when I grow up?"

"Well, you and Gert have more experience out in the big bad world than the rest of us three combined, so if you two don't know what you're doing, what hope do we have?"

"Seriously, though, Viv, you want to be a lawyer, right? And, Mary, you are going to medical school, and, Jess, I still don't understand what it is you're going to do, no matter how many times you explain it to me. Let's just go with engineering. And we all know Gert is going to be president."

"What's your point? I want to work at a world-class law firm and make partner by the time I'm thirty and then have plenty of time to do pro bono work. So what? Mary wants to be a doctor and set up medical clinics in developing countries. I don't know what Jess does either. I still don't get what your point is."

"My point is, everyone at this school could say the same thing we're saying. How many twenty-somethings actually change the world in the way they think they will in college?"

"Dylan, you need to take the buzzkill down a few notches," Jess said. "Why can't we be special and defy the odds? Your parents are rich and powerful. They must have done something right out of college."

"You know how my parents got all the money they have?" Dylan asked. "They were born. How special is that? This place is a cesspool for unrealistic and unattainable expectations, and it's making me crazy."

"I think that's something we can all agree on," Mary said quietly.

"Maybe we can change the subject?" Viv said. "Dylan, for the love of all things holy, tell us just one tidbit about Seneca King. I was the one who forced you to the bar that night, after all. I wanted to sleep with her. You got to dance with her. Give us a piece of something." Viv settled into her chair and crossed her arms. She didn't look like she was going to take no for an answer.

Dylan didn't know where to begin, or what to share. She was happy for the subject change, though, and thinking about Seneca was always welcome. "Well," she said, "she has a limp."

Viv, Mary, and Jess booed her loudly. "We all know that. We need something you can't tell from seeing her across campus. You also can't tell us she's hot."

"Why don't you tell me what you already know about her and I'll see what I can fill in for you?" Dylan said, feeling a little defensive. She had been about to explain how the limp wasn't a problem while wrapped in Seneca's arms dancing, but now she was going to keep that morsel to herself.

"We know she limps. We know she's damn hot. She works in the athletic training room. And she goes to the bar where you met her, sometimes picks up women and sleeps with them, but never the same one twice. And the rumor is she's really good in bed, but never takes her clothes off. That's unconfirmed. She also might belong to the mob, or be a drug dealer."

"Unconfirmed as well?" Dylan asked, annoyed. She didn't know why, but she was positive Seneca wasn't into anything shady and it felt awful to listen to her friends list facts about her so casually when they didn't know a thing about her. Granted, she didn't really know anything about her either, but when Dylan saw her in so much pain, Seneca didn't seem capable of hiding much of anything. She might not have been entirely pleasant, but she wasn't any of the things Dylan's friends, or others on campus, implied she was.

"So what can you add about the mystery woman?" Jess asked.

"I guess that about covers it," Dylan said. "I really don't know much more than you do. It was just one dance." She left out the dinner they shared, that they had a class together, that she'd spent some time in her dorm room, and that Seneca had called her not long ago. Those probably weren't the kinds of details they were looking for anyway. Sharing that information would be as good as strapping bacon to her ass and letting the dogs loose.

In truth, there wasn't much else to tell, even if she had wanted to. Since Seneca had called to apologize, they hadn't spoken much in class. Instead of sitting silently and quite awkwardly next to each other, Dylan had taken the childish approach and started avoiding Seneca. She showed up to class late and sat at the back of the room, disappearing quickly when the lecture was over. Seneca's silence bothered her more than she wanted to admit. The connection she had felt ever so briefly was absent, and she missed it. This was exactly why she refused to sleep with someone casually. She was sensitive and knew she would get hurt. After only one dance and dinner with Seneca, she felt the loss. It would be far worse if it had gone further, so maybe it was for the best after all. She sighed. If only she could really believe that.

Seneca stood outside the old, comfortable classroom, working up the courage to enter. She was already late for the lecture, but that hardly mattered. She figured the professor probably hadn't found her notes yet, and even if she had, she would be repeating what they had covered last class. Sometimes Seneca was amazed they covered any new material at all.

Despite the interesting professorial organizational technique, Ancient Inventions was Seneca's favorite class. But it wasn't so much the subject matter she found fascinating, though there was that too, as it was another student in the room who made her heart race.

Since the night of the apology, Seneca had been having dinner two nights a week with Kate and Lisa like clockwork. In that time she had started to realize how wonderful a true mentor and ally could be. Kate was nonjudgmental and soft-spoken but didn't mind telling Seneca when she thought she was out of her mind. In fact, Kate had done just that the previous night when Seneca admitted she still hadn't asked Dylan out on a date.

Seneca didn't want to ask Dylan out with nothing to give her in return. She didn't feel like a person worthy of dating, and she certainly had no idea what Dylan saw in her. Watching Kate and Lisa had shown her just how deficient she truly was. She felt like Dylan deserved better. The only problem was Seneca couldn't get Dylan out of her head, and not asking her out was as torturous as the thought of a date was terrifying. And Dylan was avoiding her, which sucked. It sucked even more than having Dylan see her at her lowest.

Last night, she had paced a rut into the carpet in Kate's bonus room and had ruined what probably would have been a rather enjoyable Red Sox playoff victory. Kate was patient to a fault, but Seneca felt bad and had finally come upon the only solution she felt comfortable with. It would be up to Dylan to see for herself that Seneca wasn't worth dating; she simply had no idea how to be a partner. But at least she could say she tried, which was more than she could say now.

Squaring her shoulders in what she hoped was a confident posture, she prepared herself to face Dylan. In truth, Seneca wouldn't really be facing Dylan at all. She was taking the easy way out by doing the asking during class when Dylan couldn't make a scene and tell her to kiss her ass. With that rather unpleasant thought in mind, Seneca ducked into class and made a beeline for Dylan's desk.

Dylan looked surprised to see Seneca and even more shocked to see her heading toward her, but she didn't look like it was an altogether unpleasant surprise. Seneca took comfort in that and picked up her speed. She hurriedly limped forward, gently set a stargazer lily and a small envelope on Dylan's desk, and limped past her to a seat farther up the room. Her heart was racing, and she knew her face was bright red. Her palms were sweaty, and she didn't like having all eyes in the class on her. But what mattered was what Dylan was thinking. She was too chicken to look at her, so she slumped behind her desk and focused on the book in front of her. She felt like a middle schooler passing a note in class, but it was the best she could do.

❖

"I finally did it," Seneca said almost as soon as she set foot in the training room for work.

Kate was at the computer, catching up on some paperwork before the influx of athletes arrived needing to be taped for practice and games. She looked up as Seneca bounded in.

"Finally did what, kiddo?" Kate was the only one to call Seneca that, but Seneca enjoyed the endearment. It made her feel loved and special. Both were new feelings. They were nice.

"Finally asked Dylan for a date. Remember how I told you she said her favorite flowers were lilies? I got her one of those too." Seneca looked around the training room to make sure they were alone. Many of the athletes had warmed to Seneca, some even chatting with her while she taped an ankle or applied a heat pack, but the rest of the school still harbored unknown fears of her, her past, her limp, and anything else they could think of that might somehow explain why she was such a loner.

"A date, huh? That's great. Where are you going?" Kate looked happy for her. "I'm glad you finally asked her out. I thought you were going to worry yourself into an ulcer last night. Or that I was going to have to chuck you out the window to stop the pacing." There was no censure in Kate's voice.

"Well, it's not really that kind of date. It's probably not technically a date at all. I asked her to be my partner in our class. We're going to make our invention together. See, after we learn all about the cool stuff the ancient people did, we have to re-create something just like they did. Should be pretty fun actually, but probably not a date. Not really." Seneca felt dejected. Saying it out loud made her feel silly. Sitting in the machine shop hammering away at a piece of sheet metal wasn't very date-like.

"Sounds like a study date to me." Kate continued with the paperwork in front of her.

"Are those real dates?" Seneca asked hopefully. She could see the questions in Kate's eyes, but she didn't ask them out loud. Mostly she seemed curious about Seneca's complete lack of understanding of the dating world. Maybe someday she would be able to share some of her past with Kate, but not today.

"A date is anything you make it," Kate said. "But I happen to be partial to the studying kind. That was how I met Lisa. It was the only way I could ask her out because I thought she was way out of my league."

"You did? But you two are so totally made for each other. I bet she saw that right away."

"Well, she says she did, but I took a little more time to believe it. I just didn't think I was good enough for her. But to be honest, after the first couple of study dates, we didn't get much studying done and she convinced me."

"Yeah, sometimes it takes a while to…Oh! You mean you two…and that was how you…oh." Seneca was flustered and ran her hand unconsciously up and down her abdomen, feeling the irregular bumps and crevices that now made up the anger-inflicted topography of her skin. She never let anyone see her less than fully clothed. She flushed and felt a little panicky.

"Hey, slow down, kiddo. It's just a study date. There are a lot of things that have to happen before you even think about getting to that. I doubt it will come up on the first date, especially if you're in class."

"Yeah, sorry, I just…sorry." Seneca's arms hung loosely at her sides, and she looked around desperately for something to do to keep her from having to meet Kate's eyes. Sometimes Seneca wanted to tell Kate about her past and about Shannon, but she always stopped herself. Kate was without a doubt the person she admired and trusted the most. Telling her about all that would probably drive Kate away, and Seneca didn't think she could take it. If she gave up some of the burden, only to lose Kate in the end, the memories and pain would feel twice as heavy. She didn't want to risk it.

She busied herself folding a fresh load of towels and tried not to think about Dylan. However, the harder she tried not to think about her, the more she intruded on every thought. Kate was right; dating eventually led to sex, and Dylan already knew Seneca wasn't picky with her partners, so she couldn't say she was waiting for marriage or was scared of sex. Somehow she didn't think that her usual rules of "I touch you, you don't touch me, and all my clothes stay on" would work very well with Dylan. *One thing at a time. You're getting way ahead of yourself.*

Seneca was violently folding the towels, slamming each one so hard on the stack that she threatened to topple the entire pile after each folding. She was really just moving unfolded towels from one pile to a slightly more tidy pile as she took out her stress on the defenseless linen.

Her unusual technique was clearly more than Kate could ignore. She started across the room, looking like she wanted to comfort, or at least reassure, Seneca. She approached slowly and made sure Seneca could hear her so as not to startle her and gently put a hand on her shoulder. The only reaction was an almost imperceptible flinch, much improved from the six-foot-high reaction she used to have when Kate surprised her.

"Kiddo, the only thing you have to worry about is having a good time. The rest will work itself out if you both want it to."

Kate probably expected Seneca to nod in agreement and continued folding towels, working out her demons silently and on her own, the way she usually did. She looked completely shocked when Seneca turned around and enveloped Kate in a bone-crunching hug. The reaction actually surprised Seneca as well, as she started to almost immediately pull out of the embrace, but Kate held her firmly and let her have a few minutes of safety and calm before letting her go.

"Thank you," Seneca said, almost too quietly to be heard. "I've never, it won't happen...thanks." She turned back to her towels, embarrassed.

"I'm always available for a chat, a meal, or even a hug."

She left without saying anything else. Apparently, the embrace had left her speechless. Whether it was the hug or just the emotional relief, Seneca no longer beat up the towels. Maybe, just maybe, Kate was right. Things would work themselves out.

CHAPTER TEN

Dylan held her breath as she opened the letter Seneca had left with the flower. She was amazed that Seneca remembered her flippant remark about her favorite flowers being lilies.

As she read Seneca's short, precise request, she didn't know what to make of it. It was not the date she had hoped for, but Dylan suspected it was Seneca's way of holding out the olive branch. Perhaps it was all she could manage. She took a moment to decide if a friendship with Seneca was what she was willing to sign on for. Whether "yes" was the right answer or not, it was the one she kept coming up with. She looked down at the note again. Of course she would be Seneca's partner for their ancient inventions project. If nothing else, it meant they would get to spend much more time together, and Seneca had said she knew her way around a metal shop. The formality of the request was also adorable. All week, Dylan had heard other classmates calling out to each other, seeking partners for their project, but Seneca had brought her a lily and a formal, written request. Hard to say no to that.

Seneca flew out of the classroom so quickly after the lecture, Dylan didn't have a chance to accept. She waited until after dinner and called Seneca's room phone.

"I accept and thank you for the lily," Dylan said when Seneca answered.

"What should we make? What's your major? What are you going to do when you graduate? We could do something for you to take with you," Seneca said.

"I'm a math major and I'm planning on going to business school. I don't think we should make an abacus."

"I'm not totally sure I agree. Those are pretty cool. I never would have guessed math major, Bob. And business? If I had any money or a business, I would totally trust you with it, but it doesn't seem like you."

Dylan agreed. "My cousins are doctors, lawyers, successful fundraisers for non-profits, even the rogue artist just showed her work at one of the most prestigious galleries in New York City. The corporate ladder was missing in the family tree." Perhaps that wasn't quite fair, but lately that was how it was starting to feel.

"Is it what you want to do?" Seneca asked.

"It's a good, respectable career with lots of options that will pay well and has good job security," Dylan said. She sounded like her father.

"You didn't answer my question," Seneca said.

"I know," Dylan said, feeling a little defeated. "I'll see you in class. Maybe we can do something that involves welding."

❖

Dylan put on her safety glasses and hunched over the scraps of metal she was about to weld together. She held the torch in her right hand and visualized the seam she wanted to create. Before she started, she snuck a glance at Seneca, who was resting her right hip against a pile of scrap metal and shielding her eyes from the glare of the welding torch. They weren't arc welding so they were both getting by without full-face shields. Dylan had been concentrating on the little puddle continuously forming between the two pieces of metal she had been working on for the past hour, but she'd been acutely aware of every subtle movement Seneca made.

She thought it must have something to do with the heat of the tiny space they had been working in together for the past few weeks, since they had started on their project. Dylan had been surprised by their reactions to each other. The first few "study dates" had taken place in the library as they pored over every book they could get their hands on, looking for the perfect combination of ingenious design and intriguing craftsmanship. Once she got the idea in her head, Dylan had been adamant about doing a project that required at least some welding. It was a skill she didn't feel she could graduate from college without, though she knew in real life she'd probably never use said skill. She didn't think corporate America had many uses for a welding torch. If it did, she'd be much more willing to join that particular workforce.

When they had settled on making an armored breastplate, Dylan had grabbed the book, opened it across her chest, spine out, and galloped around the room, fighting imaginary enemies with an unseen sword. In the end, Seneca had slain the good knight, catching her unawares with a well-directed and giggle-inducing poke to exposed ribs. Dylan laughed so hard she stumbled over Seneca's legs and ended up in her lap. She had felt terrible when she saw Seneca's face screw up in pain momentarily on impact, but when Dylan tried to get up, Seneca wrapped her arms around her waist and held her in place. Seneca looked even more shocked by the gesture than the pain, but Dylan had been thrilled by her impulsive gesture. They'd parted company quickly after that, and she'd wondered what Seneca spent the rest of the evening thinking about. She hadn't been able to stop wondering why she hadn't taken advantage of their proximity and kissed her.

Since then, every day she had spent in Seneca's company had reinforced her initial impression that Seneca was far more than she let people believe. She also had a sneaking suspicion she was completely smitten. What might come next was anyone's guess. Luckily, the slow pace that their flirtation was taking seemed to be working for both of them.

"Seneca?" Dylan asked, looking up at Seneca grinning madly down at her. "You okay?"

"What? Oh yes, fine," Seneca said quickly, looking guilty. "Did you need something?"

Dylan sighed in exaggerated frustration and pointed to the grinder sitting on the pile of metal scraps Seneca was leaning against.

"Oh, my turn already? Sorry, Bob." Seneca grabbed the grinder and picked up the still warm mass of metal Dylan had been working on. "Is it cool enough for me to grind yet?"

"It was a long daydream you were having. It's practically cold," Dylan said teasingly. She didn't mention just how easy Seneca's face was to read or the undisguised desire her eyes held. It was enough that they were spending time together, and Dylan wasn't ready for much more either. The idea of dating Seneca was exciting and terrifying.

Seneca's face reddened, but Dylan noticed she didn't draw away as violently or as quickly, physically or emotionally, as she had in the past. Maybe she finally knew Dylan was only teasing.

"Bob, I think I have you all figured out. You're a tease," Seneca said, as if reading Dylan's mind.

"Whatever took you so long to notice?" Dylan asked, keeping her voice light and batting her eyes dramatically.

Seneca's face grew serious and she looked earnestly down at Dylan, who was still crouching over their workspace. "I'm a little new at this. I'm trying. Just please be patient."

The pleading sound in Seneca's voice made Dylan want to pull Seneca into her arms and promise to protect her forever. Somehow, she knew that wasn't what Seneca needed and wasn't the basis for a relationship, or even a very good friendship. She smiled and nodded and pretended as if they were only talking about the teasing, but Dylan suspected Seneca was also asking for patience in any relationship they might have. Dylan was content with that, because she saw the way Seneca looked at her, and it made her feel like the most beautiful woman on the planet. For now, that was more than enough.

"Are you going to grind this down for me so I can see how we're doing? I think I might need your uber muscles again for some more hammering."

"Bob, I think you make me do that just so you can watch me sweat," Seneca complained half-heartedly, the lightness on her face giving away her true feelings.

"Maybe I do, or maybe I like those sexy arms of yours. Think you could wear a tank top for me tomorrow?"

Dylan surprised herself with her candor and watched in fascination as Seneca grew still and paled slightly before trying to hide her reaction by messing with the tools. This time Dylan didn't apologize for her comments or even mention Seneca's reaction. Seneca probably got told all the time how hot she was, but Dylan doubted Seneca ever believed it. Maybe she would if it was coming from Dylan.

"Well, in that case, stand back and let a woman get to work." Seneca puffed her chest out importantly and pushed off the metal heap. She ignored the tank top comment.

"And where would you like me to stand, ma'am? How about over here?" Dylan positioned herself directly in Seneca's line of sight and smiled her most alluring smile.

"Bob! I take it back. You're a flirt, not a tease." Seneca laughed. "How am I supposed to get any work done?"

Seneca ground down the extra metal from the novice weld and then heated another section of the metal armor and used a small hammer to pound it into the desired shape. The work was time-consuming, as the metal cooled quickly and had to be reheated often and the large gloves were bulky and awkward. After getting a shape she seemed happy with, she held up the armor for Dylan's inspection.

"Time for a test run," Seneca said as she handed the contraption to Dylan.

Dylan rolled her eyes and obligingly put it on. The breastplate slid perfectly over her shoulders and fit snugly around her waist. Seneca had made it the perfect size.

"You only do this because you don't want to be the tin can everyone feels the need to tap on."

Seneca nodded. "True. And the armor looks better on you."

Whenever either one of them tried the armor on and walked out into the main section of the shop to look in the mirror, their classmates felt it their duty to test the strength and authenticity of the armor. So far, Dylan had been tapped with a soon to be metal sword, and the handle of an imperial umbrella, and she had been shot with a small cannonball.

Early on in their attempts, one classmate had tried the same technique with Seneca donning the armor, and Seneca had bolted from the room. The incident seemed to reaffirm everyone's beliefs that Seneca was a lost cause, despite the way she acted when Dylan was around. They had decided it was safer to make the armor Dylan-sized, and, as usual, she hadn't asked Seneca why someone's touch bothered her so deeply. She let it go and they moved on. Eventually, she knew she needed to stop doing that if they were going to have any kind of future together. Seneca was going to have to trust her enough to share a bit more deeply with her. But a crowded workshop wasn't the place for that, and she could be patient.

"What do you think?" Seneca asked as Dylan returned unscathed from her harrowing trip across the larger room.

"Probably need to work on this side a little more. It sits off-kilter on my shoulders, but we can do that tomorrow. Also, someone has switched to bow and arrows for their project, and I was shot twice. We might need to consider a helmet with this thing because the shooter has terrible aim." Dylan glanced at her watch, wondering how long they had been trapped in the dungeonous machine shop. "Seneca! You're going to be late for work. Kate isn't going to be happy." Dylan hadn't met Kate, but Seneca spoke highly of her, and Dylan could see the changes in Seneca since she started working in the training room.

"I can call her and tell her I'm going to be a few minutes late. We still have to clean up." Seneca indicated the tiny metal shop behind her.

"I'll do it. Don't be late. Tell Kate hi for me."

"But, Bob—"

"Seneca, out of here now!" Dylan pointed at the door for emphasis.

"Fine. Thank you. But you know, I've worked up quite an appetite working so hard, and now you're being nice to me. I think I owe you dinner."

Dylan couldn't believe Seneca had just asked her out to dinner. She ignored just how happy it made her.

"When you smile like that, I want to reach out and touch it. I think if I could make contact with that ray of pure happiness, it could wrap a shield around me and sustain me through any hardship that might come," Seneca said quietly. "Wow, that just sounded a lot cheesier out loud than it did in my head."

"Have you been storing that one in your back pocket for just the right moment?" Dylan asked. The words were incredibly cheesy, but also rather sweet. "I happen to like a little cheese. I'm the one who wants to be wooed, remember? And there's nothing cheesier than that. Are you expecting hardship?"

"Are you implying I practice pick up cheeseball lines so I can whip them out when the time is right? You should know I'm not nearly skilled enough for that," Seneca said sweetly. "You never know when you might run into hardship. Is that a yes for dinner?"

"Yes. You are so sweet, Seneca King. Don't let anyone ever tell you otherwise."

Seneca leaned in to place a gentle, quick kiss on Dylan's cheek, then she pulled away hurriedly, looking embarrassed, and mumbled she would call after work before she limped as fast as she could from the room.

Dylan touched her cheek and glared at the few people who were openly staring at her or the doorway Seneca had just exited through, and she walked back into the metal shop feeling like she was floating ten feet off the ground. Because they were so infrequent and so out of character, special gifts like the kiss from Seneca took on more tenderness than they otherwise would have. Dylan knew Seneca had no idea, but she was subtly and ever so slowly beginning to sweep Dylan off her feet.

CHAPTER ELEVEN

I t's gonna rain tonight," Seneca said as Dylan walked up to greet her on the porch of Razor House.

"Really?" Dylan hadn't heard anything about rain, and she wasn't dressed for a downpour. Although the way Seneca was subtly trying to sneak a peek at her ass, she was glad she had chosen the outfit she did, even if it wasn't waterproof. "How do you know?"

Seneca hesitated and then pointed to her leg, lifting it off the ground just enough to emphasize her point.

"You come with a built in barometer? Well, why didn't you say so? Now I'll have to take you everywhere with me," Dylan said.

Color crept up Seneca's neck and face, but she didn't look upset.

"Does it hurt more in the rain?" Dylan asked, realizing that the weather might make it harder for Seneca to walk downtown.

Seneca shrugged. "A little, I guess."

Dylan figured that was about as clear an "it hurts like hell and I can barely walk" as she would ever get.

"Anything I can do?" Dylan knew Seneca was extremely independent, and while she didn't want to make her uncomfortable, she genuinely wanted to help if there was something she could do to ease her pain. That Seneca didn't react defensively was a good sign indeed.

"Britt tried to get me to bring my cane," she said.

"Is that code for, 'Bob, would you go upstairs and get my cane?'"

Seneca laughed. "You said it, not me. If Britt asks, it was all your idea and you made me use the damn thing."

"Be right back," Dylan said, taking the steps two at a time on her way to Seneca's fourth-floor room.

Britt looked surprised to see Dylan, out of breath and smiling, when she opened the door.

"She already left. Said she was going to meet you downstairs. I don't know how you would have missed her," Britt said.

"She did meet me downstairs. Apparently, it's going to rain," Dylan said matter-of-factly. "Do you mind if I grab something for her real quick?"

"I see you've adopted Seneca's habit of explaining things in one nonsensical sentence. Excellent." She ushered Dylan in.

"Do you know where she keeps her cane?" Dylan asked, looking around the room but not seeing it.

"Ah," Britt said, looking shocked. "It's in the closet. That's where she usually flings it when she considers actually using it. How in the world did you convince her to use it?"

Dylan heard the annoyance in Britt's voice at Seneca's stubbornness, but also noticed the concern in her eyes. Clearly, she cared about Seneca a lot. Wild, boiling jealousy gurgled up so fast Dylan barely had a chance to recognize it. It was like a bad case of heartburn, unpleasant, unwelcome, and too advanced for a couple Tums.

"You two don't….is there anything?" Dylan tried to clamp down the uncharacteristic emotions. So what if Seneca and Britt had had a thing? Britt had said there was nothing between them.

"Nope, never was, never wanted there to be, and never will be," Britt said quickly. She could probably see the crazy monster Dylan was morphing into. "I care about her as a friend only. Not sure why. She's drop-dead gorgeous, but my hormones have never taken me in that direction."

"Oh, good," Dylan said awkwardly, realizing she had been caught being insane, especially since this was only their first real date. She dove into the closet to look for the cane before she could embarrass herself any further.

"Be careful with her though. She likes you a lot. She's just so…be good to her."

"She likes me a lot?" Dylan said, all the other words fading into the background. "Did she say that?"

"She doesn't say much of anything about anything, but I think I can tell. If you live with someone long enough you pick up on things."

Dylan said good-bye and bolted down the steps feeling bulletproof. *She likes me a lot, she likes me a lot, she likes me a lot!*

"What took you so long?" Seneca asked in mock exasperation. "I'm wasting away down here."

Dylan handed Seneca her cane and cautiously ran her fingers along Seneca's side. She could feel every rib and each tight sinew of the wiry muscles beneath her hand.

Seneca saw the touch coming and Dylan could feel her brace for the contact, but instead of continuing to stay tense, she relaxed and pressed her side into Dylan's palm. She pulled away too quickly for Dylan's liking, almost seeming to realize what she was doing, but that brief moment left Dylan's fingertips tingling. Seneca was like a wild thing, and like all wild things, standing close to them electrified your soul.

"So where ya taking me?" Dylan asked.

"Don't know. Thought we could stroll around, see what smells good."

That would be you. "Lead the way." Dylan followed Seneca as she descended the porch steps, noticing that the cane significantly diminished the limp. Although she leaned heavily on the wooden aid, it appeared to make walking easier for her.

As they made their way across campus, Dylan became aware of the curious stares and outright shock on peoples' faces as they passed. Each one stared unabashedly at Seneca and continued to watch her even after they had passed. Dylan knew Seneca was quite the curiosity on campus, but she had never really noticed the gawking.

"If they don't stop staring at you, I'm going to take your cane and smack someone with it," Dylan said angrily, and not all that quietly as yet another passerby paused for a thorough inspection.

"They're pity stares," Seneca said as if that explained it. "Happens every time I use this damn thing." She indicated the cane, but rushed to continue when she saw Dylan about to apologize for insisting she use it. "The problem is it helps so much I have a hard time not using it. When my leg feels okay, I leave it at home though. I get tired of their pity."

"They're pity stares? Why do they pity you? You are the strongest, most wonderful woman I know. Your leg is about the last thing they should notice about you." Dylan flushed as the words tumbled out, but she held her ground. Someone had to tell Seneca how amazing she was.

"I…thank you." She reached out and pulled Dylan's smaller hand into her own, smiling when Dylan's fingers entwined with hers. "There. Now it'll be looks of jealousy, not pity, and I don't mind those one bit."

Dylan wanted to kiss Seneca so badly it took all her force of will to keep her lips to herself. The gesture was so tender and strong and was just the type of sweetness Dylan had come to expect from Seneca in their short time knowing each other. She was constantly opening doors, lifting heavy things in the machine shop, or trying to protect Dylan from the strange looks and rude comments that came her way because of her association with Seneca. Dylan was sure Seneca didn't think she noticed, but she did.

"You know holding my hand is going to get you pulled into all the crap they say about me," Seneca said.

Dylan felt Seneca's fingers loosen their hold on her own and she fought the sting of disappointment. "Do you want your hand back?"

"No, not really," Seneca said, sounding a little sad. "I just didn't want you to—"

"I don't give a hoot what they say about me," Dylan said, gripping her hand tightly and rubbing her thumb lightly up and down the back. Maybe it was time Seneca didn't have to face the gossip girls alone.

"Oh, that's good then," Seneca said, sounding a little shaky.

"Besides," Dylan said, gently swinging their joined hands, "I always wanted to be the girlfriend of a pirate queen, or was it a mob boss, or an inner city gunrunner? I forget what the hottest rumor is this week. Either way, it sounds more fun than being the daughter of a stuck-up debutant."

"Pirate queen?" Seneca said incredulously. "Do I look like I've ever been on a boat?"

Dylan laughed as she pictured Seneca at the helm of a vast, dark-sailed pirate ship with an eye patch and a parrot. "Okay, so maybe I haven't heard pirate queen rumors, but it is kinda funny to think of you with a parrot."

"Bob!" Seneca laughed too. "I couldn't even stand on a rolling deck."

"The other ones, though, pretty sure I've heard those."

"Really?" Seneca sounded curious. "What else have you heard? No one says any of this to my face."

Dylan was uncomfortable. She wasn't sure if she should repeat some of the horrible rumors that had spread around campus.

"I won't be upset. I'm just curious. It's not like I don't know people talk," Seneca said gently.

"Well, there was the mob boss, although I think you might be a little young for that. There was the gunrunner, drug dealer, CIA agent, and I think I even heard mention of a female James Bond. People say you were in a car accident, that you were shot, that you killed someone and were in jail. That you slept with someone you shouldn't have and her husband tried to kill you. Last week, someone in my house was insisting that you were a world-class dirt bike racer but had wrecked real bad. And of course, don't forget pirate queen."

She wanted the smile that had left Seneca's eyes to return. Her hand was sweaty where their palms met, and her face was pale and taut, like the look someone had when they were trying to unstick a pickle jar, part futile struggle, part stress at your lack of real strength. Dylan watched the conflicting emotions rush through her eyes, which finally settled into resignation.

"I definitely don't have a parrot," Seneca said, clearly trying to lighten the mood. She looked like she wanted to say more, but she didn't. Dylan felt like they were on the brink of sharing things a lot lately, but they both always clammed up before anything slipped out.

Dylan desperately wanted to know what demons Seneca kept hidden so well and struggled with so deeply. She realized that was asking a lot, but she wanted, at least for an evening, to add her hands to the burden Seneca carried.

"So were they close with any of them?" Dylan asked. She was willing to let Seneca keep her past to herself, but she wanted her to know it wasn't going to bother her, no matter what Seneca revealed.

"A couple, I guess," Seneca mumbled before pulling Dylan into the local pizza joint. "How does this sound? Being a pirate queen is hungry work."

They dropped the subject and returned to safer, more mundane topics during the meal, and Dylan was glad to see the relaxed happiness return to Seneca's expression. After dinner, they walked hand in hand through downtown, enjoying each other's company and the quiet evening. Neither seemed in a particular hurry to call it a night.

"Oh my God, that one absolutely takes the cake," Dylan said, staring in disbelief at the back of the woman who had just passed. "What was her problem? I thought she might start weeping over your head or something." On their walk, they had made a game of the inevitable pity stares directed at Seneca and her cane. There was a ranking system and points awarded based on the duration, transparency, and overall emotion behind the stare. Seneca had really warmed up to the game and Dylan was beginning to suspect she was cheating to win some extra points.

"I bet I could get a better one, if I just limped a little more when a cute old lady passes. Maybe I could lean on your arm and look all tired and worn."

"Oh you are bad, very, very bad," Dylan said, nudging her shoulder, carefully, so as not to startle her. "You have to get those pity stare scores fair and square, no playing anything up. If you want to act, sign up for the drama club."

Dylan looked at Seneca and was surprised to see the tired and worn look that Seneca had just teasingly described. Suddenly, she saw how hard Seneca was trying to hide her fatigue. Her face was drawn and there was definite tension in her body. Dylan knew she must be in a great deal of pain. The expected rain had come just as predicted, but as was often the case in New England, the storm had been fast and left the air sticky with humidity.

Making a quick decision, Dylan navigated the busy street and led them to the ice cream shop on the next block. She didn't want to draw attention to the fact that Seneca was hurting, but she couldn't stand by and let her suffer needlessly. Besides, ice cream always helped everything, or so she had come to believe.

"Where are you taking me now?" Seneca asked as Dylan started off purposefully down one of the many side streets.

"Ice cream," Dylan said, leading the way to the popular shop. "We've had enough pity stare contests for a while. It's time to get down to some real important business."

"And that would be ice cream?"

"Yup, but I have to warn you, don't get in the way when I get my bowl. That was part of the sharing concept I never learned, and I'll gladly take off someone's hand if they try to jack my sundae."

"I consider myself warned," Seneca said. "But I do have an advantage." She waved her cane slightly in front of her. "I'm armed."

When they approached the small picturesque shop, it was overflowing with patrons. Even in the late fall, it was packed. The crowd parted as they saw Dylan and Seneca approaching and one man jumped out of his group of friends to hold the door.

Dylan felt Seneca tense next to her. She knew from dancing at the bar that Seneca could be a little jumpy in crowds. She wondered if this was a bad idea. Then the idiot holding the door opened his mouth, and she thought it was a bad idea for a whole new reason.

He pointed out the step and assured her he had the door as if talking to a special needs child. He spoke in a slow, exaggerated way and much more loudly than was necessary. Dylan had had enough for the evening. She put a reassuring hand on Seneca's back and then turned on the man.

"She is not blind, deaf, or dumb, you asshole. She walks with a cane because of an injury, which did not affect her ability to make it up one step without an idiot like you making her a spectacle. You want to be a gentleman and hold the door, fine, but keep your condescending comments to yourself."

The poor man looked like he had no idea what had just hit him. Dylan was a whirling dervish of anger and energy, and the rude man quickly retreated to get away from her seething rage and poking finger.

When Dylan turned around, Seneca looked like she was having a hard time deciding whether to laugh or cry. Just as Dylan thought they were safely out of harm's way and ready to enjoy their ice cream, she pulled Seneca to a stop once again and confronted a middle-aged couple and their teenage son.

"Would you like us to pose so you can take a picture?" Dylan said, her voice dripping with venom. "It would last a lot longer. You could even take it home with you and stare at it more, later."

The woman had the decency to blush crimson and her husband mumbled a quick apology. The teenager looked horrified to be with his parents, but Dylan thought he had looked that way before she confronted them.

When they finally got in line, Seneca rested her hand cautiously on Dylan's shoulder.

"You okay?" Seneca asked.

"Me, of course, why?" Dylan asked.

"Well, because you just yelled at a guy back there and ripped a family to shreds. I'm not sure that teenager is going to go out with his parents again until his thirties. And everyone is kinda staring at us. I'm used to it, but this time they're staring at you."

"I just don't like the way people have been treating you tonight, Seneca. I've been watching it all night and I've had it. He had no right. None of them do."

"I don't really know what to say," Seneca said. She looked taken aback.

"May I hug you?" Dylan asked.

There was no answer. Instead, Seneca hooked her cane over her arm and pulled Dylan into a bone-crushing embrace.

"Thank you, Bob. No one has ever done that for me before," Seneca whispered.

"That's the most tragic thing I've ever heard."

"You clearly don't know me very well," Seneca said, then looked like she regretted it immediately.

Dylan stood on her tiptoes and gently placed a kiss on Seneca's cheek. "Well, you deserve all that and more," Dylan said, pleased when she felt Seneca shift and bring a hand to her cheek where Dylan had kissed it. She really had no idea how sweet she was.

Once they had their ice cream, Seneca left the cane on her arm and leaned on Dylan for support, although Dylan suspected it was an excuse to stay close to her. She wasn't complaining. When they got to the table, they deposited their ice cream on the tabletop, but Seneca didn't let go of Dylan's arm. Dylan turned until she was in the circle of Seneca's body and leaned into her. Seneca wrapped her in a hug and kissed the top of Dylan's head.

"Dylan, I've really had a good time tonight," Seneca said.

"Me too," Dylan said, leaning back in Seneca's arms, feeling like there wasn't anywhere else she wanted to be at that moment.

Dylan gently kissed Seneca on the cheek and put both hands on Seneca's shoulders. Ice cream was the last thing on her mind. She didn't know what she had planned, they were in the middle of the ice cream parlor after all, but as she ran her hands down Seneca's arms, the uneven pebbling of hard scar tissue distracted her. Everywhere her fingers traveled, she found it.

Seneca tensed and looked at the ceiling, but didn't pull away, something Dylan considered a major victory. She flattened her palm against Seneca's arms and traveled up to just under the sleeves of her T-shirt. When she came across a long, jagged, wide patch of scar tissue, she hesitated. She looked into Seneca's expressionless face, her eyes shut tight against whatever emotions were boiling inside. Dylan slid her hands out from under the shirtsleeves, seeing how uncomfortable the exploration was making Seneca. She pulled Seneca into her arms and hugged her fiercely. Dylan heard a sob catch in Seneca's throat, but when they pulled apart, her eyes were dry.

"Dylan, I, well, there are—"

"Hold on, not here," Dylan said. She scooped up their ice cream and got them both moving toward the door. Seneca didn't like crowds, and Dylan didn't particularly want an audience right now either. This was between her and Seneca and no one else.

Once they were outside and sitting on the curb across the street, tucked away from streetlights and heavily trafficked areas, Dylan turned to Seneca, who hadn't said a word.

"I want to know the memories that haunt you and I want to know what made those scars, but I don't want to know because you feel like you have to tell me. If you want to tell me right now, then you should, but if you feel like you have to, because I happened to discover that you have scars, then wait. We'll get there, okay? You'll feel when the time is right. I don't want to rush this."

Almost subconsciously, Dylan's hand started to move back toward Seneca's shoulder, the one where the largest concentration of scar tissue was palpable. She stopped herself, but Seneca guided her hand the rest of the way. Dylan slowly lifted Seneca's T-shirt sleeve to reveal a vicious five-inch long scar. Her heart caught as she realized the pain this injury must have caused, and she ran her lips tenderly over the puckered skin. No one deserved that much pain in her life, least of all a woman as wonderful as Seneca King.

"God. What did I do before you?" Seneca rested her hand on Dylan's hip, her eyes closed.

"I don't know, but I'm not sure what I did without you either," Dylan answered sincerely. It felt like they had known each other forever.

"I totally said that out loud didn't I?" Seneca said, rolling her eyes.

"Yep." Dylan ran her fingers through Seneca's hair before they got to work on their melting ice cream, allowing a moment for them to get their bearings once more.

Dylan was amazed at how much things had changed between them. She never would have imagined getting the chance to touch Seneca as much as she had in the past few hours. Instead of pulling away, Seneca had seemed to enjoy, maybe even welcome, the interactions, and Dylan didn't want to let her out of her sight or out of touching range. Now that she had felt Seneca's skin, her hands burned with the memory and she wanted to continue her explorations.

"So," Seneca said, looking at her hands, clearly a little embarrassed. "I don't know that I can share everything tonight, certainly not here, but that part of me represents the landscape of my checkered past. It's just one area, but it messes with me. Please don't tell anyone else about this."

"Seneca, you don't really think I would, do you? Do the scars have something to do with why you don't like to be touched? Why you left in the middle of our dance the night we met? Do they hurt?"

Seneca cocked her head and shook it slowly. "No, of course not. I know you wouldn't tell anyone. I'm kinda embarrassed. I'm also afraid you're going to think I'm too much of a lost cause to take a chance on. I think that sometimes, you know? The scars don't hurt, but they do make me jumpy, as you've seen. That's only the half of it. I didn't want to date anyone because I've got issues, a whole mess of them, and I'm still not sure if I'm any good at it, but I've had a lot of fun tonight."

Dylan took Seneca's hand and intertwined their fingers once again. It still felt wonderful. "I don't think you're a lost cause, and if you're willing to take a chance on another date with me, I'm willing too."

Seneca looked relieved. "What are you doing for Thanksgiving?"

Dylan raised her eyebrows at the change in subject but didn't say anything. Instead, she shrugged and shoved a heaping spoonful of ice cream into her mouth. She tried to answer around the enormous bite, but everything came out muffled.

Finally swallowing, Dylan managed to answer coherently. "Probably head to the parents'. They always make enough food for a small army and invite over their friends to show off their home, their food, and their daughter." Dylan indicated herself with a flourish and gave a mock bow. "What about you?"

"Kate invited me to join them, said it was low-key."

"I wish I could bring you home with me, but I wouldn't subject you to all that that entails." Dylan saw the question in Seneca's eyes and didn't want her thinking she was ashamed of her in any way, especially now, when she was probably feeling pretty vulnerable. "I want you to meet my parents, but I would be so embarrassed if you saw them on full display. My mother is enough to handle when she's not in hostess mode. Maybe we could do the first introduction at a slightly less formal event."

"Oh, of course," Seneca said. "I completely understand. I was looking forward to spending it with Kate anyway. I'd like to meet your family though, and it means a lot that you want me to come." Seneca was beet red.

Dylan let her off the hook and the conversation turned back to school, their armor, and the class they shared. Dylan realized it had quickly become her favorite, even if she had initially signed up only to annoy her mother. She knew Seneca's presence was the reason for that. She was going to miss her when they didn't have that guaranteed time together.

"I'm going to miss not having class with you," Dylan said quietly, wanting Seneca to know how she was feeling, but not wanting to scare her.

"Yeah, me too. I've gotten used to having you around. We can keep up the tradition, sign up for some crazy class next semester. I've always wanted to take horticulture."

"Yeah, maybe." Dylan was lost in thought, not able to fully comprehend she was less than a year from graduation.

"Or not." Seneca pushed her ice cream away.

Dylan snapped back to the present. "What? No, I would love to take another class with you. I was thinking about graduating. I don't feel ready. And I don't want to lose you when I do."

"I'd like that too, Bob. Not losing you, I mean."

"Good," Dylan said. "Maybe I can show you all the potential jobs I've got on my radar and you can choose the one you think is best to ensure that for us." Dylan was only half kidding, and her pulse sped up at the prospect of making a decision so big based on something so tenuous.

"Aren't you supposed to choose a job after college based on a bit more than being close to the person you're dating?"

"I don't know how you're supposed to choose," Dylan said. "I've spent my life, my school life, at least, as one of the smartest kids in the room, and being told I would 'change the world.' Even here, we're at a prestigious women's college and are supposed to be doing amazing things with the gifts we've been given once we graduate. We're told all the time about how alums go on to change the world. I have no idea how to do that. My goals are much smaller. I want to have my own apartment and not have to eat ramen every night. I don't know how to change the world." Dylan spooned another mouthful of melted ice cream into her mouth to shut herself up. She hadn't meant to unload.

"There are a lot of ways to change the world, Bob. If you cure cancer, sure you've changed the world in a really dramatic way, but if you rescue a puppy, you've changed the world for that dog. Or if you're nice to someone who limps badly when no one else is, you just might have changed their world too." Seneca looked at Dylan shyly. They were still holding hands. Seneca squeezed Dylan's. "I can't think of anyone more equipped to figure out how she is going to make her mark on the world, even if it's just paying your rent on time and eating egg noodles instead of ramen."

"How is it you know the perfect thing to say?" Dylan asked, feeling buoyed by Seneca's vote of confidence.

"It's the ice cream. It brings out my wisdom. Is business and corporate America really what you want to do? You never answered me when I asked."

"It doesn't really matter that I would rather do something else entirely, unfortunately. There are expectations to live up to. I had my chance to be free of them in Australia. Now I'm back to the real world. The world I have to change, I guess."

Seneca didn't look like she was satisfied with that answer, but she didn't push. Instead she stared down at their hands, a frown forming. "No matter what you do, I'm not sure about what I said earlier. I don't know if I'm the one to be with you while you take on the world. You don't want me, Bob. I've got…issues…I wouldn't be any good to you." Seneca looked immensely sad, but managed to get all her words out without stopping. "What if you get a fancy job and you have to bring a partner to a work event? You couldn't bring me. I know that's a lot of steps ahead, but it doesn't change the truth of the situation."

Dylan didn't say anything as she watched Seneca's eyes fill with regret and emotion. She wasn't sure what had happened between their sweet moment and right now. Something had wiggled its way into Seneca's head and was causing her doubt. Dylan wasn't going to stand for it. "You done?" she asked, not letting go of Seneca's hand.

"What? Oh, um, yeah." Seneca threw her napkin in the semi-empty cup and stood.

Dylan guided Seneca's hand to her waist. She didn't want the physical connection they had been sharing to be lost just yet. "I'm only going to say this once," Dylan said, moving even closer to Seneca, pleased to feel she didn't shrink away as their thighs brushed. "You don't get to tell me what I want. I get to decide that…AND," she said loudly as Seneca started to protest again, effectively cutting off Seneca's response. "Don't let me ever catch you talking bad about my pirate queen. Saying she's not fit for corporate dinners and stuffy golf outings. I simply won't allow it. I get the sense you don't like to be told what to do, or forced into something you don't like. Who does? But don't do that to me either."

She saw a flicker of amusement in Seneca's eyes, and then a smile crept across her beautiful mouth. Dylan was powerless against that smile, the way it lit up Seneca's face, changing her hardened features into focused, chiseled beauty. She stood on her tiptoes to reach Seneca's lips with her own.

The kiss was not long, and by most standards conservatively chaste, but it left them both breathless all the same. Seneca reached a tentative hand to her own lips and touched them as if to make sure they were real.

"Shh." Dylan kissed Seneca lightly on the lips again before grabbing her hand and stepping back, swinging their joined hands gently in front of her. "I feel it too. There's some kind of magic that happens when you kiss and you're both smiling."

"No," Seneca said, shaking her head and giving Dylan's hand a squeeze. "There's something magical about kissing you."

Chapter Twelve

Dylan looked around the crowded formal living room of her parents' house and felt completely alone. She wished she hadn't been so stupid as to exclude Seneca from this gathering. She had said she didn't want Seneca to see her family in full display, which was true, but she was also worried how her family would react to Seneca, something that very well could have shown their truest, darkest colors.

"Don't worry, Dylan. I don't like most of them either." Her cousin, the no longer struggling artist, brought over more silly sized nibbles for them both.

"How did you know that's what I was thinking?"

"The look of revulsion that makes it look like you'd rather be anywhere but here was a bit of a giveaway. Same look your mother makes."

Her cousin kissed her on the forehead and was off again. Dylan pondered the comment about her mother. Given that all of this was her mother's idea, how could she want to be somewhere else? Dylan wandered toward the kitchen, Lady Walker's domain. Even on Thanksgiving, despite desperate pleas from Dylan's father, they didn't hire help, order prepared food, or change the way Thanksgiving had been done since the beginning of time. Dylan was secretly glad, because after all, what would be the tradition in having people cook and serve you? Oddly, though,

Dylan had never been allowed to help her mother with the cooking on this, the most important of family holidays.

"Dylan, what are you doing in the kitchen?" her mother asked as soon as she walked into the beautiful, sprawling space. "You should be out, enjoying our guests, helping your father with hosting."

"You're not looking so good, Mom. You okay?"

"Of course I'm okay. It's Thanksgiving. What better day is there? What do you mean?"

Dylan saw her two aunts and a few cousins laugh behind her mother. There were a few other women in the kitchen as well, but none of them seemed willing to laugh at Lady Walker.

"You have flour on your cheek and all over your shirt, you have what I'm going to assume is potatoes on your pants, and I'm going to leave your hair well enough alone. Aside from looking like you're wearing our meal, you look stressed."

"Cooking is messy work, Dylan."

"I see that. Anything I can do to help?"

"You can get her out of the kitchen," at least three women shouted in unison. Everyone laughed, including Dylan's mother. It was an ongoing joke, and every year, at some point, she was booted from her own kitchen so she could go clean up and take a breath.

Dylan took her mother's hand and led her from the whirring stand mixers, hot ovens, and bubbling pots. "Time to let it go."

"Not really a strength of mine."

"You don't say."

They made their way quickly upstairs so her mother didn't get waylaid by guests looking like she'd been frolicking in the Thanksgiving dinner. She left Dylan in her dressing room and went to shower, leaving the door cracked so she could shout to Dylan. "Anything new at school? Are you seeing anyone?"

Dylan froze. That was what her mother chose to lead with? There wasn't a more loaded topic for them to discuss. She took a deep breath. Now that the door was open, she may as well step through.

"I am," Dylan said.

"And what's his name?"

Dylan rolled her eyes. Of course her mother would be purposefully obtuse.

"*Her* name. Her name is Seneca. Seneca King. And she's wonderful."

"I can't hear you, darling. You're going to have to speak up if you want me to hear the gentleman's name."

"You heard me just fine," Dylan said. "Pretending I didn't say it won't change anything about the way I feel about her. I wanted to bring her today, but I didn't think anyone here would treat her very well so I didn't invite her."

The water shut off abruptly and Lady Walker appeared in her robe, still mostly dripping wet. "You told her we wouldn't treat her well? Dylan, why would you do such a thing?"

"I see your hearing has returned."

"Dylan." Her mother didn't seem to be in a joking mood.

"I didn't tell her that. I made another excuse. But I would have liked to have her here today. I'd like to think that you would want to meet someone important to me. But she came from a different background than I did, and you get all, whatever it is that you just did, when I mention women and me in the same sentence, so I didn't bring her."

Her mother looked thoughtful, a little embarrassed, and cold.

"I don't do the best job with the idea of you dating women, it's true. What did you say her name was?"

"Seneca King."

She smiled slightly after searching Dylan's expression for a moment. "It's hard to argue against your daughter's happiness when her face lights up that way. If I promise to try a little harder, will you promise to stop disparaging the family's good name?"

"How about you get back in the shower before you freeze to death and we can go from there?" Dylan said. "Your lips are turning blue."

"I think there's still soap in my hair."

"I'll see you downstairs, Mom. And, thanks."

Dylan wasn't sure what progress she had made with her mother, but it was the first time they had directly addressed the fact that she was going to date women and might want to bring them home. Australia was one thing, Sophia and after-college life was another, but clearly, it might not be as big a deal as she thought it would be. She fished her cell phone out of her pocket. Talking and thinking about Seneca wasn't enough. She wanted to hear her voice.

Kate answered but put Seneca on the line. "Happy Thanksgiving," Seneca said, sounding happy and relaxed. Dylan missed her even more.

"Happy Thanksgiving. I wish I were spending it with you. My family is in full Walker mode, but I still should have brought you here, or refused to come home and stayed with you."

"Is everything okay? Are you all right?"

"Of course it is. But on Thanksgiving you're supposed to make a list of the things you're thankful for, and given the choice, I'd prefer to spend my day with the person at the top of my list."

"Thank you," Seneca said. She sounded a little shy. "You're at the top of my list too. And just so you know, Kate and Lisa are following me around the house trying to eavesdrop on everything we're saying. Even Hank is in on this."

"Who's Hank?" Dylan was glad that Seneca was being so well cared for, but she ached to be part of the relaxing scene she could imagine.

"The dog. He might be after my turkey rather than good gossip."

Dylan's father called her name from downstairs and she frowned at the interruption. "Seneca, I have to go. I hear the masses looking for me in the other room. I just wanted to hear your voice and tell you that I miss you. Say hi to Kate and Lisa and take pity on poor Hank. It's Thanksgiving. Give the boy some turkey."

Dylan hung up the phone to Seneca's sweet laughter. Her artist cousin was immediately by her side.

"The wolves are in there looking for fresh blood. You're up."

"Geez, thanks."

She hadn't even found a seat in the living room, near her father at least, before her family started in with the questions.

"How's college treating you?"

"Why are you going into business? There's no future in that."

"That women's school isn't going to make you a homo, right?"

"You should really consider law school. It pays much better."

"Have you talked to your uncle about getting an internship after school is over?"

"Do you have a job lined up after graduation?"

"Did you hear about your cousin's promotion?"

Dylan wanted to flee, but there wasn't anywhere to go. She knew everyone meant well, or at least everyone except whoever was worried about her coming down with a case of the homos.

"Dylan is rather insistent on the business path," her father said kindly behind her, putting his hand on her shoulder. "I always thought she was the one most likely to do something wild like open a small business or become a chef, but I was clearly wrong. I have no doubts that whatever she chooses to do, she'll be wonderful at it."

"A small business?" Dylan asked, looking at her father. She couldn't believe he was serious.

"Sure, why not? You'd be great at it. It just seemed like the kind of thing you might take a stab at. The corporate rat race surprised me."

"I think it's a sound decision," one of her uncles said.

"Small businesses are too unpredictable. Do you know how many of them fail?"

"And how many of them end up having a lasting impact on the world?"

Dylan wasn't even sure who was talking anymore. She felt like she needed to raise her hand and be called on to have a chance to speak. "A good friend told me if you cure cancer, you've changed the world in a really dramatic way, but if you rescue a puppy, you've made a difference in that dog's life."

"What's your point?" her cousin, the corporate tax lawyer said.

"My point is, there are lots of ways to have a lasting impact on the world," Dylan said.

"So true," her father said. "The hard part for each of us is figuring out how to carve out enough meaningful space for ourselves to do it."

The rest of the room kept buzzing on, but Dylan was lost in thought. Her father had just given her a whole new way of looking at her plans after college. Maybe she should think a little more carefully about Seneca's question of whether the business world was really where she wanted to end up. She'd always assumed her parents wanted her to be some big, successful hotshot. It hadn't even occurred to her they might be okay with her actually doing something she wanted to do. She smiled at her mother when she entered the room, suddenly far more proud of her family than she'd ever been before. Maybe she really could have it all.

CHAPTER THIRTEEN

Seneca lounged in the golf cart, enjoying the crisp late fall air. The khaki pants that were part of her work attire were less threadbare than her own jeans, and with the neat fleece pullover Kate had given her, with Sophia College embroidered on the chest, she was quite comfortable. The fall sports season was starting to wind down, but a few teams were making last-minute playoff runs and needed to practice.

She was parked at the top of the small hill overlooking the fields below. It gave her the best perspective to watch the athletes going through drills and wind sprints. She could hear the shouts of teammates and the encouragement of coaches, but her vantage point left her far enough removed to not get caught up in the drama playing out on one field or the other. It was her job to watch over them all, making sure she was available if someone got injured.

Kate, she knew, was overseeing a tennis match on the courts behind and to the right of Seneca's position. Kate hated tennis matches, complaining they continued forever and she couldn't keep track of the score. She had played volleyball and softball in college and didn't understand tennis' appeal. Seneca would have gladly traded with her, but she wasn't a licensed trainer, and one had to be at every home contest. Kate had told her to head over to the tennis courts when practices were over, to keep her company, or there would be no more weekly dinners. Although she knew

Kate would never make good on the threat, she was happy to stay late and hang out with her.

As practices dragged on, players occasionally stopped by for ice or scissors to remove tape from a sore body part, but for the most part Seneca was free to let her mind wander. As usual, her thoughts headed straight to Dylan. It had been almost a month since they had kissed, but the memory still made her lips burn and her heart race. Although they had gone out together a few times a week since then, they hadn't shared another kiss. Seneca cared about Dylan way too much to screw things up, and she worried that heading that direction meant an inevitable screw-up on her part. Then there was the old-fashioned courting idea, which Dylan seemed to want, and Seneca knew nothing about, not to mention the whole issue with sex. Just thinking about it made her queasy. It was easier to move excruciatingly slowly than face too many demons at once.

She had finally confessed the kiss, after much prodding from Lisa, over Thanksgiving dinner. She didn't know if now, without a follow-up, she should be worried. It had been so spur-of-the-moment, but Dylan hadn't tried again. God knew Seneca wanted to try again, even if fear held her at bay. It had been bliss, and she knew it could be even better.

She jumped slightly as her radio crackled to life.

"Kate, there's something wrong with your student," Jane, the athletic director, said over the radio, only a hint of laughter in her tone.

Seneca sat up straighter on the cart, looking around sheepishly, not sure if she was about to be reprimanded for her leisurely positioning.

"Oh, is that so?" Kate asked, seeming unconcerned with Jane's assertion.

"Indeed. That kid is smiling like a goof in that golf cart on the hill. I think she must be running a fever or something."

Seneca started laughing, realizing that they were pulling her leg. It was true she didn't smile much, and the few times she had interacted with Jane she had been too nervous to say anything. Besides, she *was* smiling like a goof.

"I am not," she said, trying to save some of her dignity.

Laughter from both Jane and Kate assaulted her from the radio. Obviously, they were together, using the same one.

"How can you see me from way down there anyway?"

"Jane just walked by the field house and saw you up there grinning from ear to ear," Kate said. "Hey, you got plans tonight?"

It wasn't their normal weekly dinner night, but Dylan was busy working on a project so Seneca was free.

"Nope."

"Mind staying late? I've got something I want to teach you," Kate said cryptically.

Seneca was intrigued. Kate never shared more than she felt she needed to, and it took forever to get something out of her, so Seneca didn't bother. She would find out after work. "Sure, I got time."

"Good. Are practices done yet? You know how I feel about being down here by myself," Kate said, almost whining.

Seneca laughed. "Soon, soccer's just finishing up."

"You know where to find me."

An hour later, they were finally done with tennis. The number one singles match had dragged on long after everyone else had finished. The two women went through more tiebreaks for the final point than Seneca had needed to witness. Kate had almost run on the court to end it herself. Four hours of tennis made her want to start lobbing balls at the players, or shouting obscenities at the moment of serve, anything to get the pace moving.

Seneca followed Kate back to the gym, and they both dumped their equipment in the training room. Kate tossed Seneca a pair of gym pants and a T-shirt and pointed her toward the bathroom to change. Once Kate was similarly attired, they headed upstairs. Seneca had no idea why she was in gym clothes or what Kate had in mind, but she was content to walk in blind. She trusted Kate.

They stepped off the elevator on the top level of the athletic building, and Kate let them into a large room dominated by a rock-climbing structure that covered one long tall wall.

"Are we doing that?" Seneca asked in disbelief, not thinking her leg would handle climbing two feet, much less to the top.

"Nah," Kate said, "I'm scared of heights."

She rummaged through her gym bag and pulled out a pair of boxing gloves and hand wraps for herself and another pair for Seneca. She tossed them to Seneca and then went to the closet and pulled out an eighty-pound heavy bag. She attached it to the waiting stand and turned to look at Seneca, excitement and question in her eyes.

"You interested?"

Seneca looked down at the boxing gloves, not at all sure how she felt about holding instruments of violence. Her fists had never been the ones doing the punching, and she didn't know how she felt about the opportunity.

Kate seemed to sense her hesitation and perhaps the reason behind it.

"It's a great workout, Sen, and you said you wanted to start back at the gym. This is better and will be good for your leg too. Besides, every butch girl should be able to box. Makes you feel powerful, like you can defend what is yours and protect your woman."

"That sounds a little caveman, Kate," Seneca said. It was sort of appealing though. It would be good to feel she had the power to defend herself. No one had ever thought her capable. She thought of the first dance she shared with Dylan and how she had run out when she was jostled. It was tiring always being scared in a crowd, and if this could help then it might be worth giving it a shot. She just wasn't sure today was the day to take a flier.

"Can you explain it to me first, and maybe we can try it out after that?" Seneca asked.

Kate explained some of the intricacies of boxing and why she loved it so much. She made sure to highlight that they wouldn't be hitting each other, which Seneca was relieved about.

"Do you want me to show you?" Kate asked.

"Yeah, sure. Thanks." Seneca thought it might help to watch Kate do it first. She didn't know why the idea of hitting the heavy bag and getting the kind of workout Kate described was scaring her.

Kate showed her how to wrap her hands and helped her into the gloves.

"These gloves and wraps I borrowed from a friend, but we can get you your own if you like it enough. I come up here almost every day, so we can work out together if you want."

Seneca looked at Kate, impressed. She'd had no idea and felt honored to be invited to share.

Kate stretched her arms a bit and moved in front of the heavy bag. She bounced lightly on the balls of her feet and shifted her weight easily from one foot to the other. She looked like she was dancing. Seneca watched as Kate lifted her hands in front of her face, keeping her gloves in protect mode. A knot formed in Seneca's stomach. Kate reached one hand out gently and tapped the heavy bag, judging distance, her feet constantly moving. Seneca felt bile rise in her throat. Kate unleashed a rapid three-punch combination, striking the heavy bag with accuracy and tremendous power. Seneca felt her airway constrict, and panic begin to set in. Her stomach churned, and she ripped the gloves from her hands. She made it to the trash can across the room before she threw up.

She sank to the floor next to the trash can and covered her head with her hands. Shame replaced panic. Even though Kate made plenty of noise to let her know she was coming, she still jumped when she sat down next to her.

"Seneca, what happened, kiddo?" Kate asked.

"I'm sorry, Kate." She hated that she had just ruined an amazing gift Kate had tried to give her. "I've, um, been punched before." Seneca couldn't explain more than that. "I thought it would be okay, but I couldn't handle seeing you hitting that thing."

Kate wound a finger under Seneca's chin, gently encouraging her to look up. She did. She didn't want to look Kate in the eye, but she always wanted Kate to tell her it was going to be okay. The look on Kate's face said all that and more. Seneca hugged her. She held on for a long time and Kate held her tightly in return, saying nothing. When they parted, Seneca felt better.

"I really do want my leg to get stronger. You said boxers do all kinds of workouts. Are there other things we could do that don't involve hitting things?"

Kate nodded. "If you're up for it. Why don't you go grab some water and I'll get us set up?"

When Seneca returned after washing out her mouth and drinking some water, Kate had put away the heavy bag and pulled out two gym mats, some free weights, a few exercise bands, and she had strung a rope across a ten-foot span about chest height.

Kate explained the stations: push-ups and sit-ups, simulated punching with the free weights, hooks with the exercise bands, and diagonal shuffle steps with a squat to get under the rope. The last one was the one Seneca would have the most trouble with physically. Kate knew it, Seneca knew it, but they both left it unspoken. They'd modify if needed.

Seneca found the workout challenging but invigorating. She hadn't pushed her body like this in years and was excited to feel powerful, even in a very small way. She could barely get under the rope, but she used her good leg to do most of the work and at least bent the balky one. Her arms felt like wet noodles when Kate called an end to their workout.

"I think that's probably good for day one," Kate said. "You did great, kiddo. How did everything feel?"

"What time is it? I've got to tell Dylan about this!" Seneca wanted to share her new triumph with Bob.

"About seven thirty I think," Kate said. "I'll take that to mean you enjoyed yourself?"

"Of course," Seneca said. She figured Kate could see that. "Bob's probably still at that stupid project meeting. Don't understand why they can't just do it by e-mail."

"You're really over the moon about this girl aren't you?" Kate asked.

Seneca debated the merits of telling the truth. The truth scared her, a lot, but she didn't know if she wanted to avoid the question.

Kate made it possible for her to share her feelings and her fears safely, and Seneca did have a few Dylan-related questions.

"How do I know if I am?" she asked finally, sliding down the wall into a sitting position. "I've never felt like this for anyone, so I don't know what it's supposed to feel like."

"I think you might know all there is to know already," Kate said gently, sliding down the wall next to her.

"I don't know what to do." Seneca didn't know how to admit her insecurities or her inexperience to Kate.

"I'm going to have to assume you aren't asking for my advice in the bedroom. Because I've been with the same woman since the Jurassic Age, and the rumors about you that have trickled my way are enough to make Hank blush."

"You shouldn't believe everything you hear." Seneca was horrified.

"Hey, kiddo, if people were saying that stuff about me, I would be taking out full page newspaper ads, erecting monuments to myself, and doing whatever was necessary to make billboards happen."

Seneca wasn't convinced.

"I'm just saying, walk proud, my young friend."

"You're ridiculous. But that isn't the kind of advice I was hoping for. I'm no good for her. She is beautiful and smart and worldly. She's literally been around the world. She deserves someone better than me. I mean look at me, I'm damaged...I've got secrets and demons and I can't make it through the night without waking up screaming. I can't even watch you hit a stupid heavy bag without freaking out. I'm...broken."

If it had been possible, Seneca would have melted into the floor. What in the world had prompted her to unload all of that on Kate? It was true, and it was how she felt, but she never imagined she would say it out loud to another human being. She had spent too many years alone, fighting for survival, to trust easily, but here she was, laying out her greatest fears to her boss.

"How did your leg feel during our workout?" Kate asked, seemingly straying off topic.

Seneca was relieved that Kate was apparently going to let her off the hook. She was, however, a little hurt that Kate didn't even want to address the issues she had broached. Was she so messed up that Kate didn't want to talk about it?

Seneca tried to shift gears and remember if she had felt any more pain than usual during her workout. "Actually, it felt pretty good. Only going under the rope hurt. I felt it then. I was having too much fun to notice any other time I think."

"Do you think someone watching your workout would have been able to tell you have a bad leg?" Kate asked.

In the months they had worked together, Seneca had come to understand Kate's habit of asking questions that didn't seem to make sense and eventually getting to a meaningful point. Maybe Kate was going to answer her fears about Dylan after all.

"I don't know. Maybe not, it's hard to tell. I think they probably would have noticed all the weird stuff we were doing first."

Kate nodded as if that were the conclusion she had come to as well.

"I would imagine they would see you punching the air holding dumbbells and trying to duck under a rope first too. Everyone sees a situation differently. One person sees damage, others might see survival, growth, or a challenge met and overcome. Sometimes people just see the workout, sometimes they see the boxer."

Seneca digested that for a while. She looked at Kate thoughtfully, and realized Kate was only partially with her; another part of her was far away, likely drifting with her own experiences and memories.

"So you're saying that other people might not see me as damaged?" Seneca asked cautiously. Sometimes the problem with talking to Kate was that she never knew if they were talking about the same thing.

"I'm saying it's unfair of you to force Dylan to see you how you see yourself. I haven't met her, but if you're smitten with her, she must be amazing. Why not let her show you what *she* sees when she looks at you?"

Kate focused on Seneca completely for the first time since they had started talking and Seneca was surprised by what she saw. It was as if Kate was letting her see, for the first time, the woman Kate saw when she looked at Seneca. She saw respect, admiration, caring, and love in Kate's eyes, and she didn't know what to say. She knew then that Kate was giving her a great gift. Kate was showing Seneca a path toward getting her life back. All she had to do was believe in the woman Kate saw in her. Maybe Dylan saw that woman too. It was the strangest thought that had ever crossed her mind, and yet, she felt a little silly for not ever thinking it before.

Seneca didn't say anything for a while, contemplating her options, options that until a few moments ago she didn't know she had. It did seem unfair to both Dylan and herself to cut off the chance of a relationship before it happened. She hadn't been aware she was doing it, but what Kate said made sense. It wasn't up to her to tell Dylan how to think or feel. The world of new options felt a bit overwhelming.

"May I ask you a question? You don't have to answer," Kate said.

Seneca tensed slightly. The way Kate asked, the tone of her voice put Seneca on guard, but she nodded anyway.

"What happened to your leg?" Kate asked quietly. "I don't want to hurt you when we workout and, well, I'd like to know."

Seneca only hesitated a moment. If Kate had only been asking because of the workout, she might not have answered. The honest question, however, swayed her. Most people made up excuses to find out what happened, not because they really cared, but out of morbid curiosity and to feed the gossips. But Kate had done no such thing. She hadn't insisted on knowing the moment they started working together, and she probably could have, given the physical nature of what they did. Seneca didn't feel the need to hide that truth from her, and she probably owed it to her.

"A few years ago I was shot. Once in the leg, and twice in the abdomen."

Kate opened her mouth to say something but closed it again. Instead, she rubbed Seneca's stubby hair, kissed her gently on the forehead, and slowly pulled them both up.

Dumbfounded didn't begin to explain how Seneca felt at Kate's reaction to her shocking news. Awestruck, perhaps, was a better description. She had told a few other people that she had been shot, but usually it was to scare them into leaving her alone. Kate hadn't shied away, hadn't tried to mutter some clichéd sympathy, or babble on about the past and how we all had to look to the future. Seneca knew Kate was uncomfortable with her admission, but Seneca was as well. It was natural to be upset by that kind of news.

"Not even a follow-up question?" Seneca asked with a shaky laugh.

"Would you like me to ask you one?"

"Not really," Seneca said, relieved.

"Cause I could think of one, but I don't think there's a good one after that, and you don't look like you're in a talking mood."

As they stood up, Seneca leaned in for a hug, wanting to be close to Kate and thank her for her reaction. A hug was the only way she knew how. And even that was a hell of a long way from when she'd started working for Kate not so long ago.

"So," Kate said after a moment, a hint of mischief in her voice, "have you decided what to do with your beautiful Dylan?"

Seneca laughed at the change in subject, happy for the chance to move away from the emotional exchange they had just shared. The topic of Dylan was always welcome.

"In fact, I have," Seneca said, gathering the hand wraps and boxing gloves and giving them to Kate. "I'm going to kiss her for as long as she lets me."

CHAPTER FOURTEEN

Dylan tapped her pencil against the binder balanced on her lap and tried to engage in the conversation happening around her. Her study group, four other French students and herself, were all gathered in her small dorm room, talking about the project due at the end of the semester. She loved her French class and was even excited about this project, but right now she didn't want to be trapped in her room with these women.

What she really wanted to be doing was sitting across the table at the ice cream shop with Seneca, or walking hand in hand across campus with her. The quickest flicker of Seneca's face could send Dylan's heart racing and give her goose bumps.

Lately, she had taken to picking Seneca up at work. They would silently walk next to each other on the trip back to either of their houses, and somewhere along the way, their fingers would intertwine. Dylan knew other people noticed and she had been getting some odd stares and cryptic warnings from those around her, but she didn't care. Holding hands with Seneca felt like the most wonderful achievement of her life. Although she was frustrated that they hadn't really moved the physical part of their relationship along, she was willing to take things as slowly as Seneca wanted. The last thing she wanted to do was scare her away by moving too quickly.

When the room grew silent and Dylan felt all eyes on her, she realized she had been caught in her daydream. Each expectant face was looking at her, probably expecting her to share some profound insight on their project. She had nothing. She wasn't even sure what they had been talking about.

"Uh, what—"

She was saved from answering by the knock on her door. She put the binder down and flew to answer, glad for any excuse to avoid the awkward silence.

When she pulled the door open, her knees went weak and the breath whooshed out of her in one quick, amazing exhale. Seneca was standing there, looking stunning in black nylon athletic pants and a crisp white T-shirt. Her hair was delightfully mussed, as only a good workout could produce, and her cheeks were red and glowing from the chilly night air.

"Why don't you have a jacket?" Dylan asked, before silently berating herself that that was the first thing out of her mouth. It wasn't what she wanted to say, but what she wanted to say couldn't be said with curious onlookers.

Seneca was grinning and it was disarming. Dylan reached out a hand to softly stroke Seneca's cold cheek.

"Bob," Seneca said quietly, her eyes tender and her face relaxed.

Dylan stepped closer and wrapped her arms around Seneca's neck. Their torsos weren't touching, but the heat they were producing was enough to warm the air around them. They would have fogged up a pair of glasses, if either of them wore them.

"You have company," Seneca said, looking behind Dylan.

Dylan didn't even have to turn around to picture the scene of stunned faces and open-mouth gawking happening behind her.

"I just wanted to see you for a minute. Call me when you're done."

Dylan didn't pull away. She pulled the door shut behind her without a backward glance, leaving her classmates to their gossip in her room, blind to the activities in the hall.

"Is that the only reason you came over, wandering around in December without a jacket?" Dylan asked.

"No," Seneca said, looking like she was finding it hard to breathe with Dylan so close. I wanted to give you this."

She pulled Dylan to her and kissed her without hesitation, without holding anything back.

Their first kiss had been magical and eye-opening, but this kiss put the previous one to shame.

"That, my pirate queen, was a most amazing gift," Dylan said, feeling a little wobbly in the knees.

"*Your* pirate queen?" Seneca asked.

"If you want to be, sweet girl," Dylan said, holding Seneca even tighter.

Seneca looked down at Dylan shyly. "I think I might."

Dylan didn't say anything. She kissed Seneca on the nose, causing them both to laugh. She turned and laced her fingers through Seneca's and gave her hand a tug.

"You don't have to leave, right?"

Seneca looked down at their hands. "I like not being able to tell which are your fingers and which are mine," she said.

"Come inside," Dylan said, pulling on their joined hand again. "Please?"

"You have company."

Dylan didn't think she really wanted to leave, but she did feel her hesitation. "We won't be long. You can sit at my desk, or on the bed."

Dylan wasn't sure what was scaring her so much. Dylan knew she was ready for anything the night brought, but she had a feeling Seneca wasn't. The kiss had been a wonderful surprise, and now Dylan couldn't seem to think of anything but getting Seneca's lips against her own again. Her body had finally ignited, and what had been a slow burn was quickly turning into a full-blown fire. Imagining Seneca across the room, however small the dorm room, was excruciating. Envisioning her sitting across campus, out of Dylan's sight and touching range, was beyond comprehension. It was hard getting Seneca's foot off the brake pedal, and if there was a chance of getting her to relax, Dylan didn't want to lose a second of momentum.

Seneca smiled shyly and nodded. Spontaneously, she swept Dylan off her feet and lifted her off the ground so she could kiss her again.

Dylan giggled and swung her legs in a mock effort to get free. Seneca laughed with her and gently set her down. Dylan grabbed her hand, opened her dorm door, and pulled Seneca into the room.

The four women Dylan had shut out of their private moment instantly tried to look as if they hadn't been straining to hear every word exchanged between Dylan and the campus outcast. The expressions ranged from forced disinterest to the look of someone whose hand got caught in the cookie jar.

Dylan noticed the unusually calm demeanor of her classmates and stifled a chuckle. It wouldn't do to rub in their faces that she had just kissed the most amazing woman on campus. She hurriedly introduced the four women, feeling it necessary to be polite. Seneca plopped down at the desk and muttered something about checking her e-mail and Dylan returned to her study group. She perched on the bed, amused that Seneca had avoided it like the plague. All she could think about was getting Seneca into it. For weeks now, she had wanted to speed up their courtship, and finally Seneca had come and literally swept her off her feet. Forget wooing, she would lose her mind if Seneca didn't start acting like every other horny college student in a new relationship. She was tired of slow.

❖

Seneca listened in amazement as Dylan's dorm room filled with questions asked rapidly in French. She didn't understand the questions, but from the fact that they seemed directed almost entirely at Dylan, who obviously refused to answer, and when she did, she sounded annoyed, Seneca guessed they were about her. She made a show of checking her e-mail and looking up an assignment online. She resisted the urge to turn around and watch the interrogation.

She finally turned around when she heard Dylan's exasperated sigh and her response to the last question. The four other women were still speaking in French, but Dylan answered them in English.

"We're done for the night. If you all want to talk about our assignment or the class, then feel free to set up camp in the dining room and I'll be there in a minute. If you have other questions, don't let the door hit you in the ass on the way out."

Seneca started to stand up and comfort her since she was so clearly agitated, but Dylan held up a hand to stop her. She seemed to be asking for the space to handle her classmates on her own. Seneca shrugged and wondered if any of the women had ever seen Dylan's fiery side. She turned her attention back to the computer, content to let Dylan handle her own friends. It wasn't like Seneca would have any idea what to do with them. Within two minutes, the room was silent, and everyone, including Dylan, had left.

After closing down the computer, Seneca took some time to look around the small dorm room. As an upperclassman, Dylan had a single. The twin bed was neatly made and sat under the window. The small desk and dresser took up space on two of the other walls. Seneca's eyes lit up when she saw the small television perched on top of the dresser, angled to face the bed.

Not knowing how long Dylan was going to be gone, Seneca kicked off her shoes, grabbed the television remote, and settled on the bed. She had never owned a television, and the freedom to watch whatever stupid show caught her attention was strangely exciting. She settled on *Mythbusters* and was completely engrossed when Dylan opened the door and snuck back in.

"Whatcha watching?" Dylan asked as she shed her sweatshirt and shoes and landed in the chair in front of her computer.

"*Mythbusters*. Have you ever seen this show?" Seneca asked, not able to drag her eyes away. "These crazy guys say they're testing all these urban legends and myths, but secretly, I think they just like to blow stuff up."

"Thank you for staying," Dylan said. "I'm really sorry about the French inquisition."

Seneca looked at Dylan and noticed the worry lines around her eyes and mouth. She could see she was embarrassed about her classmates' behavior and her eyes still held some of the fire of earlier.

Wanting to reassure her but not knowing how, Seneca reached her hand out toward Dylan, her long arms able to close most of the distance in the small space. Dylan moved the rest of the way and they linked fingers. Dylan looked down at their joined hands, and some of the worry left her face. Seneca thought maybe she would be okay at this after all.

"Thank you for sticking up for me," Seneca said sincerely. "I don't really care what they say, but I'm sorry they interrogated you because of me. If we…you know…are a…well, you know—"

"Couple?"

"Right, that…if we are a couple, you're probably going to get that a lot," Seneca said, realizing once again the handicap she brought to any relationship.

"Why don't you let me decide whether you're a burden, or a drag, or not worth the fuss?"

Seneca looked at Dylan, shocked at how transparent she apparently was. "Bob, I'm not sure how I feel about dating a mind reader."

Dylan laughed long and hard. She scooted out of the chair and bumped Seneca out of the way on the bed with her hip, sitting down next to her. She rested her hand slowly on Seneca's stomach. Seneca flinched like she always did, but then her muscles relaxed incrementally under her touch. Without moving her hand, she leaned down and kissed Seneca gently, and then less so.

"I'm no mind reader. You don't have to worry about that," Dylan said, her mouth hovering inches above Seneca's.

Seneca lifted off the bed enough to close the distance between their lips and kissed Dylan soundly before pulling her down on top of her. She expertly flipped the curvaceous body and settled Dylan against her side, allowing the red hair to float across her chest while she held her.

"Wanna watch *Mythbusters* with me?" Seneca asked in her most charming voice.

"As long as that's not all I get to do."

Seneca stiffened anxiously but tried hard to hide the reaction. This was one of the things she had been worried about. What would Dylan think when she saw her without clothes? She'd already seen the scar on her arm, but could she handle a body covered in them? This had been one hell of an emotional day.

"What's wrong, sweetie? I only meant I want to kiss you…a lot."

"Oh," Seneca said, feeling like an ass for assuming Dylan might want more.

Her body was betraying her once again, and as hard as she tried to push it aside, the past was invading her present. The women at the bar were easier because she didn't care about them. Physically, she didn't disappoint them, and emotions were never part of the bargain. Being with Dylan was completely different. Part of her wished she could call Kate and ask for advice, but she knew she was on her own.

"Is that okay?" Dylan asked, sounding less confident.

By way of answer, Seneca pulled Dylan against her and kissed her with every emotion she was too afraid to speak, and in most cases, too afraid to feel.

When they pulled apart, each a little breathless, Seneca tried to explain. "I want to kiss you a lot too, Bob. I just don't know that I can go any further tonight." Honesty seemed like the only option. Dylan nodded, but Seneca could see she had questions.

"Is kissing all we're ever going to do, Seneca? Because I know you were sleeping with women you didn't even know… and with me, it's been forever and I can't even get your hands to wander. I just need to know what I'm in for here and how you feel about me."

"Bob, I used to let women take me home from the bar because I needed someone to know I was alive. I wanted a bit of human connection, but that was all. They never got more of me than you do. They actually got less, a lot less. I was there, but not really. No kissing. I kept all my clothes on. Sometimes I didn't even bother taking off my shoes. I can't do that to you, but I don't know how to do anything else. I just need a little time to figure it out." Seneca saw the relief cross Dylan's face. *Maybe I'll be okay at this relationship stuff after all.*

"Oh," Dylan said, looking like she wasn't sure what else to say. "Well, that's okay then. I was worried you didn't think I was—I know there are a lot of pretty women at that bar."

Seneca was horrified that Dylan had even considered that possibility. "Bob, you are the most beautiful woman I have ever laid eyes on. I don't know how to prove that to you, but I'll think of something." *Can I? What if I can't figure out how?*

"Will you stay?" Dylan asked. She looked as scared as the question made Seneca feel. "I just want you to hold me. It took me weeks to get you to kiss me again. I don't want to let you walk out just yet."

Seneca blushed and started to apologize for her delay, but thought better of it and instead detoured to Dylan's mouth.

"Fair warning, it's a small bed and I don't plan on using more than half of it."

"I don't know if you remember, but I happen to have the same bed. I don't know how we're both going to fit and only take up half of this thing. It's not that big."

Dylan pulled the covers back and indicated Seneca should get in. "Lay down and I'll show you."

"Bob, I'm still fully dressed."

"This first time, I'm letting you stay in your comfort zone. Next time, significantly less clothing."

"Whoa," Seneca said under her breath, feeling heat pulsing through every part of her body. "At least let me take off my boots."

CHAPTER FIFTEEN

Dylan came awake slowly in the darkness, her senses filled with unfamiliar stimuli. She realized first that someone was in her bed with her. A split second later, she felt her bed partner squirming, pushing her away, and whimpering. Sounds of pain and terror filled the room. As she woke more fully, she realized Seneca was in distress. She came fully awake and tried to figure out what to do.

She placed a comforting hand on Seneca's forehead in an effort to calm her, but Seneca reacted violently to the touch. She didn't wake, but pulled away as if slapped and cried out louder in her sleep. She kicked, trying to propel herself away from Dylan's hands. She was sweating, and her face was contorted grotesquely.

Dylan sat up in bed and moved out of Seneca's thrash zone. She wanted to know what Seneca was dreaming about and hold her until the nightmare went away, but she realized she would have to wake her before she could provide any comfort.

With difficulty, she bit back a sob as Seneca started fighting an imaginary assailant, begging and pleading for her attacker to leave her alone. Seneca's face was always expressive, but Dylan had never seen it so twisted in terror. She could feel the tension radiating off Seneca's slim form in waves as she writhed, trapped in her nightmare. She was practically vibrating as she squirmed on the bed.

When Seneca screamed, a sound filled with sheer, un-adulterated agony, and reached for her injured leg, Dylan couldn't sit, paralyzed by indecision and disbelief, any longer. Seneca was curled on her side, cradling her damaged thigh between her hands, still kicking with her uninjured leg. The pain she was experiencing seemed to have transcended the fear, as now her energy was solely focused on her thigh and a moaning request to be left alone.

Dylan tried to make contact again, this time resting her hand on Seneca's back. The T-shirt beneath her fingers was drenched in sweat. Seneca didn't pull away this time. It was as if she were incapable of feeling anything but her cradled leg. Encouraged by the non-reaction, Dylan pulled Seneca to her, wrapping her in a tight embrace. She kissed her temple, rubbed her back, and quietly begged her to wake up.

"It's okay, sweetie. Wake up. It's just a dream." Dylan rocked their joined bodies back and forth. "Wake up, my pirate queen. Wake up. Please wake up."

Eventually, Seneca's body tension eased and her breathing signaled she was waking. Dylan held her more tightly and resumed her gentle kisses.

"Please stop," Seneca said, her voice hoarse and pain filled. "Shannon, stop. I'm sorry. I'm sorry."

Dylan froze. Gut wrenching, agonizing, unidentifiable emotion ripped through her system before she was able to quell it. She had no idea who Shannon was, but if she had ever held Seneca this way, or if she was the one who caused the nightmares, Dylan hated her.

"Shannon's not here, Seneca. It's me. It's Dylan."

She comforted herself by thinking Seneca didn't sound particularly happy with the idea that Shannon was the one holding her now. However irrational, she didn't want another woman, even one from Seneca's past, interfering with their present.

"Bob?" Seneca asked, opening her eyes and taking in the unfamiliar surroundings.

Seneca groaned, looking sad, ashamed, and angry. She let her damaged leg stretch free of her grasp and tentatively put a hand over Dylan's, which were still wrapped around her middle.

Seneca struggled to pull free of Dylan's hold, but Dylan held tighter. She expected Seneca's withdrawal.

"Bob, please, just let me go."

"No," Dylan said emphatically, although she loosened her hold around Seneca's middle.

"You have to. Don't you see now why you have to?" Seneca asked, her voice wild, desperate.

"No, I don't."

"I'm no good for you. Just let me go. It's better this way. We can't do this. I can't do this," she said. Seneca looked so defeated, her eyes glossy with unshed tears. "What would happen if we were at your parents' house and I did this? Or we were at a fancy business retreat of yours?"

"That's really not your decision to make. And if any of that came up in the future, we would deal with it," Dylan said. "But I'm not holding you back anymore, Seneca. If you want to walk out the door, I won't stop you. But you should know I don't want you to go."

Tears streamed down Dylan's face, and she didn't bother to wipe them away. Her hands rested on either side of Seneca, who had moved to the edge of the bed. She was terrified that Seneca was about to shatter the fragile bond of trust and tenderness they had built over the past semester. Dylan knew she couldn't force her to open up, couldn't force her to stay, but she wanted to try.

"Bob, you don't know what you're asking me," Seneca whispered.

"Yes, I do, sweet girl. I'm asking you to trust me and to be with me." Dylan tentatively closed the distance between them and rested her head on Seneca's shoulder.

"You don't understand—"

"No, I don't. I can't unless you tell me. Help me understand, Seneca. Tell me what you need. Tell me what happened." Dylan placed a kiss on Seneca's shoulder and felt her trembling.

"I'm sorry. I just can't. Not tonight," Seneca said. "Not right after. After, that." Seneca waved her hand in the direction of where she had been sleeping.

"Well, it's the middle of the night. Not the best time for talking anyway. My mother always told me nothing good ever happens after midnight." Dylan wrapped her arms around Seneca's waist, and when she leaned into her embrace, Dylan's heart swelled.

"Your mom is a smart lady," Seneca said.

"She has her moments," Dylan said, thinking how humorous it was that premarital, lesbian bed sharing probably wasn't what her mother's advice had been intended for. "Do you think you'll be able to sleep if I get you another shirt and we snuggle back up?"

"I don't think your shirts will fit me, Bob," Seneca said, her eyes already heavy with exhaustion.

"Is it terrible that I wouldn't mind you in a tight T-shirt?"

"Bob."

"All right, fine. I have at least one that I won as part of a raffle. It's unisex huge and ugly as anything, but at least it will be long enough for you."

She dug it out and handed it to Seneca. She was well on her way to helping pull off the sweaty shirt, when Seneca stopped her.

"Not tonight. I don't want to give you nightmares. You've seen the scar on my arm."

Though the remark stung a bit, Dylan accepted it, glad that Seneca hadn't simply run from the room. If this was the limit for tonight, but it still included them sharing a bed, she was okay.

Seneca moved across the room, turned her back to Dylan, and quickly stripped off her wet T-shirt. She pulled the clean, dry shirt on as fast as she could, but even in the dark and the brief exposure, Dylan could see that Seneca's skin wasn't smooth, but rather an intricate network of white pockmarks. She desperately wanted to ask about it, but knew now wasn't the time. Instead, she slid to her side of the twin bed, pulled back the covers, opened her arms, and invited Seneca in. Seneca slid into bed and fell asleep almost immediately. They both slept through the rest of the night peacefully, Dylan wrapped protectively around Seneca, warding off the demons that had left their terrible traces on her body.

CHAPTER SIXTEEN

"Enough," Seneca said, rolling onto her back, her head resting on Dylan's lap. "No more action movies. Don't you have a nice comedy, or romance, or sports highlight film we could watch? C-SPAN? Anything?"

"Hey, you said I could pick all the movies. Next time think that one out a little better." It was one of the rare weekend days that Seneca didn't have to work and neither of them had an overwhelming amount of unfinished schoolwork. They had been lounging in Dylan's room watching movies together most of the day.

"I will," Seneca said, nuzzling the top of her head into Dylan's palm, clearly begging her to continue the head rub that had been interrupted by the end of *Lethal Weapon 4.*

"Oh no, you can't expect a head rub after insulting my movies. Not even pirate queens can get away with that. Don't you know it is the pirate queen's woman who really runs the ship?"

Seneca opened one eye. "I think I might be learning that. Kate may have hinted at something along those lines too. And how does a pirate queen get back in the good graces of the pirate queen's woman?"

"They don't insult action movies, that's for sure. It's definitely going to cost you," Dylan said, eying the stack of unwatched movies, focusing on the one she had been waiting for all day.

Dylan saw Seneca getting ready to leap at the stack of movies, but she was quicker. She grabbed the movie and held it triumphantly above her head, spinning and dancing her way to her computer.

Having assured her damaged leg wouldn't collapse beneath her, Seneca caught up to Dylan and wrapped her in her arms, lifting her six inches off the ground. It took only a second for their lips to meet and for Dylan to wrap her legs around Seneca's waist. *Terminator 2* clattered to the hardwood, completely forgotten.

Dylan shoved her hands roughly into Seneca's short brown hair, holding her head close as their tongues waged a delicate, passionate battle. She felt Seneca's hands on her ass, holding her up as well as pulling her close. Seneca's tight, flat stomach against her crotch, after months of buildup, was almost all she needed to shoot over the edge. She slid away enough to lessen the pressure enough to ensure the tease remained, but the threat of orgasm did not.

Seneca bumped them into a wall. They lingered there, Dylan resting her back against the flat surface, feeling the plaster and paint as a cool counterpoint to the heat against the front of her body. With one hand, Seneca tugged Dylan's shirt as far up her back as she could without help, her intention and desire for the shirt clear. It was off and on the floor in a matter of seconds.

Seneca stopped a moment and took in Dylan's breasts, covered only in a sexy, lacy bra. She seemed to like what she saw. She ducked her head and ran her tongue along the line of fabric on each side. Dylan arched toward Seneca's touch.

"Bed," she managed between a stifled moan and a hiss of desire as Seneca's mouth roamed over one painfully erect nipple.

Seneca placed her on the bed with care, a look of reverence in her eyes that nearly made Dylan weep with joy. Never in her wildest dreams could she imagine such awe directed toward her. Seneca's weight on top of her felt so utterly perfect. As their bodies fused, lips, breasts, and thighs, Dylan could think of no greater pleasure. She was so glad they'd waited for the right time.

Dylan reached for Seneca's shirt, trying unsuccessfully to tug it up and off. Seneca's strong hands gripped her wrists and gently pinned her hands over her head. Dylan didn't argue.

She arched eagerly as Seneca reached behind her for the clasp, both of them eager to shed the final barrier to Dylan's breasts. When they were revealed, Seneca sucked in a breath, and Dylan had never felt more beautiful.

"Oh, Bob," Seneca said, flicking her tongue over first one, and then the other flushed pink nipple.

Dylan enjoyed the attention until her nerve endings were so raw she was afraid she wouldn't get to experience everything else Seneca had in mind for her. In a moment of clarity, she had an overwhelming urge to see Seneca as well. She shivered in anticipation of finally laying eyes on the hard planes and rippling muscles she had felt so many times beneath the cover of Seneca's T-shirts.

"Wait, baby. You'll make me…just slow down for a minute." Dylan gasped as Seneca tugged forcefully on her nipple, making her stomach clench in the first signs of just how close she was. "I want to see you."

Dylan pulled on Seneca's shirt, but again Seneca resisted. Dylan tried again.

"Let's worry about you right now," Seneca said, trying to remove Dylan's hands from her shirt hem.

"I have nothing to worry about," Dylan said in her best bedroom voice. "I want to see you. I want you to feel this too."

"I am feeling it, sweetheart. It's wonderful." Seneca looked anxious.

"It can be better." Dylan tried one more time for Seneca's shirt, but Seneca pulled away.

"That's not how this works," Seneca said, her voice high and hard.

Dylan felt like someone had poured ice water over her. She wiggled free of Seneca's weight and sat at the end of the bed, her knees pulled up to cover her exposed chest.

"What do you mean that's not how this works?"

"I…" Seneca looked lost. "I want to make you feel good. I want to finish what we started."

"And what about you? You stay fully clothed while I'm naked and coming?" Dylan was losing the battle to keep her voice from rising.

"Yes, but…" Seneca looked confused and scared.

"So I'm just like them? The women at the bar you had sex with?"

"Of course not. Dylan, you're amazing. But I can't…I mean, I won't…"

"Wonderful, so I'm no better in your eyes than they are. I don't deserve any more trust than some woman you pick up in a bar." Dylan's eyes swam with unshed tears.

"Bob, you're everything to me. The other women didn't mean anything, even then. You're all I care about. And I haven't been there in months." Seneca looked like she was trying to dig herself out of a hole while blindfolded, but she had no idea which way was up.

"Is that supposed to make me feel better? I don't go there anymore because now I have you to take their place?" Dylan demanded. "Do you love me?" She retrieved her shirt and stood fully clothed, hand on hip, looking down at Seneca on the bed. Her anger was cut slightly by how small and terrified Seneca looked. Every time Dylan started to speak, Seneca visibly flinched and looked as if she might cry. Tears swam in her eyes, something Dylan had never seen before.

"Do I love you?" Seneca repeated.

"Yes, do you love me?" Dylan knew it wasn't a fair question. She knew, but she had to ask anyway.

"I don't know," Seneca said.

"Fine."

Dylan turned and walked out of her dorm room door, slamming the door hard behind her for good measure.

"I don't even know how to tell." She heard Seneca's words before she stormed away from the room. That nearly broke her heart and made her rush back into the room. She was embarrassed, both at being the only one vulnerable and possibly the only one feeling as strongly as she did, but also at the way she had reacted.

Seneca had told her she always kept her clothes on, and maybe she shouldn't have expected her to change just because they were getting hot and heavy. Dylan went into the bathroom and splashed water on her face. Seneca wasn't worth losing over this. She knew Seneca had a long and complicated past, and this was clearly part of it. If she wasn't willing to understand that, she shouldn't have taken on any of it. When she put it to herself that way, she felt horrible for her outburst. But she also really needed Seneca to meet her partway too. They couldn't have a future together where they either never slept together or Seneca hid in the closet to change her clothes.

When Dylan slipped back into her room, Seneca was clearly packing up to leave. Her shoulders were slumped and she looked like she had just hopped a marathon on her one good leg. Her limp was more pronounced, something Dylan had come to recognize as a sign of either pain or emotional turmoil, and her face was anguished.

"I'm going to leave you alone now. I'm sorry I ruined our day. Please call me when you're ready."

"Please don't go," Dylan said softly. "I'm sorry I reacted the way I did. You warned me. I moved us too quickly."

At the smallest hint of hope on Seneca's face, Dylan rushed headlong at Seneca and threw herself into her arms. Seneca hung on as Dylan sobbed loudly against her neck.

"I don't think I'm ever going to understand relationships," Seneca said. "Is that how this is supposed to work?"

"Come to bed with me?" Dylan asked when she finally got her crying under control. She had Seneca's hand gripped tightly in hers.

"I thought—"

"Just to snuggle…and talk. I think maybe we should talk." Dylan pulled gently, getting Seneca moving, one jerky step at a time. "Then maybe we can have dinner."

"I'm sorry," Seneca said. "I've ruined everything."

"Shh, we'll get there. Right now, I need you to hold me,"

When they were settled together, Dylan kissed Seneca's arm and then asked, "Why wouldn't you let me take your shirt off?"

"I have…scars," Seneca said, choosing her words carefully. "I don't like to feel exposed."

"You seemed like you were feeling better and—" Dylan snuggled closer, feeling comfortable and whole when she was this close to Seneca, even when she was confused and still a little angry.

"Not those kind of scars. I guess I have those too, but I mean scar scars. Real, physical scars. You felt one of them, on my shoulder. You've seen the one on my arm."

Her voice had crept below a whisper. Dylan got the sense she hadn't ever talked about this with anyone.

"And you what, don't want people to see them? Don't trust me? Worry I'll think they're ugly?" Dylan knew she needed to try to understand. Seneca wasn't rejecting her; they were both learning as they went along.

"Yes, I guess all of those things. Please just give me a little time. I do trust you, or at least, I really want to. I've never had anyone who cared about me, so this is all a little new."

"Well, you do now."

Dylan leaned over Seneca and kissed her. They were gasping for breath and needing a cold shower when she was done. Seneca let her hand stray up and down Dylan's back. She stopped and lingered over her legs and ass.

"I'd like to finish what I started. I'm sure you're as worked up as I am. I'm practically dying over here, which is new for me. I was never really all that invested in my part with the women at the bar."

"Can we stop talking about them?" Dylan asked.

"Oh, yeah, just so you know that I'm done with them for good."

"Are the same rules in effect if my shirt goes flying again?"

"I'm sorry, Bob. I just need a little more time," Seneca said. "I don't know that I'll react all that well if I just dive in. I think about it, and then...Well, it's not pretty."

Dylan kissed her on the cheek gently and then cupped her palm where her lips had been. "I'm willing to wait. Besides, I can't have sex with you while you're wearing that raffle T-shirt." Seneca wore the T-shirt Dylan had let her borrow at every opportunity, the awfulness of it a part of their understanding now.

"You sure do give me a whole lot of motivation to get over this problem of mine." Seneca pulled Dylan closer, and once again, Dylan was content to wait. Seneca was hurt in ways Dylan didn't yet understand, but she was too amazing to let go.

They ended up skipping dinner and falling asleep together.

Long after Seneca drifted off to sleep, Dylan lay awake and thought about the evening. She knew without a doubt that she was falling in love, and she hoped Seneca would let herself follow. When the nightmares claimed Seneca, as she suspected they might after their emotional evening, Dylan soothed away her fears and quieted her back into peaceful slumber. She refused to think about the possibility that Seneca wouldn't let her walls down enough for them to really be together.

CHAPTER SEVENTEEN

"You okay, Senny?" Jenny Collins asked.

Jenny played on the squash team and was a friend of Britt's. Word had spread, first through the squash team, and then across other teams, that the wildly good-looking and slightly intimidating student trainer who prowled the sidelines with Kate, was actually really nice. Or at least, that's how Britt had reported it back to Seneca.

Seneca glared at her, trying to look tough and intimidating, but the sophomore wasn't taking the bait. The ridiculous nickname was a small price to pay for people talking to her instead of staring at her.

"Fine, why?" Seneca asked innocently, pulling the ACE bandage tight around Jenny's strained quad. She applied the tape, securing the compression wrap in place, and stood up, gingerly testing her leg before turning to toss the supplies back under one of the treatment tables.

"Don't know. You've got that look that says you've got romantic trouble," Jenny said knowingly. "If you need help with that, I know a few women around here who wouldn't mind helping you out."

Jenny said some outrageous things, but everyone knew she wasn't flirting, despite how it sounded. Jenny was straight and quite happily partnered.

"Leave the poor girl alone, Jenny. And pull your pants down already," Kate said, placing her hand on Seneca's shoulder. Jenny quickly lowered the leg of her shorts that she had pulled up to allow Seneca access to her quadriceps.

Seneca could hear the squash team's laughter and a few frantic admonishments about time as they finished getting ready. She followed Kate into the small office space of the training room, and she caught Britt's eye through the glass separating the offices from the treatment area. Britt winked.

After the team filed out for practice and the training room was mercifully quiet, Kate turned to Seneca. "I know Jenny was just messing with you, but are you okay? Everything good with you and Dylan?" Kate's face showed nothing but concern, but Seneca had long ago stopped looking for something other than caring and kindness.

She and Dylan spent every available minute together, and for the most part, it was wonderful. After their awkward fight, they hadn't talked again about the incident, but neither had there been a repeat of the passion of that afternoon. She was coming to realize that the next step in that part of the relationship would be left to her, just like last time. All these steps were hers to take, and it was getting progressively harder. Dylan hadn't pushed, nor, it seemed, would she. It was wearing on Seneca, and it couldn't be easy on Dylan either.

They slept in the same bed, cuddled and kissed, but Seneca knew she wanted more than that. Then there was the question of being in love. She hadn't been able to stop thinking of that since Dylan had asked.

"I don't know," Seneca said, realizing Kate was waiting for an answer. "Things were great, but I kinda screwed it up again. I don't know how to make it better. Or actually I do, but I don't. It's complicated."

Kate didn't say anything, but continued to give Seneca her full attention. Seneca recognized that as Kate's "if you want to talk I'm here to listen" face.

"We were…uh…this is embarrassing—" Seneca didn't get to finish because a worried first year squash player came careening through the door, her eyes wide and her face pale. "Someone got hurt upstairs. We need you."

Seneca grabbed a radio and put a calming hand on the young woman's shoulder. "Who's hurt?"

"Jenny. She got hit in the head."

"With what?" Seneca asked as she scooped up her small kit filled with essential supplies and slung it over her shoulder. Kate did the same and they hurried out of the training room.

"A racket, or maybe Britt's elbow, the ball, I don't know." She looked close to tears.

"Is she conscious?" Seneca asked, trying to keep her calm.

"Yes." A smile slowly crept across the woman's face. "She's pissed as hell. Said you were going to see her all busted up."

Seneca and Kate laughed. That didn't sound life threatening.

"Head on up. Radio if you need me. Sounds like this doesn't require both of us," Kate said. Seneca noticed Kate had slowly been giving her more responsibility and autonomy in situations that weren't emergencies. It seemed to be part of some master plan for her training, and it felt good. Kate kept giving her new challenges, so she figured she must be passing them. Well, maybe. She never really could tell with Kate's master plans and Yoda-type lessons.

Upstairs in the squash complex, Seneca fought her way through the crowd of women surrounding their coach and Jenny, who didn't look pleased to see Seneca.

"Go away. I'm fine."

"I can see that," Seneca said mildly, taking in her already swollen cheek and puffy eye that seemed to be blackening darker by the second.

She assessed Jenny's immediate state and convinced her to head down to the training room.

"Aren't you all supposed to get out of the way when another person is going to hit the ball? Gentleman's game or something like that?" Seneca still hadn't figured out the rules to squash.

"It's a small court," Jenny said, her uninjured eye not completely focused. "We're supposed to wear goggles too."

"That was going to be my next question."

"It's that big hulk of a roommate of yours that's the problem. She ran into me. Or my face ran into her. I'm actually not really sure. She could probably tell you better." Jenny swerved a little in the hall and Seneca grabbed her shoulders to steady her.

"Here." Seneca offered Jenny her arm. "Hang on. We're almost there." Seneca was already mentally making a checklist of the next steps in Jenny's care. Apparently, a concussion assessment should be a high priority.

"You're tall," Jenny said suddenly.

"That I am." Seneca held Jenny a little tighter, wanting to get her to the training room as quickly as possible.

Jenny was silent a few moments and then looked up again. "You're tall."

Seneca groaned; it was classic concussion behavior. With her luck, Jenny would be commenting on her height until they got her shipped off to the hospital for an evaluation.

"You're hot too. Has anyone told you that?"

"I think you got hit in the head harder than you think," Seneca said under her breath.

"Well, you are. I'm just saying."

"Jenny, you're straight." Seneca knew reasoning probably wasn't going to work.

"Doesn't mean I'm blind," Jenny said before falling silent. "Was practice over?" She asked as they made it through the door into the training room.

"It certainly is for you."

Kate was on her feet as soon as she saw the look on Seneca's face. They ran through the concussion assessment quickly, pretty sure what they would find. They didn't bother with the computerized version since Jenny wouldn't be able to do it in her current state anyway. It only took a few minutes for the ambulance to arrive and transport her to the local hospital for evaluation and testing. Concussions weren't treated lightly. As they loaded Jenny into the ambulance, she said to Seneca, "You're tall. And hot." Seneca just waved, and Kate chuckled.

The rest of Seneca's shift wasn't much calmer. It had been steady work after Jenny's concussion, with a random assortment of blisters, bumps, strains, bruises, and one badly sprained ankle. Some days were just like that. Seneca had seen enough black-and-blue skin for the day, though.

By the time she and Kate had time to head upstairs for their customary workout, they were both dragging a little.

"Busy day," Seneca said casually, trying to assess whether Kate remembered their earlier conversation and that it had been interrupted.

"Yep. You still liking it?"

Seneca felt the weariness of the day lift. "I love it. It's, I don't know, perfect, I guess."

Kate nodded and seemed to know exactly what Seneca meant. She looked like she was making a mental note about something, but Seneca knew it wasn't worth asking. Kate would tell her when she was ready, if it pertained to her. Besides, she had a more important question.

"Kate," she asked softly, "how do you know if you're in love?"

Kate stopped mid-stretch. "Shall we take a break for a minute?" Kate asked. They'd only just warmed up, but Seneca figured it was the kind of question you had to pay attention to. They lowered themselves against the wall and gulped down a few mouthfuls of water. "Do you think you might be?" Kate finally asked.

"I don't know. I don't even know what it's supposed to feel like. I haven't ever…no one has ever…" Seneca didn't know how to begin explaining her past and its influence on her present. She didn't know what being in love was because no one had ever loved her.

"Do you like her?" Kate asked seriously.

Seneca figured this must be another one of Kate's riddles.

"Yes, very much. I like her a lot."

"Well, that's a good start. Test out saying 'I like you, Dylan' and 'I love you, Dylan' in a private place and see how it feels. I bet one will feel a bit more true than the other, after you say it a few times."

"That's it?" Seneca asked. "Aren't you supposed to tell me what being in love feels like? How I should be able to tell because my stomach does strange flippy things every time I think about her and I sometimes can't form a coherent sentence when she's around? Or that all I can do sometimes is stare at her?"

Kate laughed. "I think if you're feeling all those things that's probably a pretty good sign, but no, I can't tell you what symptoms to look for. This isn't like an injury in the training room, Sen. It's different for everyone."

Seneca didn't like that answer. "I thought being in love was being in love. That everyone just knows."

"Being in love *is* being in love, and it is as simple as that. And it's so very much more complicated. I thought I was in love once," Kate said. "I said 'I love you' to her, and I meant it and it felt good. And I got my heart broken when she left me after seven years. But then I met Lisa."

"And you knew you weren't in love before?" Seneca was trying to understand.

"No, I was. It was just very different than being in love with Lisa. It started differently, and I reacted differently. Most people would say that I was in love with both women, but the feelings didn't look or *feel* anything alike. Does that make any sense?"

"Yes and no," Seneca said. "But I'm not sure that's much help deciding if I'm in love with Dylan. All you told me is that if Dylan was someone else it would feel completely different and I wouldn't recognize it."

Kate glared at her with one eyebrow cocked. Seneca knew she wasn't really upset and started laughing.

"I told you to say it out loud," Kate said defensively.

Seneca was still laughing, releasing some of the tension she had been carrying since her fight with Dylan.

"What brought all this on?" Kate asked.

"Dylan and I got into a fight." Seneca's laughter died down as the details of the night came back to her.

"Ah, yes, fights always make me wonder if I'm in love, and they give me the warm fuzzy feeling you were describing earlier," Kate said. "Although the makeup sex is a nice bonus."

Seneca felt her face heat up and knew it was probably very red. "Aren't you my boss? I thought we weren't supposed to talk about that sort of thing."

"I probably wasn't supposed to invite you to live with me over the winter break either, but I did and you're going to, and besides, I'm not your boss up here, just your workout buddy. So was I right about the makeup sex?"

Seneca figured, if possible, she turned even redder. "Um, that was kinda what the fight was about."

"You got into a fight about makeup sex after a fight? I don't understand young people."

"We didn't…there…no sex. I wouldn't let her…she-wanted-to-take-my-shirt-off-and-I-wouldn't-let-her," Seneca said, turning the admission into practically one unintelligible word. Her face was on fire.

Seneca took a deep breath, mortified. She couldn't look at Kate for a long few seconds, but when she finally did dare to sneak a peek, Kate was looking at her as she always did, with love and no judgment.

"When I got dumped, I didn't go out with anyone for a long time. I thought if I stayed locked away from everyone, even my friends, no one would disappoint me, and I couldn't get my heart broken again."

"Why did she leave you?" Seneca was happy to have the focus on something other than her failure with Dylan.

"We grew up. The paths we were on just started to veer away from one another. They would occasionally meander in the same direction and we would rediscover what we liked about each other, but in the end, we simply grew apart. I was just blind to that happening." Kate's face grew sad as she thought about her younger self.

"But you found Lisa," Seneca said.

"Yes. Well, actually, her dog found me. She had gotten out and ended up in my neighborhood. I called to return her and ended up with a date. I almost didn't go."

"Why?" Seneca asked, horrified. "You and Lisa are about as perfect for each other as I can imagine."

"Too scared."

Seneca couldn't imagine Kate being scared of anything, let alone mild mannered and cute as a button Lisa. Sure, she could lay down the law when Seneca or Kate stepped a toe out of line, but still, not worthy of terror.

"Sometimes the past interferes so much with the present that it risks screwing up the future too. That was my problem. Good thing for me, Lisa is persistent, and damned stubborn." Kate's eyes sparkled and her mouth curled up a little more on one side when she thought about Lisa.

"So you're telling me that whatever the problem is in my past, I shouldn't let it mess up my future with Dylan?"

"I don't remember saying that."

"I'm starting to figure out these riddles of yours."

"Riddles? I don't speak in riddles."

Seneca rolled her eyes good-naturedly. "I want to get over it, but I'm scared. I've got these." Seneca lifted up one side of her shirt, exposing her heavily scarred abdomen. "No one wants to look at someone whose body looks like mine. I've got them all over."

"Who did this to you, kiddo?"

Kate's tone was light, but her eyes were deadly serious. Seneca was afraid for the people responsible if Kate ever learned their names.

"Doesn't really matter," Seneca whispered, dropping her head.

"Okay. For now, I'll accept that," Kate said, lifting Seneca's chin with her index finger, forcing her to look her in the eye. "Do you think Dylan loves you?"

"I think, maybe. I don't know. She asked me if I loved her after I wouldn't take my shirt off. I think she was maybe saying she did love me. I do know that I feel loved when I'm with her. That's nice." Seneca couldn't help but smile. The thought of Dylan did that to her.

"If she loves you, then she loves all of you, even the parts you think you're keeping hidden from her and the parts you might not love so much about yourself. I feel like we've had a similar conversation before. About your inner scars. She seems to have handled those pretty well, right?"

"So far she has. I took your advice about letting her show me how she sees me. I like it. But how do I know she won't break my heart?"

"That, kiddo, is the million dollar question, one to which I have no answer. Relationships are work. You have to keep them healthy. In the good ones, though, the hard work feels an awful lot like play." Kate gave Seneca's arm a light squeeze. Maybe she was silently encouraging her to fight off her fears.

"You think she could handle seeing the scars? She saw one already and didn't freak out too much," Seneca said, not sure how serious Kate had been about Dylan loving all of her.

"Probably. She may not know what they look like or where they are, but she knows that you've been hurt in the past and that makes you cautious. She knows you're tall and thin and strong, and she seems to like that combination, so I don't think it would matter if you were covered head to toe in tattoos, scars, or painted blue. The woman is on your side."

Seneca sprawled back on the floor and looked at the ceiling. What would Dylan do if she saw everything Seneca kept hidden under her clothes? Seneca didn't know what she would do if Dylan wasn't okay with it. She also didn't know what she would do if she was. If Dylan didn't mind her body as scarred and damaged as it was, if she was able to peel off that exterior layer and see what was underneath, what else might she see that Seneca tried to keep hidden, not under her clothes, but deep inside? It felt so vulnerable and soft and raw. Could she even risk it? Could she not?

CHAPTER EIGHTEEN

I'm going to brush my teeth," Dylan said. "Try not to miss me too much while I'm gone." She wandered out of the room and down the hall to the communal bathroom that was a staple of every college dorm.

Seneca paced the room, waiting for Dylan to get back. She didn't even glance at the pajamas that were hanging neatly on the back of the desk chair across the room. She knew she was making a bigger deal out of this than she needed to, but she had never been in love before. It certainly felt like a huge deal. Aside from that, she had screwed things up so completely with Dylan before, she wasn't sure she deserved another chance. She needed to make the first move if they were going to move forward, and damn was it hard.

"What's wrong, my sweet girl?" Dylan asked, walking up behind Seneca and wrapping her arms around her.

Seneca startled at the unexpected contact. She hadn't heard Dylan come back into the room. She spun around in Dylan's arms and clung to her for a moment, drawing strength from her steadiness and wonderful calm.

"Ask me again what you asked me when you were mad, after we tried to...you know. I want to answer you now," Seneca said, her face still pressed against Dylan's shoulder.

"Ask you what, sweetheart?" Dylan sounded confused. She guided them both to the bed and sat them down facing each other. "What did I ask you—Oh."

"The answer is yes," Seneca said quietly, feeling incredibly happy, knowing what she was saying was true.

"Yes, what?" Dylan asked, a smile sweeping across her face.

"Yes, I love you," Seneca said, louder this time.

"Again." Dylan laughed, her hands in Seneca's hair, their faces just inches apart.

"I love you."

"I love you too," Dylan said before closing the distance between their lips.

The kiss was sweet and tender, conveying their love and deeper level of commitment. It didn't stay that way. Soon the sweetness was overcome by passion and the tenderness with urgency. Their tongues battled in the first attempt to show physically what Seneca knew words would never be able to fully express.

When Seneca reached for Dylan's shirt, Dylan pulled back. Despite the new assurances of love, she clearly wasn't going to be the only one lying naked in bed. Seneca felt the withdrawal and stilled her hands. She took a huge breath and held it. She reached for her own shirt but paused a moment. She blew the breath out, drew the soft cotton T-shirt over her head, and tossed it to the floor.

Dylan drew a rasping breath. She stood and pulled Seneca to her feet and stepped back to get a better view.

Seneca squirmed under Dylan's intense scrutiny. She resisted the urge to hide her stomach, to cover the scars and blemishes that she saw every day in the mirror, or at least the days she was brave enough to look. When Dylan didn't say anything immediately, she thought her gamble a terrible mistake. It would be impossible for anyone to see past the ugliness. That was why she always remained clothed, partly for the control it afforded, but mostly to stop the gaping stares she always expected would accompany the unveiling of her body.

"Bob?" Seneca asked, hating the uncertainty in her voice.

"God, Seneca, you are absolutely beautiful. It is criminal to have a body like yours."

"But what about these?" Seneca motioned at her stomach.

Dylan unabashedly stared at Seneca. She took her time looking her up and down. She started with her shoulders, lingered on her sports bra, took in the curve of her ribs, and licked her lips as she moved along her abs and stopped at her waist. Seneca had never had anyone look at her like that. It was as if Dylan didn't see, or didn't mind, the hundreds of small round scars that covered her upper torso. Dylan had already seen part of the long, jagged scar that slashed across her shoulder blade and ended just below her armpit, but Seneca was most self-conscious about the raised patch of scar tissue that stood out on her belly and the multiple smaller linear gashes that were their companions.

"Your body is beautiful, Seneca. *You* are beautiful." Dylan ran a finger along the scar on Seneca's stomach, the one she worried would repulse Dylan the most. "I want to spend hours getting to know all of it. I want to be the only one who has the map to this stunning landscape. And," Dylan said, "someday, I want to know what happened to you."

Dylan kissed Seneca, who deepened the kiss and pulled Dylan close. Seneca had no idea how anyone could find her beautiful, but she felt very lucky that Dylan did, and when Dylan looked at her the way she just had, she felt beautiful in a way she'd never even considered possible.

"I thought you'd think I was ugly," Seneca said.

"Never. But I'm ready to not be wearing a shirt either."

Thinking about Dylan's gaze on her skin fired her libido. She deftly removed Dylan's shirt, barely breaking kissing contact to do so. Lips still locked, they tumbled backward onto the bed, Dylan on top in a tangle of arms and legs.

In the places Seneca was long and angled, Dylan was soft and curvy, and their bodies fit together perfectly. Seneca held Dylan to her tightly, each hand cupping a cheek of Dylan's wonderfully seductive ass. Seneca was content to stay as they were, kissing each other until suddenly that wasn't nearly enough.

Eventually, the feel of Dylan's weight pressing against her breasts and against her center was more than Seneca could stand.

She moved her hands from Dylan's backside, along the side of her abdomen, and finally rested on the curve of her breasts, which were still hidden behind another lacy bra. Dylan propped herself up on her elbows, dragging her lips away from Seneca's, letting her breasts dominate Seneca's vision. Seneca got the message loud and clear, and the bra was off as quickly as Seneca could unclasp it.

She pulled Dylan further up her body, taking a moment to admire the beauty before her. Tenderly, she flicked her tongue over first one, then the other of Dylan's hardened nipples, forcing them to stand at attention. Dylan lowered herself over Seneca's mouth, encouraging her to spend more time acquainting herself. Seneca pulled a nipple into her mouth and Dylan cried out in pleasure. Her arms gave out at the touch and she landed in a heap on top of Seneca.

With a practiced thrust of her hip and the gentle guidance of her hands, Seneca flipped them so she was on top. She removed her own sports bra and kissed Dylan again, groaning into her mouth as their breasts met skin to skin for the first time.

Dylan, apparently dissatisfied with Seneca's lack of attention to her chest, tried to gently direct Seneca's attention. When that failed to yield the desired results, she shimmied up the bed as far as she could with Seneca's full weight on her, in an effort to put her breasts directly under Seneca's mouth.

"Impatient?" Seneca asked.

She flicked her tongue across a nipple and watched the pleasure ripple across Dylan's face. She flicked again and then ran her tongue in increasingly wider circles around the dark pink center. Dylan rose off the bed, her body reacting to every sensation. Seneca repeated the teasing touch with the other breast.

"Oh…Sen…please." Dylan begged her, twisting her fingers in Seneca's hair, trying to guide her back to her hard nipples.

Dylan's fractured pleading was Seneca's undoing. They had barely begun, but she was wet and in danger of coming. Knowing Dylan reacted so strongly to her and that she, in turn, reacted the same way to Dylan was an incredible turn on. She realized this was what it felt like when you were in love. Emotions heightened every touch, strengthened every sensation, and Seneca decided it was well worth the wait.

She moved one leg between Dylan's and pressed intimately into her. At the same time, she finally took one irresistible nipple in her mouth and ran her palm over the other one. Dylan exploded off the bed, her back arched and her hips thrusting. She tangled one hand in Seneca's hair, the other ran up and down Seneca's back, digging in slightly with pleasure as Seneca's tongue wandered over a particularly sensitive spot.

Seneca eased the pressure between Dylan's legs but continued to ravish attention on her breasts. They were round and full and so perfect they took her breath away. She followed the pattern of Dylan's breathing, lingering in places that made her moan. As she began to wonder if Dylan could come just from this stimulation, she felt a petite, determined hand slide under the waistband of her jeans.

Dylan fumbled with the button fly on Seneca's jeans, but they were baggy enough to slip her hand inside even with the buttons fastened. Seneca rose until she was on her knees, her upper body propped on her elbows. Her breath caught as Dylan dipped into her waiting wetness.

Normally, Seneca would have protested. She never went first. Hell, most of the time she didn't go at all, but this time was different. It sure felt different. They were in love. Seneca would do anything Dylan wanted. When Dylan ran her fingers along Seneca's throbbing hard clit, she lost all resolve of going slow and savoring the moment. It took all her concentration not to explode in Dylan's hand.

"Come with me?" she rasped.

Dylan nodded and used her free hand to undo the fly of her own jeans. She kept a steady rhythm on Seneca's clit as she shimmied out of her pants.

When Dylan's pants passed her knees, Seneca couldn't wait any longer. She gently took Dylan's hand and encouraged her inside. Dylan kissed her fiercely and then returned the gesture, taking Seneca's hand and guiding it to her wet and waiting center. Seneca groaned at how ready Dylan was. She stilled her own pumping hips and focused solely on Dylan's pleasure. For now, having Dylan inside her was enough. She wanted them to come together the first time.

Seneca watched Dylan's face as she got close to coming. She wasn't focused and her face was incredibly beautiful.

Dylan slipped another finger into Seneca. They moved together, breathing heavily, in unison, sharing the physical pleasure and tender intimacy their love brought.

"I'm going to…"

"Me too…oh, baby, now…baby!"

Seneca collapsed on top of Dylan, her body feeling unlike her own. She felt electric and powerful, and sexier than she could ever remember. Dylan slowly extracted her fingers, and Seneca whimpered at the severed connection. She gathered Dylan into her arms and kissed her. She knew she had no words to describe what she was feeling so she concentrated every emotion Dylan brought out in her into their kiss. It was searing, sweet, tender, and torturous.

"Oh my God," Dylan said, trying to catch her breath, clinging to Seneca. She was holding Seneca so tightly, Seneca felt like she might be trying to crawl under her skin.

"Is it going to be like that every time?" Dylan asked.

"I hope so," Seneca said.

Dylan ran her hands along Seneca's back and legs, lingering over the scar on her right thigh. Seneca tensed but let her continue her exploration. Dylan pushed her gently onto her back. She caressed the scar carefully and kissed it softly, gently. "What happened to you, baby?"

"There's no reason to ruin something so beautiful with something so ugly. All that can wait," Seneca said.

She kissed Dylan solidly, flipped her once again onto her back, and pinned her hands above her head. She trailed kisses down Dylan's abdomen and gently parted her legs. She took a moment to savor the gift she had been given as she tasted Dylan for the first time.

❖

Dylan was usually a sound sleeper, but she suspected almost anyone would be wakened by the fool currently trying to gain entry to her room by breaking down the door. What could possibly be so damned urgent? Considering Seneca was lying naked next to her, she couldn't think of anything dire enough for her to get out of bed. Until the siege machine on the other side of the door started talking, and she realized it was her mother making all that racket. Then Dylan was up and full of urgency. She wanted Seneca to meet her mother, but she didn't think either of them wanted to be introduced like this.

"Seneca, sweetie." Dylan didn't want to startle Seneca too much. "Time to get up. And get dressed."

"Getting dressed sounds like a terrible idea," Seneca said. "How long did it take you to get me out of my clothes? What's the rush to get them back on?"

Seneca grabbed Dylan around the waist and tried to pull her back in bed. Despite the slight panic that was rising in Dylan's chest, it nearly worked. Seneca was so sexy, with her floppy morning hair and her soft, sleepy face. It wasn't like her mother had a key, after all. The doorknob rattled as her mother tried to barge her way in.

"Do you hear that banging just outside my door?"

"It's really annoying. We should make whoever it is stop. I bet they'd go away if I answered the door like this," Seneca said, getting up and making for the door.

Dylan considered letting her do it, for just a moment. "It's my mother," she whispered.

Seneca froze mid-step as if making any more noise would give away the fact that she was there and buck ass naked in the middle of the room.

"Care for these?" Dylan held up Seneca's pants.

"I'm contemplating going out the window, but I don't like my chances for survival if I fall."

"Since I live on the fourth floor and it's snowing?"

"Yeah, something like that. Maybe I could hide?"

"Pants and shirt is the best you can do, cutie. We're in this together." Dylan threw her clothes on, kissed Seneca, and opened the door with bated breath. She had no idea how her mother was going to react to finding Seneca in her room, having clearly spent the night. She reached back and grabbed Seneca's hand. She wanted the support and she also wanted her mother to know this was her girlfriend and it wasn't open for debate. If only she thought that would actually work. Despite their conversation at Thanksgiving, she wasn't convinced her mother would actually play nice.

"Hi, Mom. I wasn't expecting you."

"Dylan, we go Christmas shopping this weekend every year. We talked about it at Thanksgiving, although I can see why you might have had reason for it to slip your mind." Dylan's mother eyed Seneca and moved into the small dorm room. Dylan looked around at the unmade bed, scattered shoes, and what she was pretty sure was her bra hanging over the lamp in the corner. This wasn't exactly how she would have wanted to welcome her mother.

"I'm Patsy Walker. Dylan's mother. You must be Seneca King."

Seneca looked startled, but she held out her hand and seemed to be taking in the woman Dylan always referred to as "Lady Walker." Poor Seneca probably didn't realize her first name wasn't actually Lady.

"Yes, ma'am," Seneca said. "It's nice to meet you. I'll let you and Dylan get to your shopping. We had forgotten you were coming this morning."

"I can see that," her mother said, looking a little too amused for Dylan's liking. "But don't be ridiculous. You have to come with us."

Dylan felt her heartbeat increase roughly tenfold at her mother's suggestion. Her mother and Seneca spending the day shopping together seemed like a terrible idea. Her mother could be judgmental and classist, and Seneca didn't exactly scream upper middle class. She immediately felt horrible for the thought, but it was all true. She loved Seneca, but even if her mother was willing to see past Seneca's lady parts, there were a few other sticking points to their forming a lifelong bond.

"I'm sure Seneca has things to do, Mom," Dylan said.

"Is that true?" her mother asked, fixing Seneca with one of her signature stares. Dylan knew Seneca was screwed. You couldn't lie when faced with that stare.

"Well, I, sort of, have." Seneca was looking at Dylan for help. She looked so unsure of herself it hurt Dylan deeply that she was causing some of this.

"Sounds important. Unless Dylan has some reason to keep the two of us apart, I would love to get to know you better, Seneca. I love buying things for new people. And you look like an excuse to go to the men's department."

"Oh, you don't have to buy me anything, ma'am," Seneca said quickly. Dylan recognized the look on her face. She was scared and looking for a way out the door. Her mother had just made her uncomfortable without meaning to. This was going to be so much fun.

Dylan was still holding Seneca's hand. She gave it a tight squeeze and pulled her closer. She put her arm around Seneca's waist, careful to go slowly so she didn't startle her with the touch. "My mother loves to buy people clothes. It's the only way you can truly get 'in' the family. She has to see what kind of taste you have and if you're compatible shopping companions."

"And I thought finals were going to be tough," Seneca said. "Good thing we finished our armor already. At least I passed something with an A since this afternoon might not go so well. I don't know what kind of shopping companion I am."

"Oh, Seneca, you'll be fine," her mother said. "I don't know why Dylan always makes things so dramatic and puts so much weight on everything. She's done this since she was a child. Her father and I tried to shield her from all the family expectations of her uncles and cousins, but she added twice as large a helping on her own head. Did she tell you she's going to join the rat race in corporate America? Have you ever heard anything so crazy? I try to keep her out of the kitchen every Thanksgiving so she doesn't feel the pressure to do the big family dinner, but she wanders in every year. She's impossible. But anyway, I just like to shop, and it's enjoyable to take along new people I've not met before, or people I've not spent a lot of time with. I buy because I have the money and I don't assume everyone else does or wants to indulge in my insane hobby. That being said, I do already have a few items in mind for you."

Dylan dropped her grip around Seneca's waist in shock. What was her mother talking about? She didn't put the pressure on herself. Did she? She could tell Seneca had quite a few questions, but they would have to wait. She couldn't get into it now with her mother right there. Besides, how would she begin to explain how different her world looked right now?

She barely registered most of the shopping trip as she reevaluated her goals. She was too busy with her own self-evaluation to be shocked at how well her mother and Seneca were getting along. She probably shouldn't have been so surprised, but it was still a bit of a jolt when they finally returned to Dylan's dorm room and Seneca's arms were filled with packages. Patsy Walker only outfitted a shopping companion like this when she really took a shine to them. Dylan felt like she had entered the twilight zone.

"I don't know, Bob, your mother is nothing like you described," Seneca said, surveying the piles of new clothes.

Dylan had to agree.

CHAPTER NINETEEN

Seneca was tired of sitting on the couch. She was tired of the winter break, tired of Dylan being away, tired of all of it. She was about to stomp down the stairs and tell Kate all of that when she overheard Kate and Lisa in the kitchen.

"She's driving me crazy. I don't know what to do with her," Kate said. Seneca felt terrible. She had been a grump. She started to head down to apologize, but stopped as Lisa worked to soothe Kate's irritation.

"She's falling in love. Leave her alone. She has a right to need her own space."

"Falling in love, oh no. When you fall in love you are not mopey and impossibly grumpy. As for needing her own space, she's in our house and she hasn't talked to me in three hours. We were in the same room! Maybe it's you she's falling in love with."

"Sweetie, you know I love you, right?" Lisa didn't wait for Kate to answer. "You're a gigantic idiot sometimes. You've done amazing things with that girl. She adores you and you've been good for each other. I know you carry the burden of passing along mentorship, and I would have to say you have done yours proud. That said, you're an idiot. She's not falling in love with me—"

"Better not be."

"And the way you're stomping around here, even I'm having to work to find things to love about you."

"Yeah, so?"

"So when we first fell in love, did you enjoy our time apart?"

"Uh, that would be a no," Kate said, sounding a little less grumpy.

"Well, I'm guessing she isn't enjoying her time away from Dylan, either. Now get your butt back upstairs and keep her company. Or take her for a walk and for once make sure she wears a jacket, or do one of those torturous workouts you two call fun."

Seneca tried to look like she hadn't been eavesdropping when Kate returned.

"Hey, kiddo," Kate said. "Seem a little quiet. Everything okay?"

"Guess so."

"Up for a walk? Lisa said we both have to wear jackets, though. The snow and all." Kate vaguely indicated the window behind her head.

"Actually," Seneca said, thinking maybe getting out of the house would do her some good. "Maybe a workout? I also kinda need to go downtown to finish shopping, if you're headed that way later. Dylan's mom said we were going Christmas shopping, but she just bought a bunch of clothes for me. I didn't get any gifts for anyone else."

Kate and Lisa had been wonderful to her the past few days. She was staying through Christmas, and it was the first time she could remember looking forward to the holiday. If Dylan were here, everything would have been perfect. But she wasn't. She was with her family. As much fun as she'd had with Mrs. Walker, she was a little worried about Dylan. Her mom's comment about Dylan putting too many expectations on herself had really thrown her, and she hadn't been able to shake it since. It was like her whole career path was now up for reevaluation, which Seneca actually thought was a good thing. Dylan didn't seem like she would be happy in the corporate life, but at least for now, she was pretty miserable as she tried to figure out what she really wanted from life. Maybe some time away from school would be good for her.

"I think we can arrange a little of each. We can head to Sophia for a workout and then hit the shops. You and I ought to be quite dangerous alone with a naughty and nice list, a credit card, and no supervision."

"Quite a sight, is more like it," Seneca said, regaining some of the good mood that had left her as she watched Dylan's parents drive her away for the break. Things were just getting good between them. A month seemed like a long time apart. Dylan seemed like she was committed to Seneca and what they had together, but Seneca was still nervous about how long they had to go without seeing each other. Her mom had seemed to really like her when they were shopping, but Dylan said she wasn't thrilled with the idea of her daughter dating women. Maybe she would try to talk Dylan out of it. Or maybe this career path crisis would make her rethink other parts of her life. Seneca was making herself crazy. Kate was looking at her, clearly picking up on Seneca's contemplative turn and she tried to refocus. "I don't see you as the shopping type."

"What gave me away?"

Seneca shrugged. "Lucky guess." If she couldn't be with Dylan, spending the day with Kate seemed like a decent alternative, and while they were shopping, she could have Kate help her pick something out for Dylan.

❖

After their workout, they showered quickly and decided to walk downtown. Although it was only a few days before Christmas, it was unseasonably warm. Lisa had made sure Seneca was prepared for an arctic blizzard, but Seneca begged Kate not to tell as she stripped off the gloves, scarf, and large coat.

"Keep the hat. She worries about your ears," Kate said, agreeing to the subterfuge, removing some of her extra layers as well.

"My ears?"

"Hair's short. Doesn't cover them. See mine? Covers the ears. No one said she isn't quirky." Kate pulled off her ball cap and displayed the longer hair around her ears. "I'm gonna run in for some coffee. You want anything?" Kate asked, stopping in front of the small local coffee shop.

Seneca shook her head and indicated she would wait outside. The weather was too beautiful to spend any extra time indoors. New England had a way of redefining just what beautiful weather was. Forty-five degrees and sunny in the middle of December could take your breath away. The crystal white snow glistened at every angle, and there was no wind chill to drop the temperature. In a few days, the snow would be slushy and brown and no one would pay it a second's notice, except to wish it weren't slowing their travel and sticking to their boots and pant legs. Today, Seneca wanted to enjoy it. Besides, the coffee sucked there anyway.

She plopped on a bench and watched the world go by. The Christmas spirit infused the air, and other last-minute shoppers walked by looking happy, or stressed, or a strange combination of the two. She had an overwhelming urge to share the moment with Dylan, but she wasn't there. Seneca pulled out the brand new cell phone Kate and Lisa had given her, ready to call Dylan and explain the fabulous feeling of peace that had settled over her. She wished the feeling could last forever.

She was interrupted by Kate returning from her coffee errand. When Kate came out of the coffee shop, her latte in one hand, her cell phone pressed to her ear in the other, and a confused, slightly worried look on her face, Seneca's stomach dropped. She didn't know what it was about the look on Kate's face. Maybe it was something about the way her mouth was barely moving when she spoke, or how intensely her eyes were focused, but Seneca knew, just knew. Her peaceful world was about to come crashing down around her. She stood shakily to face the truth.

"Someone's on the phone for you, Sen," Kate said. "They won't tell me what it's about. They're calling from California."

There was only one person that would be calling on Kate's phone from California. She had had to put two contact numbers down and since she didn't have a cell phone at the time, Kate had said she could put hers as the alternate. Seneca didn't think this call would ever come. Seneca was sweating, even though she had stripped off enough layers and had been sitting long enough that the chilly winter air had penetrated her clothes. She tried to back away from the phone, but backed into the bench and ended up sitting again. She waved off the phone, but Kate held it out insistently.

"They won't talk to anyone but you. I'm sorry, kiddo. I tried."

Seneca took the phone and held it lightly, shrinking her body size down as small as she could on the bench. Even if it wasn't Shannon on the other end of the line, it had to be about her. She didn't know anyone else in California. She brought her knees to her chest and wrapped her free arm around them. She took a deep breath.

"This is Seneca King."

She listened to the man on the other end of the line. He hadn't finished, but she couldn't take anymore. She dropped the phone on the bench and ran. She had to get as far away from that link to her past as she could. The man on the line was a link to Shannon, and if Shannon was linked to her, then she was also linked to the people Seneca cared about. Which put everyone in her life in danger.

She could hear Kate yelling after her, even chasing after her, but Seneca was running on fear and adrenaline and pain. Not the kind of pain that usually held her back, however, the kind of pain so deep it fuels you and allows for feats of inhuman magnitude. The pain in her leg seemed to feed the inner pain and make it stronger. There was no stopping her. Kate had no chance.

CHAPTER TWENTY

Dylan twirled happily when she saw Kate's phone number pop up on her caller ID. It was earlier than she expected Seneca to call her, but she certainly wasn't complaining. Being away from Seneca felt like torture, so any chance to talk to her was welcome.

"Hello, gorgeous," Dylan said happily.

"I'm sorry, Dylan." A woman who was most certainly not Seneca was on the other end. "It's Kate, Seneca's friend and supervisor from the training room."

Dylan felt like a black hole opened in her chest.

"Of course, Kate. Seneca adores you," Dylan said. "What's wrong?"

"I don't know what's wrong," Kate said. "Seneca got a phone call from some guy. I don't know who because he wouldn't say anything except that he needed to talk to her. She got extremely upset and took off at a sprint and I can't find her. Have you heard from her? I've been looking for an hour."

Dylan was scared. She could tell by Kate's voice that she was scared too. She felt wild with fear. What must have happened to send her running from Kate? And now she was alone somewhere, facing whatever nightmare that phone call had brought, by herself.

"No, I haven't heard anything. I assumed it was her calling me on your phone. I'm less than an hour away, and I'll be there as soon as I can."

Kate gave Dylan Seneca's new phone number, and she promised to keep calling it, and to let Kate know right away if she heard anything. Dylan rushed to get ready and was out of the house in record time. She barely remembered to leave a note for her parents.

❖

Dylan found Kate pacing in front of the Sophia College gates, where they had agreed to meet. It had taken everything in her power to go to the meeting point instead of running around campus wildly yelling Seneca's name. As it was, she had practically sprinted to the gates, looking left and right searching for the familiar tall, lanky form. But no luck.

She hugged Kate tightly despite never having met her. They both loved Seneca, and that was enough to make them friends. "I called Britt, Seneca's roommate," Dylan said. "She should be here any minute."

While they waited for Britt, Dylan repeatedly called Seneca's cell phone, hoping each time it rang that Seneca would finally decide to pick up. She had called ten times before Britt finally arrived, out of breath from her hasty journey.

"Where is she?" Britt asked, her face tight with worry. She looked as distressed as Dylan felt.

"We don't know. She's not answering her phone. We have no idea where she went."

Kate ran her hands through her hair, knocking off her Red Sox hat in the process. She didn't seem to notice, and it lay on the ground next to her until Britt retrieved it and plopped it back on Kate's head. Kate let out a worried sigh.

"I don't understand," Dylan said. "What happened?"

Kate steered them toward a nearby bench and they sat. Once they were settled, Kate recounted the phone call Seneca received.

"I got a call from someone at the California Department of Corrections. They wanted to talk to Seneca and said that they would only talk to her. I tried to take a message because we were downtown and she wasn't in the mood to talk, but they were insistent. After Seneca got on the phone, I couldn't hear much, but I did hear the name Shannon Clarke. After Seneca heard that name, she turned white and looked like she reverted back to when I first met her. She was limping really badly when she took off. I tried to follow her, but she was sprinting. She was headed back up the hill toward campus, but that could lead anywhere."

"Does anyone know who Shannon is?" Dylan asked. She had heard Seneca call out that name in the night during one of her nightmares, but they'd never talked about it.

"No," Kate said.

"She, uh, sometimes Seneca talks to someone named Shannon in her dreams," Britt said, looking a little uncomfortable.

"I've heard it too," Dylan said, giving Britt's hand a squeeze. "She never seems happy to see Shannon in the dreams, does she?"

"Yeah, she's usually begging her to leave her alone. At the end of the bad ones she just curls up and holds her leg."

Dylan nodded. That was exactly what she had witnessed as well.

"She said she was shot," Kate said. She looked like she was thinking back to a previous conversation.

Dylan figured her expression must mirror the flabbergasted look on Britt's face. There were so many rumors floating around campus about Seneca, and her getting shot was one of them, but Dylan hadn't even considered it possible. She'd actually thought Seneca must have been in a terrible accident because it seemed more likely than anything else, although it didn't explain all of the scars.

"I didn't know that," Dylan whispered. She was a little hurt that Seneca trusted Kate more than she trusted her with that information.

"Me either," Britt said.

"She told me one day when we were working out. I said her limp was better and she agreed. I asked what had happened. I expected her to tell me to fuck off, but she didn't. I think she was testing how I would react so she could eventually tell you guys," Kate said.

"So are we going with the assumption that this Shannon character is the one who shot her?" Dylan asked, suddenly eager to get out and start looking.

"Not sure it matters, but hopefully, she'll tell us if we can find her," Britt said.

"Any ideas where to look?" Kate asked.

Dylan pulled out her cell phone and dialed Seneca. It went straight to voice mail.

"Shit, she turned her phone off," Dylan said, finally giving in to the overwhelming emotions and starting to cry. Seneca could be anywhere.

"Maybe we should split up so we can cover more ground," Britt said, clearly also ready to begin the search.

"No," Dylan said forcefully. "We stick together. If she's this upset, it might take all of us together to get her back. She needs us."

Dylan pulled Britt and Kate to their feet. It was time for action, and since they didn't know where Seneca was, action meant wandering around in the dark hoping to get lucky. What a plan.

Britt called a friend of hers that lived down the hall and asked her to check for Seneca. It was unlikely that she would have gone home, but they had to check.

Kate led them through the athletic building, searching any room that Seneca would have access to. She was nowhere to be found. They checked the student center, Dylan's dorm, and both libraries. Periodically, Dylan pulled out her cell phone, checked for messages, and tried to call Seneca. It was still off. Finally, she sent a text message, wanting there to be a breadcrumb if Seneca turned her phone on. It said simply, "I love you."

When they had exhausted the possibilities on campus, where it was relatively well lit, they borrowed flashlights from the training room and crossed the small bridge that lead to the athletic fields. She wasn't in the field house or on the soccer field. There wasn't anyone on the softball or field hockey fields either. They climbed the hill and surveyed the track. No one was visible, although their flashlights didn't penetrate the deep shadows created by the stand of trees edging the far straightaway.

Dylan was starting to feel desperation overtake her. It was cold and Seneca was out here somewhere, alone and afraid. It was eating at her that she couldn't find her and ease some of the fear. Suddenly, she thought of where she had first met Seneca. The thought that Seneca might have gone back to the bar to pick up a stranger made her want to vomit, but if it meant Seneca was safe, there was a part of her that hoped that was exactly where she was.

"Kate, can you call the bar and see if she went there?"

"Dylan," Kate said. "She wouldn't go there. She has you."

"I didn't think she'd take off at a sprint away from you either," Dylan said. "I just want to know where she is." She felt like crying again and couldn't quite contain the sob that broke through the silent night. Britt hugged her while Kate called the bar. Dylan was both relieved and disappointed that Seneca wasn't there.

Dylan took one final look around and turned to leave. There wasn't any reason to linger on the track any longer. As the three of them turned away, Dylan's cell phone pinged. She had a new text message. It said, "I love you too."

"Where are you, sweetheart?" Dylan asked the night, relief flooding her so quickly she nearly lost her balance.

She tapped the question into her phone and pressed send. In the distance, Dylan swore she heard a beep.

"Did you hear that?" Kate whispered excitedly.

"It was a beep. I definitely heard a beep," Britt said.

"I think it was from across the field. Send her another one, Dylan," Kate said.

Dylan wrote another message and sent it. A short time later, another beep, this time quite clear, pinged through the dark. They headed in the direction of the sound, and Dylan punched in

Seneca's number. There was no answer, but the ring tone sounded close by. Dylan broke into a run, honing in on the noise. Kate and Britt were close on her heels. When she was within ten feet of the trees, Dylan saw a huddled dark shape. She dropped her phone and sprinted toward Seneca. She vaguely registered the other two slow and then stop. It was up to her to make first contact. Who knew how Seneca would receive any of them?

Dylan dropped to her knees in front of Seneca, who was huddled inside her jacket, her head resting on her drawn up knees. One hand absently massaged her damaged right thigh. Her cell phone rested next to her feet, lit up, showing twenty missed calls. Dylan pulled Seneca to her and held her tight. She was trembling, her breathing raspy. Dylan held her and whispered that she was safe now.

Kate and Britt approached and also dropped down next to Seneca. Kate rubbed her back and Britt slipped her hand into Seneca's.

"You all right, kiddo?" Kate asked, trying unsuccessfully to hide her worry.

"I'm sorry you had to come all this way," Seneca said, looking at Dylan with pain-filled eyes. "And you two, sorry about dragging you out here, Britt. And for taking off like that, Kate. I just needed to…I don't know."

"Shh." Dylan held Seneca to her until she felt her relax into the embrace.

They sat like that a while, silently supporting Seneca until she was ready to speak to them.

Seneca squeezed Dylan tightly and then pulled out of her arms. She turned and embraced Kate and then Britt. "It's a little chilly out here don't you think?" Seneca asked. "Think we could head inside?"

Although her voice was light, Dylan still felt the tension seeping from Seneca's pores and the tremor in her hands as she grasped Dylan's for help up. As they started across the track toward civilization, Seneca clung to Dylan, squeezing her hand painfully in her fear. She was barely able to walk, probably from the pain and the cold, and leaned on Dylan for help.

Dylan and Seneca led the way to the field house and Kate let them in. They settled in the open room strewn with odd furniture and run-down couches.

Dylan settled them on one of the couches and Britt and Kate pulled up chairs nearby. All eyes were on Seneca, whose eyes were on her shoes. She looked exceedingly nervous.

Kate leaned forward and cupped Seneca's cheek in her palm.

"Would you like to speak to Dylan alone, kiddo? She was worried about you and determined to track you down."

Seneca shook her head. "Don't go. You either, Britt. Don't think I don't know about your pile of earplugs behind your desk. I don't know why you chose to be nice to me, but I am forever grateful. I probably should have told you all of this before, but I'll be honest, I was, and I still am, scared shitless."

Dylan flung her arm around Seneca's shoulders and hugged her close. Kate took one offered hand and Britt the other. Seneca held each tightly before letting go. She looked down at her damaged leg once and began.

"My parents died in a car accident when I was five. I don't have any relatives so I went into foster care. For some reason, I was never adopted and I moved from home to home. I've heard most foster families are wonderful, but I guess I had crappy luck. I ran away from the last one when I was fifteen. My foster father used me as his ashtray and whipping post when he drank."

Dylan's hand strayed to Seneca's abdomen where she envisioned all the cigarette-sized circular scars. Anger unlike any she had ever known welled inside her. She felt as if she could kill the man who had hurt Seneca so badly.

"These are his handiwork," Seneca said, raising her shirt enough to show a few of the circular scars. Kate's and Britt's eyes flared with the same anger Dylan was feeling. "Like I said, I was out of there at fifteen. I didn't know where to go, and I ended up in California, living on the streets with a group of other homeless kids. We did all right for ourselves most of the time. I was the youngest and not very good at the survival game. One of the older kids looked after me. It was through her that I met Shannon. She charmed us all. I was seventeen when I met her.

"At first, Shannon was wonderful. She was attentive and charming and made me feel taken care of. I had never known anyone who really cared for me, and I was in love with that feeling. I thought at the time that I was in love with her. Now I know that's not true. Dylan, you're the only one I've ever loved." Seneca leaned in for a quick kiss. "Anyway, the first year was great, then not so much. I didn't see it, but she was slowly controlling every part of my life. Shannon doesn't date people; she owns them. If you belong to her, there's no getting out. I wasn't allowed friends. I didn't leave the house much because I was scared of upsetting her. If I did anything wrong, she beat me up. She pushed me through a plate glass window once because I forgot to make the bed. That's how I ended up with the scar on my back," Seneca said, looking at Dylan since she was the only one who had seen it.

"Was she, I mean, did she make you…sexually…" Kate didn't seem able to finish the thought. Dylan agreed. It was too horrible to think of Seneca being treated so horribly.

"No. She lost interest in me in any way except as a possession after about two months."

"Oh, well that's good then," Kate said.

"Why did she have so much power over all of you kids? Was she a lot older?"

"Oh, right," Seneca said. "I forgot that part. She was also one of the larger drug dealers in the area, so there weren't many people who were willing to cross her, no matter how much of an ass she was to me or anyone else."

Dylan didn't know what to say. The rumors around campus didn't come close to reflecting this reality. "What did she do to you, baby?"

"She…I was going to…one of the kids from my small troupe was trying to get me away from Shannon. She had seen what she was doing to me, and we were plotting my escape. I guess she was a friend, but I have suspicions that she had ulterior motives. It didn't matter because I didn't trust anyone. Anyway, Shannon doesn't let go of what she owns and she found out. She was really paranoid and very good at finding out information that should have stayed hidden. I came home one day and she was waiting for me. Sitting on the couch so calm." Seneca stared at the ceiling. She looked like she was going to cry, but no tears fell.

"You want some water, kiddo?" Kate asked. She jumped up and went in search of water. Dylan suspected it was all to give Seneca time to collect her thoughts, or maybe time for Kate to gather hers.

"The nightmares, they're from that night, right?" Britt asked.

"Yes," Seneca said, "every one of them. Always the same dream."

When Kate returned, Seneca started again.

"She was waiting for me and she started yelling. That was when it was worst, when she yelled. Usually, she was totally in control at all times. She stood and shoved me against the wall. She pulled a gun out of her jacket pocket and waved it in my face. I hadn't ever seen her like that. Her eyes were crazy and she was babbling about loving me and if she couldn't have me, no one could. Such a cliché. I was scared to death, and so I did what I hadn't done in our years together, I fought back. I didn't attack her, but I tried to get away. Before, it was better if I did nothing, because she got tired of beating on me and let me go."

Seneca took a deep breath, leaned into Dylan's protective embrace, and kept going. "Next thing I knew, there was a deafening explosion and pain like I had never known. She fired three times; two hit me in the abdomen and the other bullet ripped through my femur and the muscles in my thigh. I would have bled to death, but Shannon had an attack of conscience. She apologized, like she always did, and called nine one one. Then she left me on the floor holding my leg and begging her to go away. She didn't leave until she heard the ambulance pull into the driveway, then she walked out the back door and was gone.

"They arrested her a few days later. I had had hours of surgery to try to save my leg and fix the problems in my abdomen. There are a lot of organs stuffed in there. I was in the hospital for months while I rehabbed. I didn't have anywhere else to go. I only left to testify at Shannon's trial. She got in trouble because she talked to me. She was crying and apologizing and said she would find me when she got out and make it up to me. They had to suspend the proceedings for that day and give special instructions to the jury. It was horrible.

"Anyway, I got to Sophia because one of the women who was part of the trial is on the Sophia board of directors. She offered me a scholarship and I wasn't so stupid that I would turn it down, even though I hated that she gave it to me out of pity. Shannon had been in prison for a few years, and it was time to make a life for myself. When I got to Sophia, I didn't like to be touched. I was jumpy and didn't trust anyone. I have nightmares, and I don't like crowds and loud noises. But you guys know all that." She squeezed Dylan's hand and looked at Kate. "And today I got a call that Shannon is being paroled. She doesn't give up what she owns. She's coming for me. That's why I ran. I got scared. I'm still scared."

Silence filled the room when Seneca finished her story. Dylan didn't know what to say. She felt sick thinking about Seneca's life. No wonder she had sprinted away from the phone call that had brought news of Shannon's release. Dylan could hardly blame her.

Dylan looked at Seneca and saw her struggling with emotions. Her eyes were red, but still no tears fell. Dylan didn't know how she was keeping it all inside. It couldn't be healthy to keep that kind of pain bottled so tightly.

"It's okay, sweetheart. I've got you. It's okay to let go," Dylan whispered in her ear, kissing her cheek tenderly.

Seneca nodded but didn't look like she agreed. The look of astonishment on her face when she raised her hand and felt the trail of wetness slide over her cheekbone and gather in the corner of her mouth was sort of adorable. She flicked her tongue out and caught the salty drop. As if sensing it was real and feeling truly safe for the first time, she cried. It started as delicate tears streaming down her face, but quickly evolved into desperate, wracking sobs. She clung to Dylan like a life raft as she let it all out.

The ringing of Kate's cell phone finally interrupted the moment.

"Holy fuck," Kate said, looking at the caller ID. "I forgot to call Lisa. She's probably out of her mind."

Seneca actually laughed and wiped away the last few tears. "Let me talk to her, Kate," she said reaching for the phone. Kate held it like it might explode and looked relieved to pass it off.

"Hi, Lisa, it's Seneca. Kate's fine. I'm the one who's a mess." She stood and retreated from the large common room, wandering down the hall of the field house looking for a little more privacy. When Seneca returned, she sat in Dylan's lap while they all decided what to do next. Everyone agreed they would spend the night being held by the women who loved them, even Britt it seemed had snuck a new girlfriend right under Seneca's nose, and in the morning they would get together and plot strategy. It scared Dylan when Seneca insisted that Shannon would be coming east as fast as she could, but there was no way in hell she'd let Seneca face it alone. Now that she knew what the demon looked like, or at least what her name was, she and Seneca would be on the lookout together.

"Shannon, go away…please leave…I'll do whatever you want…NO!"

Seneca bolted awake, sitting up in bed, sweat and tears streaming down her face. Her breathing was heavy and labored, and she looked around wildly, panic and pain unlike anything she had ever felt coursing through her. When she saw and felt Dylan next to her, clearly wakened by Seneca's nightmare but looking tousled and beautiful despite that, the sense of relief was swift and startling. The tears really started flowing when she realized Dylan was okay.

"Oh God, Dylan, I…that dream…" She couldn't bring herself to finish the thought. Instead, she pulled Dylan on top of her and kissed her long and hard.

She yanked the thin cotton shirt over Dylan's head and tossed it across the room. Dylan was on her back before she could ask Seneca what she was doing. Seneca was just getting started when Dylan shoved her off.

"Seneca, we're at Kate and Lisa's house. They're sleeping fifteen feet away, and after that nightmare, they're probably not sleeping anymore. Also, you have to talk to me, not just have sex with me, when you're scared, or sad, or lonely, or happy. You get the idea."

"For the record, I like my plan better," Seneca said. She felt like a firecracker about to go off and didn't know how to release the energy.

"Who wouldn't?" Dylan asked. "Tell me about your dream."

Seneca started crying again, remembering pieces of her dream. "Damn it, I cry once and now I'm a fucking faucet."

"You're safe here. I'm here and I've got your back. She's not going to get near you. I'm yours now and you're mine and nobody can take that from us, especially not her." Dylan spoke softly. "I'll keep you safe, sweetheart, and if I have to, I'll fight for what's mine."

Seneca believed her. The problem was that in this dream, for the first time, the gun in Shannon's hand wasn't aimed at Seneca. It was aimed at Dylan. Seneca didn't know what she would do if any harm befell Dylan because of her past. Nothing was worth that, not even her own happiness. She lay awake long after Dylan fell back to sleep. She held Dylan's soft, lovely body against her and tried to memorize every curve.

Her past was now her future. Gone from her mind was the promise of a life with Dylan and Kate's unwavering love. Shannon was coming for her. She'd tried to find an alternative, a way to keep Dylan without leaving, but she couldn't. She didn't have a passport, so leaving the country wasn't an option. It didn't matter where she went, though. Shannon would never rest until she found her. And if she found her and Dylan was with her, what Shannon did to her would look like the measured response of a clinically insane person. Shannon was bat-shit crazy with a jealous streak, which wasn't a good combination. Seneca knew Shannon would see Dylan as having stolen something of hers. Dylan would be a rival to be taken care of, nothing more. Seneca had to keep her safe. She owed her that much.

In two days, Dylan was going on a European trip with her parents for Christmas, and wouldn't be back until just before the spring semester started. She was safer a continent away, and she wouldn't know until she returned that Seneca had done what she needed to, and left. The thought broke her heart, and by morning, happiness was barely a memory.

CHAPTER TWENTY-ONE

Seneca and Kate warmed up as usual for their regular workout. Seneca had been relying on the distractions more and more. Dylan had been with her family for over a week, and Seneca hadn't told anyone that she and Dylan couldn't be together any longer. She figured Kate would try to talk her out of it. Besides, she also needed to tell Kate that aside from work, their time together was over as well. She would have stopped seeing Kate completely, to protect her too, but she really needed the money.

She felt like every day she stayed with Kate and Lisa was a twisted game of Russian roulette. She didn't have much choice. The dorms weren't open, except for a few students with no other place to go, and willing to pay, those preparing to take classes over break, or athletes staying for sports training, and she couldn't really take to the streets in New England in the middle of winter. While they still had time together to work out, she needed something from Kate. She was hoping Shannon couldn't get across the country very quickly.

"Kate, do you think you could teach me to fight?" Seneca asked. She hoped she wouldn't throw up again.

"You sure that's a good idea, kiddo?" Kate asked, looking concerned.

"Yes," Seneca said. "And can you show me how to set up the heavy bag in case I want to come up and practice on my own sometime? You know, in case you're busy."

Kate paused and looked quizzically at Seneca but didn't say anything. She retrieved her gloves and hand wraps and an extra pair of each for Seneca before speaking.

"Have I ever told you about the first time I sparred? It was my first and last time, actually."

"That bad?" Seneca asked.

"I guess," Kate said. "I was so worried about getting hurt, or hurting my friend, that I spent the entire three rounds dancing, and ducking, and weaving, and never threw a punch. My friend was so mad at me that she broke my nose after our workout."

"Why did she do that?" Seneca was shocked. "You were both safe. No one got hurt."

"Kiddo, we were supposed to be fighting. I was running away. I was wrong."

Seneca was wary. She probed Kate's expression, but it was impassive. Could she possibly have figured out Seneca's intentions?

"Is this one of your hidden, cryptic lessons?"

"I don't think it's particularly hidden or cryptic," Kate said. "In boxing, as in life, I suppose, sometimes you have to let the fight come to you. And sometimes you have to trust your friends enough to let them help you or risk pissing them off. Shall we get started?"

Seneca didn't know if she should respond to what Kate had said, or how to respond if she did. With Kate, there was no way to tell if all that really was just a boxing lesson. Even if it wasn't, it didn't change what she needed to do. Sure, maybe you needed to trust your friends. But you also needed to protect them. Wasn't that part of friendship? They didn't know what was about to come their way.

She was saved further reflection when Kate started wrapping her hands and helping her into her gloves. The large, heavy red gloves felt awkward and foreign on her hands. They were clunky and huge, but she liked the way they looked, neatly wrapping around the middle of her forearms. The sudden sense of control felt empowering, and she felt like she could breathe a bit easier for the first time in days. She took a few awkward swings and heard Kate groan behind her.

"Am I that bad?" Seneca asked.

"Bad? No, I was groaning because you're a southpaw and I hate southpaws. You guys are damned hard to box. Take it easy on me these first few times when I'm figuring it out or you'll pop me in the face."

"Southpaw? Hey, wait," Seneca said. "I can't hit you. I won't. I'm sorry. I just—"

Seneca started to pull the gloves off, but Kate stopped her, placing both gloved hands on Seneca's shoulders and looking forcefully into her eyes. "No hitting. Don't worry. You'll get to hit the mitts and I'll be holding them, but no hitting me. I promise."

"Oh, well, why didn't you say so? Let's go," Seneca said, feeling much better. She needed to learn how to protect herself. It was well past time.

"All right," Kate said, standing across from Seneca with the mitts on her hands. "You're a southpaw, so your right foot is forward. Your right hand is there to protect your face, so keep it up all the time. After you punch, bring your right thumb back to your chin, okay? The left one is like a spring and it pulls your body back into position. Keep your elbows tucked in and we should be ready to go."

Seneca paid attention and moved into position. She stood with her right foot forward, body sideways, right hand in front of her face, and left hand just under her left cheek.

"Okay, now jab with your right hand and twist your wrist as you punch. Your knuckles should be up and your palm down when you hit the mitts."

Seneca punched the mitts for the first time and was surprised at the pop that sounded as her glove made contact. She saw Kate grin and found it was infectious. And she didn't vomit, which was a major victory. They jabbed a while longer and then added the left-handed straight punch. She combined the punches when Kate requested a "one-two."

After a few more minutes of practice, Kate showed Seneca the uppercut followed by the hook. Although she liked the punch, the uppercut was the hardest on her damaged leg. It required a lower knee bend to get power, and the added muscle contractions and upward explosions were difficult and painful. She still hit hard, rolling her shoulder and using her long, lean frame to generate speed, but it didn't come easily. The purpose of all the exercises she and Kate had been doing for the past months came together. Taken out of context, they had seemed a little goofy, but the workout had always been good and Kate enjoyed it, so Seneca didn't complain. Now she understood how each part was designed to help specific parts of each explosive movement.

The hook, however, was her joy. Although all punches required her legs, the hook's power and speed was generated through her hips. She knew she had found her punch the first time she tried it. There was something magical about watching her gloved fist travel in front of her eyes and solidly collide with Kate's mitted hands. The smack of the gloves and the feeling of power were addicting.

Kate taught her a new combination, a one-two-three-four, jab, straight punch, right hook, straight punch. The first time through, Seneca put so much energy and effort into her hook she forgot to throw the second straight punch. After the hook connected, she felt so alive and invigorated she let her hands drop to her sides. They came back up quickly however when Kate made a wide jab at her ear with the mitt. In the past, that would have sent Seneca packing, but somehow she had overcome her instinct to pull away and run, at least from Kate. She knew she would never hurt her. She also felt committed to her task now that she had a taste of it.

"All right, kiddo," Kate finally said after they had been working for an hour. Both of them were covered in sweat. "I think that's it for today."

"Just a few more?" Seneca asked hopefully, keeping her hands up protecting her face for emphasis.

"That's probably good for today. I know you feel great right now, but those are muscles you haven't used like this, even if we've been working out for a few months."

Seneca considered her body, feeling how leaden her arms were and how much her leg ached. For the first time, the ache felt good. It felt like progress and it felt earned. She pulled off her gloves and flopped down against the wall, grinning from ear to ear at the new experience. Unlike the last time she had seen Kate whack the heavy bag and she'd thrown up, hitting the mitts herself made her feel capable in a way she hadn't ever before.

CHAPTER TWENTY-TWO

When the spring semester started again, Dylan was happy to be back on campus with Seneca, but nervous about what the future would hold. She didn't know how much to believe Seneca's assurances that Shannon would make the three-thousand-mile trek to find her. It seemed so stupid to break her parole and risk her freedom, but Seneca had no doubts. The minute Dylan got back to campus, she headed straight to Seneca. They'd hardly spoken over the break since she'd been in Europe with her family. Even when they had talked, though, Seneca had seemed a little distant. That worried her.

Seneca didn't look as happy to see her as she hoped.

"We need to talk," Seneca said after they had kissed hello.

Dylan didn't want to talk. Or at least, not talk about what Seneca's tone implied they were about to talk about. Nothing good followed a "we need to talk" lead-in. She had been worried about Seneca the entire time she was on vacation, stressed about how she was handling the threat of Shannon, and now they needed to talk.

Dylan's chest felt tight and she felt sick to her stomach. Instead of consenting to a chat she wasn't interested in, Dylan turned to leave.

"I don't want to talk, Seneca. Not if you want to talk about what I think you want to talk about."

"Come on, Dylan," Seneca said, looking pretty miserable. "You know this is how it has to be."

"I know no such thing. I love you. You said you love me. I have no idea why you think it has to be this way," Dylan said. Anger was easier to give in to than the terrible sadness threatening to swamp her.

"I do love you. I love you so much I can't stand the thought of anything happening to you," Seneca said. "That's why we have to be apart. Shannon can't know anything about you. If she knows you exist…" Tears streamed down Seneca's face.

Dylan was conflicted. She was still angry at Seneca for ambushing her, but her heart was still so pure it reminded her of everything she loved so much about her. And she was crying, which was more than she could handle.

"That's not really how relationships work, Seneca," Dylan said. "You face the good and the bad together. Haven't you ever heard the marriage vows, for better or for worse? Through good times and bad? I'm not saying we're getting married, but the sentiment is true. You're either in it together or you're not really in it at all."

"That's never been my life," Seneca said. "And I have to keep you safe." Seneca looked sad. More than sad, actually. She looked as if she had spent the entire time they had been apart holding her world together and now it had just fallen to pieces at her feet.

"Don't do this," Dylan said, crying. She didn't feel much of anything at the moment, but she knew it was waiting, just below the surface. It was as if her eyes were reacting out of courtesy, but the rest of her was too shocked to respond.

Seneca moved closer to hug her, or kiss her, to comfort her in some way, but Dylan wasn't interested. The only comfort Seneca could offer would be to take back this stupid, misguided sense of chivalry and bravery. Or maybe it was all fear and Seneca was using this as an excuse to run. Whatever it was, she wouldn't get a chance to kiss away Dylan's hurt.

"Shannon doesn't scare me as much as the thought of losing you. I don't need you to single-handedly keep me safe, Seneca. I want us to keep each other safe." When Seneca stayed silent, her hands thrust into her pockets, her jaw clenched, Dylan didn't want to hear any more excuses. She had heard Seneca's reasoning and she thought it sucked. That Seneca could push her away so easily, and because of an ex, even a criminally insane one, hurt more than she thought possible.

Dylan felt a bit dazed on her walk back to her dorm room. She couldn't believe the difference a few weeks could make. She and Seneca were so happy just before Christmas and now, apparently, they couldn't even see each other anymore. Anger swelled in her gut. Anger at Seneca, but mostly anger at Shannon, the woman who had ravaged Seneca's life and was still doing so.

When she got to her dorm room, she stopped before unlocking it. She felt uneasy but couldn't pinpoint why. She looked behind her and scanned the campus. She couldn't see anything amiss, but she also couldn't shake the unsettled feeling. If anything, it was getting worse. She felt like the hairs on the back of her neck were standing up. She quickly held her keycard to the door and heard it click open. She pulled it open and leapt inside. She relaxed slightly when the door clicked closed behind her, but she didn't like that she had been so freaked out.

She rushed upstairs to her dorm room and looked out the window, hoping a higher vantage point would help her identify the source of her creepy crawlies. There wasn't any obvious scary person hiding in plain sight. She did take note of a blond woman walking quickly away, her back to Dylan, but that in and of itself wasn't all that suspicious. She realized she had no idea what Shannon looked like. If Seneca was right, and Shannon was coming, Dylan should find out what she looked like. Quickly.

Dylan picked up the phone against her better judgment and called Seneca.

"I'm not saying I agree with anything you fear about Shannon or that she's coming to campus, but if you're worried, I should probably at least know what she looks like, right?"

"Dylan, what aren't you telling me?" Seneca sounded terrified.

Dylan knew this was a bad idea. "You said she was coming and I don't know what the woman looks like. Besides, if she's going to be such a fucking home wrecker and ruin what we have, I want to be able to look at her picture and curse her to her face."

"Dylan, don't lie to me, please."

"It's nothing, an overreaction. I got a little bit of a creepy feeling when I was walking back to my dorm room. Everything else is true. I think I should know what she looks like."

"Did you see anyone? Was there anyone around that you didn't recognize or that shouldn't be there? Shannon's blond. I can't come over there because I don't want her to see me near you, but I'm calling campus police to come and check the building."

"You're doing no such thing," Dylan said. "I'm fine. Send me the picture. Send it to Britt too, and any other athletes you're friends with. They're all over this campus. Let's set up a spy network. She won't be able to set foot around here without our knowing about it."

"That's actually a good idea," Seneca said. "I'll e-mail the picture now."

"Seneca, I love you. You don't have to do this alone."

"I just can't let her get to you," Seneca said. "I love you too much. I'm sorry."

CHAPTER TWENTY-THREE

No arguments, Seneca." Kate's frustration showed in the way her arms were crossed over her chest. Seneca knew she was close to crossing a line. She and Kate had been at odds more and more lately. It had started since she had begun distancing herself from those she cared about. Kate didn't approve of her breaking up with Dylan and wasn't pleased at being cut out of Seneca's life except for work and occasional workouts.

"I don't need a damned babysitter, Kate!" Seneca's voice was barely below a shout.

"If you keep acting like a two-year-old, we can argue about that, but for now let's leave it that Jay is not your babysitter. He is a licensed EMT and you two are going to be out in the woods alone. Do I feel better that he's with you? Yes, but that isn't my motivation."

Seneca took a moment to decide if she should argue further. It wasn't unusual for an EMT to be around for particularly dangerous or out of the way events, and she had to admit, it was comforting to know Jay was going to be with her. Jay was built like an SUV crossed with a muscle car, heavy on the muscle. Sophia was hosting a huge track meet this weekend. There were over thirty schools represented. The campus would be full of strangers.

"Fine, but I'm driving the whole time."

Kate rolled her eyes. "I'm sure Jay will be thrilled to hear that. He's outside waiting for you."

Seneca grabbed her pack and walked out, still fuming, but not really sure why.

"Seneca!" Kate called her back.

"Yeah?" Seneca leaned back into the training room. She felt a little bad for yelling at Kate a minute ago.

"Radio." Kate flipped one of the portable handheld devices across the room. Seneca caught it neatly and secured it to the portable athletic training pack strap resting across her chest. "Try and stay on the road with the damned cart. Follow the runners. They'll know where they're going and you won't get lost."

Although she knew Kate was mostly kidding, Seneca could feel her hackles rising again. She hated how on edge she was lately and felt like she was being a bear to those who loved her. "Yeah, okay." Today was an unusual event because the athletes would be competing through the woods behind the track. That meant they were out of sight almost the entire event. As a result, Seneca and Jay would be following the course behind the last runner in the cart. If anyone were injured, they would pick them up and transport them out of the woods. Kate's laughter followed her down the hall.

Once outside, Seneca felt a little less on edge. Although the danger Shannon presented would most likely come outside the safe confines of the training room or her dorm, Seneca didn't like feeling trapped. Lately, the buildings had taken on a distinctly claustrophobic feel. It didn't make any sense, but the fresh air felt safer than the stuffiness inside.

She spotted Jay immediately. He was hard to miss.

"Morning," Jay said cheerfully, his voice deep and warm.

"I'm driving." Her bad mood refused to go away.

"You always this peppy in the morning?" he asked with a laugh. "I'm a morning person, I gotta warn you."

Seneca just grunted.

Jay followed her as she unlocked the field house training room and grabbed the necessary gear. She threw the splint kit and crutches on the cart and then returned for the large kit containing tape, first aid supplies, and any number of other useful tools.

Seneca thought about her own recent adventure in the woods and how much the people who loved her had done for her on that night. The only way for her to show her appreciation to them was to stay away from them, and that sucked. To make it worse, she had just snapped at Jay, who had done absolutely nothing wrong and didn't know about her situation. She felt like a class one asshole.

When she turned around to apologize, Jay was leaning against the cart inspecting his nails, a deep frown on his handsome face. He was attractive in a gentle way and the day-old stubble added to his appeal.

"It's not even ten yet and already, a broken nail," Jay said, looking incredulous.

"Christ," Seneca said, trying to hide her smile, "you are such a stereotypical gay man."

Jay's face lit up. "Thanks, honey."

Seneca laughed. Perhaps today wouldn't be so bad after all. "Look, I'm sorry for snapping earlier, I've…" she thought about telling him about her personal problems but couldn't bring herself to do it. She had gotten better at sharing what she was feeling, but she was still really only comfortable with Dylan, Kate, and, occasionally, Britt. "I've got no excuse."

Jay waved her off and settled onto the passenger seat of the golf cart. "Let's go rescue us some track stars." He patted the seat next to him. Seneca wasn't sure there was room on the seat for her. She squeezed in and set off.

The women's race was uneventful and painfully slow. Sophia was a Division III school, which meant that most of their competition was as well. Division III didn't give out athletic scholarships, and many schools promoted an "everyone can play a sport" philosophy. As a result, Seneca had to crawl through the woods after the final two runners who were jogging slower than she could walk.

Any annoyance she had at going so slowly disappeared when they came out of the woods and crested the hill to the track and the finish line. The home stretch was lined with fans and other athletes, all of them cheering and screaming for the final contestants. Seneca wanted to slap herself on the forehead for being annoyed at these women. It wasn't every day you got to witness the true meaning and value of sports.

During the break between the women's and men's events, Seneca checked in with Kate and then returned to the cart to have an early lunch with Jay. He was easy to talk to and they passed the time laughing frequently. Seneca was only peripherally aware that a few short months ago she never would have let herself have this easy interaction. It was further evidence of all Shannon was threatening to take away. It was also motivation to ensure that never happened.

The men's race was run at a much quicker pace, but it was also longer, taking them farther into the woods. It was during this race that the cart was particularly important, as any runner who got injured would have to make their way almost a mile back at the farthest point.

Jay informed her early on that he was planning on enjoying the view and not to disturb him. He frowned disapprovingly when Seneca reminded him he had a boyfriend. Even Seneca could see the change that came over him when he thought of his man. All the bravado about checking out boys in their little runners' shorts was just talk. She was happy for him. Everyone should have that kind of love in their lives.

As much as Seneca hated to admit it, having Jay with her on the cart was a relief. She was still skittish any time they rounded a bend, and the noises of the woods freaked her out. Although probably too early for Shannon to have tracked her down and made her way across the country, Seneca was still wary. The Sherman tank sitting next to her was a comfort. She took a steadying breath and tried to relax, just a little.

The natural sounds of a spring day were broken by the footfalls and heavy breathing of the athletes and the rumble of their golf cart. Until a loud *pop-crack* rang out in the quiet woods.

After the loud crack, the terrified scream seemed like a foregone conclusion. Seneca didn't feel any of the hot, searing pain she had felt the first time she was shot, so she figured she hadn't been hit. All the same, she didn't start the cart again for a beat or two, taking stock and trying to calm the panic threatening to overtake her. They were parked just before a curve in the course and she steeled herself for what she would find around the bend. She could remember how she felt and how much blood there had been, but she didn't know how she would handle seeing it as an observer.

Jay's face was set and his body tense. He too seemed to know they weren't dealing with a sprained ankle, although Seneca doubted he knew the sound of a handgun crack.

She put her foot to the floor and the cart hurtled forward, propelling her toward the source of her fear. Jay could take care of the wounded and she would have to face Shannon. She felt nothing as she prepared to face her worst nightmare.

"Sounded like a bad break," Jay said, his voice tense as they hurried forward. "Good thing you brought the splint kit. I think we're going to need it."

"What?" Seneca asked, unable to understand what he was saying. Did he think the bullet had broken a bone? It was possible, she knew, but how could he tell without seeing the patient?"

"The crack. Sounded like a broken bone. Probably leg, for us to hear it all the way back here. The ride out is going to be horrible for the poor guy."

Understanding flooded Seneca's senses. "You think someone broke their leg?"

"Um, yes." Jay looked at her with a strange expression on his face. "What do you think we're about to find up there?"

"Me, oh, uh, nothing, probably leg. Tibia, probably. She wanted to hug him, but a part of her was still convinced she had heard a gunshot. Was it possible it was just a leg snapping that had sent her heart into overdrive?

Just around the next curve was a small group of runners, huddled protectively over another young man lying on the ground holding his lower leg and rocking back and forth in pain.

The group parted as the cart careened to a stop and Seneca and Jay leapt out. Seneca headed immediately for the fallen man and Jay went to the back of the cart for their supplies. She knelt next to him and quickly assessed for signs of bleeding. There was some, but not the kind she was expecting. The poor man's tibia protruded through his shin about three inches.

"My leg, I think I broke my leg." He was gasping and tears slid down his face. "I stepped on something, I think, and then I heard this really loud crack. I tried to stand up, but then it cracked again. I can't get up and it hurts so much. I thought I saw the bone sticking out, but that's just crazy, right? I can't look. It hurts so bad."

"I know it does," Seneca said, looking at his leg without touching it. "We're going to get you out of the woods and get that taken care of. Anything else hurt?"

He shook his head. "Just my leg. It's been hurting the last few days at practice but nothing like this."

Jay knelt next to Seneca with the splint kit and two pairs of gloves. Seneca covered his leg with a towel. The young man didn't need to see his bone sticking out of his leg again. There wasn't much they could do except immobilize the leg and get him out of the woods as quickly as possible. It wasn't going to be a pleasant ride.

"What's your name?" Jay asked as he too looked at the leg without touching. They would have to move him soon enough, no need to add to the pain just yet.

"Justin."

"Okay, Justin, we need to get your leg immobilized with our splint and get you out of the woods. We're going to call and have an ambulance waiting at the track when we get there. They'll take you to the hospital for x-rays and get this taken care of, okay?"

Justin nodded. He sat up, and in doing so, his leg moved. He screamed. From a point about midway down his calf, it looked as if there were no bones in his leg. It flopped freely like a sack of skin with nothing solid keeping it in shape.

They worked quickly to get the splint inflated around his leg. Although tears streamed down his face, he stayed silent, his eyes closed, his fists clenched so tightly they were white. The runners that had stopped continued with the race. Seneca wondered how many other athletes would have stopped. The men that had were guaranteed a last place finish.

Jay picked Justin up carefully, carrying him as if he weighed nothing. Seneca marveled at his strength. If she had been out here alone they would have had to perform a painful and awkward hop to get him in the cart. They settled him as best they could, trying to cushion his damaged limb, and then headed slowly out of the woods.

This time Jay drove, and Seneca radioed Kate.

"Kate, this is Seneca, over."

"Kate here."

"Ambulance needed at the west entrance to the athletic fields. We have an athlete down, open lower leg fractures." Seneca hoped Justin wasn't listening.

"Is he immobilized?" Kate's voice was calm but much more alert.

"Yes, we're in the cart heading back. Athlete's name is Justin." She paused and turned to Justin, asking him for his last name, then relayed the information to Kate.

"Okay, bring him in. We'll be standing by."

When they finally exited the woods, Seneca was exhausted. They had been on the second half of the course, but still a good way out. She had felt every bump and dip along with Justin. She had desperately wished they could do more to ease his pain. Although he tried to hide it, she could hear his pained whimpers and simultaneously urged Jay forward faster and admonished him for driving too quickly over the many rocks and divots in the trail.

As promised, an ambulance was standing by when they arrived at the track. Kate did a cursory exam of Justin's leg. Not much else was needed. The man's leg was so swollen by the time they had gotten him out of the woods that it was hard to tell where his lower leg ended and his upper leg began. It was also difficult to even see the bone protruding anymore. He raised his hand in thanks as he was loaded up and the ambulance doors were closed.

"Damn, Kate, you got a good one here," Jay said, indicating Seneca as he packed up his supplies. "She was amazing out there. Got to the poor guy before I even had time to figure what the hell was going on."

Seneca felt herself flush. She was pleased with the praise, but also embarrassed by her reaction in the woods. Jay didn't know about that.

"You two good for the rest?" Jay asked, indicating the track meet. The long events through the woods were over and he was off duty.

"We're good, thanks, Jay," Kate said, shaking his hand and sending him on his way.

Kate led Seneca back to her post at one end of the track. She always set up closest to the jumping portion of the steeplechase, as that was often where people wiped out. Her half-eaten sandwich was sitting on the bench seat of her own golf cart.

"Jay said you did a great job. So what's eating at you?" Kate asked.

"He's wrong." She looked at Kate and confessed. "I thought it was a gunshot. His leg breaking was so damned loud, I thought it was a gunshot."

"Ever heard one after you got shot?" Kate asked.

"Once, yeah," Seneca said, shivering at the memory.

"What'd you do?" Kate had her arm across the back of the bench seat. It seemed like she was purposefully leaving her arm close enough that she could wrap Seneca in a hug if she needed to but far enough away that she wasn't coddling her.

"Started screaming my head off and ran like the devil," Seneca said, cracking a smile at the memory. It wasn't funny and certainly hadn't been then, she could still feel her panic, but she must have looked quite a sight to the people around her.

"And what did you do today?" Kate had infinite patience.

"I just reacted. I thought it was Shannon, but I didn't feel anything. I looked at Jay and we drove on down the path. It was weird. I wonder what Shannon would have done if I came around the corner in a golf cart with Jay next to me. That might have been worth it, actually."

"Then I would say Jay is right. You did a damned fine job. Being scared is okay. Being scared is a good thing, especially when you think someone is popping off a gun nearby, but you reacted just like you should have. One of the things that makes me most proud of you, kiddo, is that even when you're scared you still keep your head."

"I didn't when I went running out on you the night I hid in the woods," Seneca said quietly.

"Oh yes, you did. You ran somewhere safe and when you could, you contacted us. Then, you were brave enough to tell the whole story. Don't beat yourself up. I've only heard a leg break once, but even I thought it was a gunshot and I've never heard one before."

Seneca leaned back against Kate's arm, needing the contact but not wanting to break down with everyone so close by. They were still on duty, and she couldn't let down the carefully constructed guard she'd tried, mostly unsuccessfully, to put up. Like Kate said, she had to keep her head. No matter how much she missed Dylan.

CHAPTER TWENTY-FOUR

W hat's up today?" Seneca asked, pulling up a chair and massaging her sore leg. She knew she had been doing that more since Shannon's presence started to haunt her again. The frequent boxing was also tiring her out, and at times, that translated to a tired and sore leg as well.

"Softball's practicing, lacrosse is away at a game, and track has the day off." Kate checked her schedule to make sure she wasn't forgetting anything.

"Coach getting soft?" Seneca asked in amazement. The track coach was renowned for her tough style and demanding practice schedule. A day off was unheard of.

"Nope," Kate said, her eyes sparkling with mischief. She leaned forward conspiratorially and whispered, "But ever since that attractive new lacrosse coach started dining with her almost every night, she's been much more interested in attending their games, home and away."

Seneca considered. She actually liked the track coach quite a lot. "Good for her. The newbie is hot! Hey, how did you get out of traveling with them?" There was a part of her that had trouble really being happy for anyone in love. She was in love, but was miserable. Dylan would tell her that was her own fault. Thinking of Dylan made her even more depressed. They hadn't talked in weeks, and in class she made sure to sit where she couldn't see her. Otherwise, she just sat and stared at her the whole time. She also tried to get to class late and usually took a bathroom break right at the end and never came back. Running into her was so painful she would rather hop on her bad leg for an hour.

"T wanted to go." Kate referred to the other trainer. "Besides, we're not traveling as much with the teams, budget cuts or some crap. You okay? You've got your forlorn 'Bob Face' going something fierce."

"I have no idea what that even means."

"You know I don't agree with your decision to cut ties with Dylan. You two should be facing this together. And I'm not thrilled that the only reason you didn't cut me loose completely is because you need the money I throw your way. But I hate that you won't spend time with us anymore. Lisa misses you."

"I've told you, I'm trying to protect her. You and Lisa too. I don't want Shannon to know anything about you guys. Since I distributed the picture, I've gotten five calls or e-mails this week from people swearing they saw Shannon on campus. I don't know if it's her or not, but what if it is?"

"Just my opinion here, but if you aren't careful, even if you vanquish that demon, there won't be anything left to protect. How is Dylan supposed to trust that you won't just ditch her again if things get rough? Partnership is partnership, and it means a hell of a lot more than you're giving it. Dylan deserves better than what you're doing to her. I don't care that you're calling it chivalry. You're scared of losing her. I get that. She's scared of losing you too, but you made that a reality for her. And if Shannon is here, then you two are facing it alone. I don't know what to tell you about the sightings. Take them seriously, I guess, but don't make yourself crazy."

"That's not fair," Seneca said. As she said it, she wondered if that was true. She had pure intentions, but maybe they were still wrong.

"What part, kiddo? Where am I wrong?"

"I don't know," Seneca said. "I miss her though. It's tearing me up inside." She and Kate had been going around in circles about this for the past week. "So budget cuts means no more exciting away games?"

Kate ignored the change of subject and they prepared silently for the chilly afternoon outside on the golf cart. They strolled down to the field house, squishing through the wet grass. Seneca didn't trust the nice weather. Next weekend there would probably be a blizzard.

She retrieved the golf cart from its storage shed while Kate taped the ankle of a late athlete. They bundled their supplies, training kit, splint pack, ice bucket, and radios into the back and set off for the softball fields. Seneca loved driving the cart. She knew Kate wished she would slow down.

Practice was uneventful, but their conversation was even more strained than usual. Overall, it made for a pretty miserable workday.

"Have you thought at all about what you want to do when you graduate?" Kate asked unexpectedly.

Seneca shook her head. It wasn't for at least a year, and she didn't want to think about leaving the friendly confines of this remarkable campus. She shrugged. "I don't want to have to leave here." Even with the renewed threat of Shannon, this place felt more like home than anywhere else she had ever lived.

"What about training? Would you like to keep doing this?"

"Yes. I love this job. You know I want to be you when I grow up." Seneca wasn't really kidding.

Kate smiled at the compliment. "For the record, I wouldn't have abandoned Lisa at the first sign of trouble. But I guess we've been over that enough already. What I wanted to talk to you about is a friend I've got at Springfield. He's the department head in their graduate athletic training program. I talked to him about you. If you're interested, I think we could get you caught up on required undergrad courses and step up your training with me. If you meet the coursework pre-reqs and I say you're ready, you're in. Think about it. I think you'd be great at the job."

Seneca couldn't believe what a wonderful opportunity Kate had just laid before her. She was overwhelmed at Kate's generosity and supremely happy that she had that kind of faith in her. She shook her head in disbelief for a second before recovering and launching herself at Kate. She hoped to God Shannon wasn't watching.

Kate accepted the hug easily. "Is that a yes?"

"When can I start? Do you have a list of classes I need? Do I have to take them at Springfield if they aren't offered here, or can I take them at one of the other schools that are a little closer? Oh, and summer, can I start this summer? Thank you. Thank you, thank you, and thank you. I won't let you down." Seneca paused to replenish the air she had just used up with all of her questions.

"You can take the classes anywhere. I'll give you a list, and I know you won't let me down. I wouldn't have suggested it if I didn't think you would be good at it." Kate was smiling as widely as Seneca.

Seneca didn't realize how much she had missed her equilibrium with Kate, or how much it had been a steadying influence on her life. It had been hard knowing Kate was upset with her. She took a moment to bask in this part of her world returning to normal. She reached in her pocket to grab her cell phone. She had to text the good news to Dylan. Suddenly, the euphoria of a moment was gone. Her triumph was so much less satisfying given that she had cut off the only person she wanted to share it with. Adding insult to injury, she felt tears threatening yet again. It was as if, now that she finally unclogged the pipes, she couldn't shut off the spigot.

Kate must have seen her eyes welling because she started to shift her weight and lean into Seneca as if to comfort her, or provide some meaningful advice. Or perhaps she was about to tell her she was an idiot, once again. Whatever she was going to say or do, however, was interrupted by her cell phone. She checked the display and quickly answered. Seneca was surprised. Kate almost never answered her phone while they were working.

Kate moved a few steps away from the golf cart, but Seneca could still hear bits of their conversation. Whoever was on the other end, Kate greeted them using "kiddo," something Seneca assumed was reserved for her alone. She was immediately jealous and a little hurt. Did Kate have other lost young women she was caring for?

"No, get back inside right now. Leave the bike where it is. You can call campus security later. Can you get back into a classroom where there are a lot of people? I'll be right there. And, Dylan, lock the door if you can."

Seneca started sweating. She must have misheard. Why would Dylan need to lock herself in her room? What was wrong? Why was she calling Kate?

"Kate, what's wrong?" Seneca asked. "Is Dylan okay?"

"Look, kiddo," Kate said, looking away. "Dylan doesn't want you to know she's talking to me at all, but I don't think that's fair to any of us, so she's okay. Someone slashed her bike tires. She's been getting the creeps, like someone's been following her lately, so she called me last week. Since you told her to get lost, she didn't have anyone to talk to." Kate didn't sugarcoat it, and Seneca cringed. That wasn't how she saw what happened. But now Dylan was in trouble and she was calling Kate.

"I'm not trying to guilt you into talking to Dylan, or make you feel bad," Kate said, softening her tone. She had always been pretty good at reading Seneca, so it wasn't surprising she could pick up on Seneca's feelings now. "I just want you to know what's going on. I'm going over there to drive her home from class. You're welcome to come along, but don't expect a welcome mat from Dylan. She's pretty pissed at you."

Seneca's mind was racing. This news about Dylan was upsetting enough, but it was also painting a disturbing picture when taken with reports of Shannon sightings from some of the athletes. Seneca had dismissed them because they hadn't been near her dorm room, classes, or the athletic fields, and if it really was Shannon, surely she'd be in the areas where Seneca usually was.

"I have to take care of something," Seneca said. She was scared. What if all her careful planning and attempts to keep

Dylan safe had backfired? What if it really made more sense for her to be at Dylan's side, where she might be able to protect her, rather than far away and out of the loop? *Shit.* "Can you tell Dylan I love her? I'll call her in a little while. I think I've been so stupid. Please keep her safe, Kate."

Seneca took off in the golf cart at top speed. She didn't bother heading back to the shed where they usually housed the cart during off hours. It would take her too long to lock it up and then get across campus to her room. She careened straight across the soccer field, onto the narrow jogging trail that encircled the athletic fields, and across the footbridge that separated the fields from the rest of campus. Once on the real roads of campus, the cart really picked up speed. Luckily, the small cart had a horn, something she'd never had to use before, or she would have run over more than one pedestrian.

Once upstairs, she grabbed the sheet of binder paper where she had scribbled each potential Shannon sighting. She pulled the laminated campus map off the wall and set it on her bed. Using a Sharpie, she put a dot on the map for each potential sighting. She recoiled at the finished product. There was a heavy concentration around a building where Dylan had almost all of her classes. A few of the dots were directly outside Dylan's dorm, and one was outside the office of Dylan's advisor's office. Shannon was here and she knew about Dylan. Seneca held the paper in front of her face and looked at it until her anger boiled to the point she couldn't see the ugly dots anymore. She tore the paper into four pieces and slammed them down on the table. She grabbed her cane from the closet, quickly changed into her heavier, sturdier boots, and grabbed a pair of fingerless gloves she often wore while working. They were the closest thing she had to hand wraps in her room. She picked up the phone to make a long overdue call.

CHAPTER TWENTY-FIVE

Dylan replayed the conversation with Seneca in her mind. It had been a few days, but the fear in Seneca's voice still gave her the chills. Shannon was stalking her, there was no question about that, and the police had been unable to track her down. Dylan had four websites open on her computer but couldn't remember anything about them. She was supposed to be preparing for job interviews at three companies, but her mind had been elsewhere for more than an hour. If she was honest, it had been elsewhere longer than that.

Seneca had tried to rush over and search every bush and shrub near Dylan's dorm room, but that was silly. Clearly, Shannon wasn't interested in seeing Seneca, at least not yet. And for the moment, Dylan wasn't interested in seeing Seneca, either.

It probably made sense for Seneca to keep her distance and for them to not give any indication that they knew Shannon was watching Dylan, like Kate said. But that wasn't the reason Dylan had told Seneca to stay away. When Seneca's world had come crashing down, she had used the pieces that were left to wall Dylan out. That hurt every time she thought about it. No matter how noble Seneca intended her actions.

Dylan sighed. She's been down this road too many times already. What she really needed to do was prepare for her job interviews. She looked at the first website and scanned the company's mission statement and history. She pulled up the job posting and scanned it. She started to panic. She couldn't think of a single skill she could offer this company. She had very little experience, was just coming out of school, and wasn't even sure if this was the field she wanted to be in long-term. She thought again about what her mother had said. She and Seneca had talked about what they would do if they could be anything they wanted. Maybe it was time to revisit that.

She called Gert. No answer. She scrolled through the other websites hoping they were less intimidating. They weren't. She considered calling Kate. She had been very kind lately, but she didn't want to intrude. Besides, Kate was close to Seneca, and she didn't want to put her in an uncomfortable position. She let out an exasperated breath and did what she had been wanting to do since she read the first line of the mission statement on website number one. She grabbed her dorm phone and called Seneca. Regardless of their current struggles, Seneca had given her fantastic advice in the past about all this job business. Besides, she had promised to be there from start to finish. Dylan was just making her live up to that promise.

"Hi, Bob," Seneca said, "Is everything okay? Are you all right?"

Dylan stretched the phone cord across the room until she was standing in front of the window, surveying the lawn below her window. This view had always been relaxing, doubly when coupled with Seneca's voice. But now she scanned the grounds for a stalker, someone possibly intending to hurt her.

"I'm trying to get ready for my job interviews," Dylan said.

"And let me guess," Seneca said. "You just freaked yourself out that no one will ever hire you because you have nothing to offer the company? Or are you still chewing on what your mom said when she popped in on us unexpectedly?"

"How did you know?" Dylan had forgotten how well Seneca knew her.

"Because, Bob, you always underestimate how amazing you are and how good we were together, before I messed that up."

Before Seneca could continue, a ding sounded in the background behind her, followed quickly by three more. They sounded to Dylan like the dings of a computer chat.

"What the hell?" Seneca said. Her words were slightly broken. Her cell phone signal was being disrupted. "I just got about six text messages and five chats," Seneca said. "I have no idea what that's about."

"Go ahead and check them," Dylan said, a little jealous that Seneca had so much time on her hands for that many friendships now. She stared out the window and suddenly saw her. Shannon was standing on the lawn in front of her dorm, surveying the building, searching the windows. Dylan took a stumbling step backward, her heart pounding, her anxiety ratcheted up.

"Oh my God, Seneca, she's here. She's outside my dorm. She's standing on the lawn."

"That's what all these messages are about," Seneca said. "I'm already on my way. Call the police."

"Seneca?" Dylan said. She heard the line go dead. Her stomach sank. She felt as if her last tie to Seneca was severed. She walked back to her desk, hung up the phone, picked it up again, and called the campus police. She reported Shannon on campus and Seneca's imminent confrontation. They were an unarmed security force ill equipped to handle a paroled felon. Campus police patched her through to nine one one. She relayed the same information to them. While she was talking, she moved back to the window and peered out from the side.

From her vantage point, Dylan could see the entire scene below her. Shannon was still on the lawn looking at her window. Behind Shannon and to her right, Dylan could see Seneca just coming into view. Dylan felt like she should go down to help her, get involved somehow, but it felt as impossible as entering the scene of an Imax movie.

As she approached, Seneca must have yelled, because Shannon violently spun in Seneca's direction, and when their gazes locked, her body language relaxed. She looked in control and overly confident, arrogant. When Seneca came to a stop in front of her, Dylan thought she looked smaller than she ever remembered. It looked like they were talking, or more accurately, like Shannon was talking and Seneca was receiving. Shannon clearly had a few things she'd been meaning to say for all these years. Dylan stood paralyzed by fear as Shannon lashed out, and Seneca dropped to the ground.

❖

Seneca dropped to one knee. It all felt so familiar. Shannon moved forward, her foot back, ready to kick her. What felt different was her. She got back to her feet quickly, avoided the kick, and took a few steps back. She got into fighting position, just like Kate had taught her. If Shannon wanted a fight, now, finally, she would get one. Gone were the days of beating on a helpless little kid.

Seneca held her hands in front of her face and bounced on the balls of her feet. Shannon looked surprised and stopped her advance momentarily. She put her own hands down by her side briefly, then struck out wildly.

"You looking for a fight, Seneca? Bring it on, tough guy. It's more fun for me when you fight back." Shannon rushed her.

Seneca saw Shannon's advance as if it were happening in slow motion. She timed her punch and connected solidly with the right side of her head. Kate couldn't have prepared her for the feel of fist on skull, like punching a wall. She didn't like the feeling, but fighting back, fighting back against Shannon, fighting back for Dylan, felt invigorating. Getting punched by the two quick counterpunches felt familiar, but instead of filling her with fear, they filled her with righteous rage.

Seneca could hear the sirens in the distance, but she hoped they stayed away. This was her fight to finish. She stepped back and reset. Shannon seemed to be waiting for her to make the next move. She did. She landed two solid punches to Shannon's body, one to the stomach and one to the ribs. She could feel Shannon's rapid exhale against the back of her neck. The victory was short-lived, however, because Shannon was quick. She elbowed Seneca solidly in the face. Blood started flowing freely, running into Seneca' mouth and dripping onto her shirt. She raised her hand to her nose for a second to stem the tide, and Shannon pounced.

She punched Seneca repeatedly in the body, sending her stumbling back. There was a park bench behind her, an unwelcome piece of battlefield detritus, and Seneca tripped over it, falling backward onto the cold, snow-covered ground.

Seneca knew she needed to get up. She had been in this position too many times, lying on the ground, vulnerable, Shannon standing above her, ready to strike. Shannon seemed to recognize the situation as well. She moved in slowly, mockingly.

"You knew it would end like this, King. Did you think she could keep you forever? Keep you from me? She's watching, you know. I can see her with her ugly face pressed against the window. Watching you get the shit beat out of you. Why isn't she down here fighting for you? It doesn't matter. When I'm done with you, I'll take care of her."

Seneca's leg was on fire from the fall and all the power she had needed for the first round of fighting. She was holding her leg close, massaging it and trying to work out some of the ache while Shannon talked. It probably looked like weakness to Shannon, but Seneca was really reloading. She was counting on Shannon's damned overconfidence and her assumption that nothing had changed, that Seneca hadn't changed. If only she knew that the woman watching them had finally made Seneca's life worth living. This pontificating piece of shit certainly wasn't going to take that away.

Shannon moved in and kicked Seneca in the ribs. Seneca could take it; she'd had worse. She needed another minute to get her legs back under her. Shannon knelt down, grabbed Seneca by the hair, and pulled them face to face.

"You are nothing to me. You hear me? I'm done with you. But before I go, I'm going to kill your new minder. And you're going to have to watch."

Shannon got up and started toward Dylan's dorm room.

Seneca rose as well. Her leg was going to have to be good enough.

"I don't think so," she said, loudly, stopping Shannon in her tracks.

Shannon spun around, a weird, creepy smile on her face. "Oh, you have more in you before I head upstairs?"

"No, we're finishing this here. I was never anything to you. And you will never lay a finger on Dylan. Not over, under, or around my dead body. If anyone dies tonight, it's going to be one of us. But you tried to kill me once and couldn't get that right, even with a gun."

"Well, well, look who grew some balls. Going to try and kill me. What a surprise."

"Not exactly what I said, but we can run with that. But you're right. I'm a different person. A real relationship will do that. They lift you up, make you stronger. They don't suck the life out of you and leave you to die."

"You done with the inspirational quotes?" Shannon asked, looking wild and dangerous. They could both see the police moving across the quad in their direction.

Seneca could see Shannon winding up for a vicious shot, but all that time with Kate had taught her to avoid just such a punch and she was ready. When Shannon swung, Seneca ducked under the punch. She countered with three rapid shots to Shannon's face. This time Shannon stumbled and Seneca pounced. She punched again and again and again, her fists a blur as she thrashed out her anger on Shannon's body. Rage fueled the fury of her fists, and her focus narrowed to releasing years of anger, pain, and fear on her abuser.

Shannon wasn't putting up much of a fight anymore, just covering her face with her arms, but Seneca was only barely aware of it.

"You will not touch her," Seneca said, over and over, underscoring each word with a punch.

"Seneca," Dylan said. "Stop." She tried to grab Seneca's arm. "Stop hitting her. I'm fine. It's over. It's over, baby." Seneca didn't stop, although she did slow. She didn't know when Dylan had arrived.

The police broke up the fight, pulling Seneca off Shannon and away from her. That finally snapped Seneca out of her fury.

"She said she was going to kill you," Seneca said, looking at Dylan. "I couldn't let her do that."

"I know. I saw the whole thing. From my room. I wanted to come help, but it was like I was watching a movie. I was locked out."

Seneca gingerly wiped her nose and smeared blood all over her face. Her knuckles were bloody and swollen; her face didn't feel like her own.

"How are you still standing up? I'm glad an ambulance is here. You need to get to the hospital," Dylan said, clearly worried. She looked afraid, or unwilling, to touch Seneca.

"She's not going to bother us again," Seneca said.

"I'm glad she's out of your life," Dylan said. "Let's get you checked out. We'll figure out what 'us' means later."

Seneca was confused but didn't say anything. She thought getting rid of Shannon would reset everything, make everything okay. Apparently, Dylan wasn't so sure.

"I love you, Bob," Seneca said.

"I love you too, Seneca, more than I thought it was possible to love someone. That still doesn't change the fact that you shut me out. That isn't a relationship. We need to talk about that. But not now," Dylan said. "Now it's hospitals and police questions." She took Seneca's hand and led her to the ambulance. When Seneca stumbled, she wrapped her arm gently around her waist and walked her to the waiting medical attention.

"How romantic," Seneca said, leaning into Dylan's embrace just before she lost consciousness.

CHAPTER TWENTY-SIX

Seneca was still moving with care. Her whole body was sore, bruised, and battered. She wasn't feeling tip-top emotionally either. She had expected, now that Shannon was no longer a concern, that she and Dylan would resume where they had left off. But Dylan had made it clear things weren't that easy. She didn't know why. Dylan had explained it, but it still made no sense. Seneca suspected this was what Kate had tried to warn her about. At least she was coming over daily to check on her. The time she had gone without seeing Dylan had been more painful than anything she was experiencing now.

Seneca smiled when the knock sounded at the door. Dylan was impressively prompt.

"It's unlocked," Seneca said.

Dylan took her breath away when she walked in. She always did. Seneca eased herself up and limped over to Dylan. Her limp wasn't as much due to her damaged leg as her more recent injuries. Getting the shit beat out of you took its toll.

"Stay seated, Sen. You don't have to get up and greet me," Dylan said.

Seneca kissed Dylan on the cheek and hugged her. Dylan refused to hug her back, given Seneca's two broken ribs.

"You can hug me," Seneca said. "I'm already broken, so you can't do any worse." She always said that, and Dylan always refused. It stung.

"Tell me about what Shannon said to you, before she threatened me," Dylan said.

Dylan's request caught Seneca off guard. She had thought about Shannon over and over since she had been re-arrested, but only about what it felt like to finally be rid of her. She didn't want to think about the rest.

"Why does that matter?" Seneca asked. "She's out of my life now, finally. I don't have to worry about her for the first time in a long time."

Dylan looked thoughtful, like she always did when she was choosing her words carefully.

"It matters because that was the part that you shut me out of completely. That's the part that I can't stop thinking about. I love you so much it hurts, but I can't be with you if you're going to have parts of your life that you wall off from me. I don't mean that you can't have your own interests, friends, and hobbies. But if you are going to have something that affects your life that completely, and I'm not allowed to have any part in it, then I don't know if I can do that. I want to understand."

Seneca didn't ever want to think about what Shannon had said to her, but if it meant a future with Dylan, she'd do whatever it took. "She told me I was worthless. She told me I would amount to nothing. That it didn't matter how far I ran from her, I would always belong to her. She said she should have let me die when she had the chance because it would have saved her a lot of trouble now. She said she enjoyed that I was fighting back because it made it more fun for her."

Seneca lowered herself gingerly onto the bed and stared at her hands as she talked, unable to look at Dylan. "I felt like I had never left that world. Or maybe like I was stuck between the two." Seneca shuddered at the sharp pain from her broken ribs. "I guess when she got to town she asked about me. Everyone told her about you. She wanted to see who had taken what she thought was hers. She didn't understand that I could be with you out of true love. Maybe for the second time now, Shannon saved my life.

She had won, you know, until she mentioned you. I didn't think I could get up, my leg hurt so bad. But she said she was going after you next, and that was all I needed. It felt like I was finally pushed out of the past. No more cowering, or limping, or being scared of her. I knew I wasn't ever going to run from her again. I guess I took it a little too far."

"She has plenty of time in prison to recover," Dylan said, clearly not overly concerned about Shannon's health and well-being. "I'm glad you're here. Not stuck between anymore."

"It really only means something to me if I'm here with you," Seneca said, laying all her cards on the table. "I didn't push you away or shut you out. I was trying to protect you from her. I knew what kind of person she was and what she would do to you if she knew you existed. I failed at that, but I had to try. The things she said she was going to do to you…and make me watch. You know that dream I had the night after you found me in the woods? After the phone call?"

"Of course, the same one you always have, where Shannon hurts you."

"It was the same, except in that one, she wasn't pointing the gun at me. She had it pointed at you. Since that night, I've had that same dream almost every night. I've had to watch her kill you in my sleep over and over, and I knew if she found out about you, she would do it. Tonight, she would have. She told me she was going to. I couldn't live with myself if that happened. I know I messed this up so badly. Kate's pissed, Lisa won't even talk to me, and you're mad as hell, but I did it all because I care about you and I knew what she was. Whatever you decide, I did what I did because I love you."

Dylan didn't say anything. She reached out and caressed Seneca's hand. Seneca hoped that was a good sign. Finally, she spoke. "I thought I could handle all of this. I'm not sure I could have, honestly. I don't know how you did. Why didn't you make me understand what you were trying to do? Why didn't you tell me about the dreams?"

Seneca felt embarrassed. That seemed so simple looking back now. And she had tried. "I tried to explain in my own way. Not very well. You got a little mad. If you remember, I ran and hid in the woods when I found out Shannon was loose in the world. I'm not great with emotions, but I'm getting better. Be patient with me?"

"I've never been good at saying no to that face," Dylan said. "But I've got some things to tell you. I'm not going to business school. I'm not going to get a fancy job or wear a suit. I've had some time on my hands, and I've done some thinking."

"Oh yeah?" Seneca asked, distracted by the fact that Dylan was practically sitting on her lap she had moved so close, broken ribs be damned.

"I'm opening my own business. I think I want to own a coffee shop, actually." Dylan sounded a little shy making the announcement and Seneca thought it was adorable.

"That is perhaps the most perfect thing I've ever heard," Seneca said. "You'll be so damned good at that. Your customers, especially this one, are going to love you. Were you thinking of staying around here to open up shop? There's that empty storefront right downtown, and the coffee at the other place really sucks."

"What about you, though? What are you going to do after graduation? I'm not starting a business if you move to Wyoming."

Seneca laughed. "Do I look like a cowboy to you? I guess I haven't had a chance to tell you. Kate offered me a chance to go to grad school for athletic training. I can stick around here to do it. And I ran into Jane, the athletic director, and she was really weird and cryptic, but I think she might have been offering me the second athletic trainer position in a couple years when I graduate. The other trainer is getting old and crotchety."

"Seneca, that's wonderful." Dylan was beaming.

"Will you show me your storefront?" Seneca gingerly stood and looked for her cane.

"Right now?"

"Well, will you let me take your clothes off instead?"

"You have two broken ribs and I don't even want to know how many stitches," Dylan said, looking horrified. "You have to wait."

"It's only two ribs. I have a lot of others."

"Aren't you supposed to know how many, Ms. Athletic Trainer?"

"I only need to know how many are broken. Two. Job done," Seneca said. "So, no naked time?"

Dylan just looked at her with a mixture of disbelief and disapproval, but beneath was a burning desire that made Seneca grin. Her world, a place that had been dark and lonely for so long, suddenly felt light, open, and welcoming. The future held so much promise, if Dylan weren't holding her hand and looking at her like there was no one else on the planet, she would have thought it was a dream. But it was real, and it was theirs.

"Okay fine, tomorrow then. Let's go downtown. Show me our beautiful future."

About the Author

Jesse Thoma splits her professional time between graduate school and work. She is a project manager in a clinical research lab and spends a good amount of time in methadone clinics and prisons collecting data and talking to people.

Jesse grew up in Northern California but headed east for college. She never looked back, although her baseball allegiance is still loyally with the San Francisco Giants. She has lived in New England for ten years and has finally learned to leave extra time in the morning to scrape snow off the car. Jesse is blissfully married and is happiest when she is out for a walk with her wife and their dog, pretending she still has the soccer skills she had as an eighteen-year-old, eating anything her wife bakes, or sitting at the computer to write a few lines.

Books Available from Bold Strokes Books

Timeless by Rachel Spangler. When Stevie Geller returns to her hometown, will she do things differently the second time around or will she be in such a hurry to leave her past that she misses out on a better future? (978-1-62639-050-8)

Second to None by L.T. Marie. Can a physical therapist and a custom motorcycle designer conquer their pasts and build a future with one another? (978-1-62639-051-5)

Seneca Falls by Jesse Thoma. Together, two women discover love truly can conquer all evil. (978-1-62639-052-2)

A Kingdom Lost by Barbara Ann Wright. Without knowing each other's fate, Princess Katya and her consort Starbride seek to reclaim their kingdom from the magic-wielding madman who seized the throne and is murdering their people. (978-1-62639-053-9)

Uncommon Romance by Jove Belle. Sometimes sex is just sex, and sometimes it's the only way to say "I love you." (978-1-62639-057-7)

The Heat of Angels by Lisa Girolami. Fires burn in more than one place in Los Angeles. (978-1-62639-042-3)

Season of the Wolf by Robin Summers. Two women running from their pasts are thrust together by an unimaginable evil. Can they overcome the horrors that haunt them in time to save each other? (978-1-62639-043-0)

Desperate Measures by P. J. Trebelhorn. Homicide detective Kay Griffith and contractor Brenda Jansen meet amidst turmoil neither of them is aware of until murder suspect Tommy Rayne makes his move to exact revenge on Kay. (978-1-62639-044-7)

The Magic Hunt by L.L. Raand. With her Pack being hunted by human extremists and beset by enemies masquerading as friends, can Sylvan protect them and her mate, or will she succumb to the feral rage that threatens to turn her rogue, destroying them all? A Midnight Hunters novel. (978-1-62639-045-4)

Waiting for the Violins by Justine Saracen. After surviving Dunkirk, a scarred and embittered British nurse returns to Nazi-occupied Brussels to join the Resistance, and finds that nothing is fair in love and war. (978-1-62639-046-1)

Because of Her by KE Payne. When Tabby Morton is forced to move to London, she's convinced her life will never be the same again. But the beautiful and intriguing Eden Palmer is about to show her that this time, change is most definitely for the better. (978-1-62639-049-2)

Wingspan by Karis Walsh. Wildlife biologist Bailey Chase is content to live at the wild bird sanctuary she has created on Washington's Olympic Peninsula until she is lured beyond the safety of isolation by architect Kendall Pearson. (978-1-60282-983-1)

Tumbledown by Cari Hunter. After surviving their ordeal in the North Cascades, Alex and Sarah have new identities and a new home, but a chance occurrence threatens everything: their freedom and their lives. (978-1-62639-085-0)

Night Bound by Winter Pennington. Kass struggles to keep her head, her heart, and her relationships in order. She's still having a difficult time accepting being an Alpha female. But her wolf is certain of what she wants and she's intent on securing her power. (978-1-60282-984-8)

Slash and Burn by Valerie Bronwen. The murder of a roundly despised author at an LGBT writer's conference in New Orleans turns Winter Lovelace's relaxing weekend hobnobbing with her peers into a nightmare of suspense—especially when her ex turns up. (978-1-60282-986-2)

The Blush Factor by Gun Brooke. Ice-cold business tycoon Eleanor Ashcroft only cares about the three P's—Power, Profit, and Prosperity—until young Addison Garr makes her doubt both that and the state of her frostbitten heart. (978-1-60282-985-5)

The Quickening: A Sisters of Spirits Novel by Yvonne Heidt. Ghosts, visions, and demons are all in a day's work for Tiffany. But when Kat asks for help on a serial killer case, life takes on another dimension altogether. (978-1-60282-975-6)

Windigo Thrall by Cate Culpepper. Six women trapped in a mountain cabin by a blizzard, stalked by an ancient cannibal demon bent on stealing their sanity—and their lives. (978-1-60282-950-3)

Smoke and Fire by Julie Cannon. Oil and water, passion and desire, a combustible combination. Can two women fight the fire that draws them together and threatens to keep them apart? (978-1-60282-977-0)

Asher's Fault by Elizabeth Wheeler. Fourteen-year-old Asher Price sees the world in black and white, much like the photos he takes, but when his little brother drowns at the same moment Asher experiences his first same-sex kiss, he can no longer hide behind the lens of his camera and eventually discovers he isn't the only one with a secret. (978-1-60282-982-4)

Love and Devotion by Jove Belle. KC Hall trips her way through life, stumbling into an affair with a married bombshell twice her age. Thankfully, her best friend, Emma Reynolds, is there to show her the true meaning of Love and Devotion. (978-1-60282-965-7)

Rush by Carsen Taite. Murder, secrets, and romance combine to create the ultimate rush. (978-1-60282-966-4)

The Shoal of Time by J.M. Redmann. It sounded too easy. Micky Knight is reluctant to take the case because the easy ones often turn into the hard ones, and the hard ones turn into the dangerous ones. In this one, easy turns hard without warning. (978-1-60282-967-1)

In Between by Jane Hoppen. At the age of 14, Sophie Schmidt discovers that she was born an intersexual baby and sets off on a journey to find her place in a world that denies her true existence. (978-1-60282-968-8)

Secret Lies by Amy Dunne. While fleeing from her abuser, Nicola Jackson bumps into Jenny O'Connor, and their unlikely friendship quickly develops into a blossoming romance—but when it comes down to a matter of life or death, are they both willing to face their fears? (978-1-60282-970-1)

Under Her Spell by Maggie Morton. The magic of love brought Terra and Athene together, but now a magical quest stands between them—a quest for Athene's hand in marriage. Will their passion keep them together, or will stronger magic tear them apart? (978-1-60282-973-2)

Homestead by Radclyffe. R. Clayton Sutter figures getting NorthAm Fuel's newest refinery operational on a rolling tract of land in Upstate New York should take a month or two, but then, she hadn't counted on local resistance in the form of vandalism, petitions, and one furious farmer named Tess Rogers. (978-1-60282-956-5)

Battle of Forces: Sera Toujours by Ali Vali. Kendal and Piper return to New Orleans to start the rest of eternity together, but the return of an old enemy makes their peaceful reunion short-lived, especially when they join forces with the new queen of the vampires. (978-1-60282-957-2)

How Sweet It Is by Melissa Brayden. Some things are better than chocolate. Molly O'Brien enjoys her quiet life running the bakeshop in a small town. When the beautiful Jordan Tuscana returns home, Molly can't deny the attraction—or the stirrings of something more. (978-1-60282-958-9)

The Missing Juliet: A Fisher Key Adventure by Sam Cameron. A teenage detective and her friends search for a kidnapped Hollywood star in the Florida Keys. (978-1-60282-959-6)

Amor and More: Love Everafter edited by Radclyffe and Stacia Seaman. Rediscover favorite couples as Bold Strokes Books authors reveal glimpses of life and love beyond the honeymoon in short stories featuring main characters from favorite BSB novels. (978-1-60282-963-3)

First Love by CJ Harte. Finding true love is hard enough, but for Jordan Thompson, daughter of a conservative president, it's challenging, especially when that love is a female rodeo cowgirl. (978-1-60282-949-7)

Pale Wings Protecting by Lesley Davis. Posing as a couple to investigate the abduction of infants, Special Agent Blythe Kent and Detective Daryl Chandler find themselves drawn into a battle over the innocents, with demons on one side and the unlikeliest of protectors on the other. (978-1-60282-964-0)

Mounting Danger by Karis Walsh. Sergeant Rachel Bryce, an outcast on the police force, is put in charge of the department's newly formed mounted division. Can she and polo champion Callan Lanford resist their growing attraction as they struggle to safeguard the disaster-prone unit? (978-1-60282-951-0)

Meeting Chance by Jennifer Lavoie. When man's best friend turns on Aaron Cassidy, the teen keeps his distance until fate puts Chance in his hands. (978-1-60282-952-7)

At Her Feet by Rebekah Weatherspoon. Digital marketing producer Suzanne Kim knows she has found the perfect love in her new mistress Pilar, but before they can make the ultimate commitment, Suzanne's professional life threatens to disrupt their perfectly balanced bliss. (978-1-60282-948-0)

Show of Force by AJ Quinn. A chance meeting between navy pilot Evan Kane and correspondent Tate McKenna takes them on a roller-coaster ride where the stakes are high, but the reward is higher: a chance at love. (978-1-60282-942-8)

Clean Slate by Andrea Bramhall. Can Erin and Morgan work through their individual demons to rediscover their love for each other, or are the unexplainable wounds too deep to heal? (978-1-60282-943-5)

Hold Me Forever by D. Jackson Leigh. An investigation into illegal cloning in the quarter horse racing industry threatens to destroy the growing attraction between Georgia debutante Mae St. John and Louisiana horse trainer Whit Casey. (978-1-60282-944-2)

Trusting Tomorrow by PJ Trebelhorn. Funeral director Logan Swift thinks she's perfectly happy with her solitary life devoted to helping others cope with loss until Brooke Collier moves in next door to care for her elderly grandparents. (978-1-60282-891-9)

Forsaking All Others by Kathleen Knowles. What if what you think you want is the opposite of what makes you happy? (978-1-60282-892-6)

Exit Wounds by VK Powell. When Officer Loane Landry falls in love with ATF informant Abigail Mancuso, she realizes that nothing is as it seems—not the case, not her lover, not even the dead. (978-1-60282-893-3)